THE BOOK OF
Saints

THE BOOK OF

Saints

NINO RICCI

ALFRED A. KNOPF   NEW YORK

1991

For my parents

THIS IS A BORZOI BOOK
PUBLISHED BY ALFRED A. KNOPF, INC.

Copyright © 1990 by Nino Ricci

Portions of Chapter VII appeared in a different form in *The
Moosehead Anthology* (Montreal: DC Books, 1989).

The author is deeply grateful to Terence Byrnes, whose
continuing support helped bring this book to fruition and
whose criticisms and suggestions helped shape it.

Library of Congress Cataloging-in-Publication Data

Ricci, Nino.
The book of saints / Nino Ricci. — 1st American ed.
p. cm.
"Originally published in Canada as *Lives of the Saints* by
Cormorant Books, Dunvegan, Ontario, in 1990" —
T.p. verso.
ISBN 0-679-40118-0
I. Title.
PR9199.3.R512B66 1991
813'.54—dc20 90-53397 CIP

Manufactured in the United States of America

First U.S. Edition

THE BOOK OF

Saints

~~~

*The places we have known belong now only to the little world
of space on which we map them for our own convenience.
None of them was ever more than a thin slice, held between the
contiguous impressions that composed our life at that time;
the memory of a particular image is but regret for a particular
moment; and houses, roads, avenues are as fugitive, alas,
as the years.*

Marcel Proust
Remembrance of Things Past

~~~

I

If this story has a beginning, a moment at which a single gesture broke the surface of events like a stone thrown into the sea, the ripples cresting away endlessly, then that beginning occurred on a hot July day in the year 1960, in the village of Valle del Sole, when my mother was bitten by a snake.

Valle del Sole—which was not in a valley at all, but perched on the north face of Colle di Papa about three thousand feet above the valley floor—had no culinary specialties, no holy sites, no ancient ruins; forgotten and unsung, it was one of a hundred villages just like it flung across the Italian Apennines like scattered stones. Its main street, via San Giuseppe, came down a mile or so from the high road before carving a sharp S through the village centre and ending at a 200 foot drop at the village's edge; and that July afternoon the street was deserted, the women and children walled up in their houses, the shutters closed against the flies and heat, the men out in the fields, which they had departed for before dawn and from which they would not return until after nightfall.

But in our house there were no men to go out and work the fields. My father—a native not of Valle del Sole

but of nearby Castilucci, Valle del Sole's age-old rival—
had emigrated to America almost four years before, when
I was barely three; and my grandfather, my mother's
father, in whose house we lived, had been crippled during
the first war, one leg, its bone crushed on the battlefield by
a horse's hoof, left shorter than the other, and his calves
scarred and pitted from the damage a grenade had done.
He lived now on a government pension, and on the rent he
collected from his few hectares of olives and vineyards;
and in the village he was known simply as *lu podestà*, the
mayor, because he had held that position unchallenged
since the time of the Fascists.

Before lunch my mother had received a letter from
the postman. Letters came to her every few months from
my father; but the tight blue script I'd glimpsed on the
envelope, before my mother had whisked it up to her
bedroom, had been neat and legible—not at all my father's
violent scribble, which did not resemble in the least the
shapes *la maestra* had been teaching us at school, all the
letters levelled out into a series of homogenized loops.
After lunch, when my grandfather as usual had gone up to
Di Lucci's *Bar e Alimentari* for a glass of watered-down
wine and a game of *scopa* (Di Lucci, possessed of a deep
entrepreneurial spirit, did not close up his shop during
siesta), my mother slipped out of the house, making me
promise to sit in the kitchen and study my school books.

'Where are you going?' I asked her.

'I have an appointment.'

'With who?'

'With the man who cuts the birdies off boys who
ask too many questions.'

The books had been consigned to me because I had
not done very well in my first year of school. The teacher,
a big-boned woman from Rocca Secca whose breasts jutted
out like a mountain face and whose body gave off a strong
odour of garlic and perfumed soap, had sent me home with

a note:

> Vittorio Innocente is intelligent but *lazy*. However if *la signora* doesn't interest herself in his education, there is nothing to be done.

My attendance at school had not been very regular—it had somehow fallen out that I'd spent much of class time wandering up to the top of Colle di Papa or down to the river with my friend Fabrizio, sharing with him the cigarettes he filched from his father. *La maestra* had paid a visit to my mother one afternoon, to advise her of my truancy and vices; but my mother had only laughed.

'He's just bored, that's all. Sitting in that classroom all day.'

But now, it seemed, I was to be reformed.

'We'll show *la maestra*, eh?' my mother said. 'When you grow up you're going to be a pope. This summer you'll catch up on all the lessons you missed while you were out chasing sheep with Fabrizio.'

And so I sat, now, on the stone bench in front of my grandfather's house, a book called *Principi Matematici* open on my lap to page 3. But I was not attending to it. I had slipped instead into a state of indolence which was very common at that time of year, especially when it was one o'clock and the sun was shining and the whole world seemed wrapped in a warm, yellow dream. Nearby, a swarm of flies hovered around a cluster of droppings on the cobblestones, the braver ones alighting and calling out to their friends.

'It's goat, but it's not bad!' They rubbed their hands together the way my uncle Pasquale did when he sat down to a plate of *pasta all'uovo*.

A flock of sheep came around the corner from the direction of the square, followed by old Angelo Dagnello— the Red, we called him, because he was one of Valle del Sole's few Communists; though years of faithful drinking had helped his appearance conform to his name, his nose and cheeks bright with shattered blood vessels. He moved with a measured nonchalance, his legs taking long slow strides which his upper body bobbed in tandem to; though his arms remained inert at his sides, only one hand moving, slapping a short sheep stick idly against a pant leg as he walked. The horde of flies above the goat droppings rose in unison as the sheep approached.

'Ho, Vittò,' Angelo called out. 'What are you doing out here, frying yourself in the sun like that?'

'I'm studying my mathematics,' I said, opening my eyes wide and flipping a page. 'I'm going to be a pope.'

'A pope! Why settle for a pope? Why not Jesus Christ himself?'

My grandfather's house sat at the very edge of town, set apart from the village's last straggling houses by a patch of low bush; and not far beyond it the cobblestones ended and the road deteriorated into a mere dirt path, scarred by gullies and by the ruts of mule carts. A thin film of dust rose up from the ground as the sheep moved onto the dirt, hovering round their feet like a fog. At *la fonte di capre*, the village's communal fountain, Angelo stopped a moment to cup his hands under the spout and bring a draught of water to his mouth.

I turned another page in my book, relieved for a moment by the taut crinkling of paper. The picture showed four shiny black apples, two spaced out widely and two huddled close together. Then, underneath, these markings: $1 + 1 = 2$. The book seemed to be arguing that I make some connection between the apples and the markings beneath; but the sun, reflecting off the page and filling my eyes with sleep, was arguing otherwise. Slowly my eyelids drooped and closed, while a happy host of apples and numbers, freed from the tyranny of the book, danced in my head in wild combinations.

I was awakened by a muffled shout.

The shout—it had sounded like a man's—had

come from the direction of our stable, which on the street side of the house was buried in the slope the house was cut into but on the valley side opened out at ground level. I set down my book and bounded down the crooked stone stairway at the side of the house that led down to it; but when I rounded the corner at the bottom of the steps I stopped short. The stable door was closed, but through a crack at the bottom of it a small, tapered head was flicking its tongue: a snake. I had seen it just in time; now I stood frozen as it slithered a long, slim green through the crack in the door and disappeared down a row of tomatoes in my mother's garden, a gentle rustling of leaves leading finally to the ravine formed at the edge of my grandfather's property by years of run-off from *la fonte di capre*.

Snakes, in Valle del Sole, had long been imbued with special meaning. Some of the villagers believed they were immortal, because they could shed their skin, and at planting time, to improve their harvest, they would buy a powder made of ground snake skins from *la strega di Belmonte* and spread it over their fields. Others held that a snake crossing you from the right brought good fortune, from the left, bad, or that a brown snake was evil while a green one was good. But there was a saying in Valle del Sole, *'Do' l'orgoglio sta, la serpe se ne va'* —where pride is the snake goes—and there were few who doubted that snakes, whatever their other properties, were agents of the evil eye, which the villagers feared far more than any mere Christian diety or devil, and which they guarded themselves against scrupulously, by wearing amulets of garlic or wolves' teeth and by posting goat horns above their doorways.

But while I had been staring after the path of the snake, someone had cracked open the door of the stable. Two dark eyes were staring down at me now from the shadows, concentrating their energies on me as if to make me disappear by force of will. I was about to turn and run when the stable door opened a few inches further and the two eyes suddenly swooped out of the stable like swallows, turning magically a luminous blue as they caught the sunlight, bright flames that held me transfixed and seemed to burn away all other features of the figure swooping down on me. I stumbled backwards and fell, my arms coming up instinctively to shield me against a blow; but the blow did not come, and in a moment the sound of cracking twigs told me that something had followed the snake into the ravine.

I sat for a moment dazed where I had fallen, my head pounding and my palms scraped and bleeding from my fall. The thick growth of bushes and weeds and saplings that lined the ravine cut off my view of the pasture which opened out beyond it; but up on the high road I made out a glint of metal amidst a clump of trees that rose up from the bank of a curve. As I watched, a small figure scrambled up the slope beneath the trees and a moment later an engine sputtered distantly to life and a small car pulled suddenly out of the trees' shadow, disappearing almost at once around a corner of the mountain in the direction of Castilucci.

Someone, though, was still in the stable. My mother: I came in to find her pouring water from a bucket into the pigs' trough as if nothing had happened, a lantern burning pale blue from a rafter above her.

'Ah, it's you,' she said, turning. She ran a hand through her hair to pull away a stick of straw dangling from it. 'I thought you were studying your mathematics.'

'I heard someone yelling,' I said.

'Oh, that was nothing. I saw a snake.'

'It wasn't you, it was a man.'

My mother pursed her lips and drew them to one side, the way she did when she was considering a problem. She crouched down in front of me.

'What did you see when you came down here?'

she said finally. She stared at me hard a moment, her eyes narrowed; but when I did not answer she put her hands gently on my shoulders.

'Don't be afraid,' she said, more softly. 'Maybe other people will ask you too. What will you tell them?'

Question and answer: that was how *la maestra* taught us our lessons at school and how Father Nicola, the village priest, taught us our catechism. Every question had its right response; from everything you had heard and learned you had to pick out only what was necessary, only what was required.

'I didn't see anything,' I said finally.

For a moment my mother stared at me through narrowed eyes again, as if to gauge the solemnity of my response; but finally she leaned forward to plant a kiss on my forehead. In the sanction of her kiss it seemed possible for an instant that I had told the truth, that the strange blue eyes had been an aberration, a trick of the sunlight. But I had noticed now the two small pin pricks of red on my mother's ankle.

'*Mamma*,' I said, 'there's some blood on your foot.'

My mother looked down at her ankle.

'*Gesù Crist' e Maria.*'

She touched a finger to the blood and smeared it across her shin.

'Run up quick to Di Lucci's,' she said, 'and get him to bring his car. Tell him I've been bitten by a snake.'

~~~

II

Antonio Di Lucci's bar stood at the point where the big S cut by via San Giuseppe widened into the village square, tucked back against the embankment that the church and the schoolhouse sat on. Half-way up the street I could already see my grandfather and Di Lucci, a balding, thick-waisted man whose wrinkled, loose-skinned face had a larger-than-life animation about it, as if it were a mask, playing cards on the terrace.

'*Mamma*'s been bitten by a snake!' I yelled out. The village women who had come out after their siesta to knit on their front steps stared after me as I ran; others popped their heads out of doorways and over balconies.

'Come quickly! *Mamma*'s been bitten by a snake!'

My grandfather was already hurrying down the terrace steps by the time I got to the bar, one hand gripping the rail and the other his cane.

'Andò!' he called out to Di Lucci, who was still standing open-mouthed on the terrace. 'What are you waiting for? Get your car!'

Di Lucci owned the only car in Valle del Sole, a battered orange Cinquecento which he had bought used in Rocca Secca and which he parked prominently next to his bar, despite the envy it was likely to inspire there. In a minute we were scrambling into it, I crawling into the cramped space in back while Di Lucci struggled to help my grandfather pull his legs into the front passenger seat.

'*Basta*, Andò, enough, I'm not a child,' my grandfather said, waving Di Lucci away. 'Just get in and drive.'

Di Lucci squeezed his thick body into the driver's seat and moved his hand towards the ignition.

'The keys! I've forgotten the keys!'

He scrambled back out of his seat. From the centre of the square he shouted up to a balcony above the bar's terrace, holding a hand up to shield his eyes from the sun.

'Marì! MARIA! Where are the keys to the car?'

'Oh, Andò!' Di Lucci's wife, a stout woman with the thick-boned build of an ox, had come out on the balcony. 'Why are you yelling like a madman? How should I know where you put the keys? Do I drive your car? Aren't they in the glove compartment where you always put them? Where are you going with the car?'

Di Lucci hurried back to the car. A few strands of his thin hair had fallen across his forehead and his face had flushed a deep red. He carried his belly in front of him like a huge gourd.

'Hurry up, Andò, *per l'amore di Cristo*,' my grandfather said. 'Here, I've got the keys.'

Di Lucci's wife was still watching us from the balcony.

'*Ma* Andò, where are you going, I just finished making your lunch, if it gets cold you can feed it to the pigs!'

'Look after the store,' Di Lucci called out through his open window, pulling into the square with a lurch. 'The mayor's daughter has been bitten by a snake!' From the back window of the car I saw Di Lucci's wife make a quick sign of the cross.

The front steps and balconies along via San Giuseppe were lined now with women and children. As Di Lucci tried to manoeuvre through the narrow street some of them crowded up to the windows to find out what had happened.

'Out of the way, *per favore!*' Di Lucci shouted, leaning on his horn. 'Can't you see we're in a hurry?'

By the time we had reached my grandfather's house we had a crowd in tow, women dropping their knitting or their washing to fall in behind us, diapered toddlers waddling after them, bawling at being left behind, older children running ahead and mimicking Di Lucci's curses. Even my old aunt Lucia, my grandfather's sister, who seldom moved out of the comfort of her kitchen, had come out to her front door to see what the commotion was, her club-footed daughter Marta staring out of the shadows behind her. But when we pulled up in front of my grandfather's house the noise of the crowd fell down to a murmur, because there was my mother sitting calmly on the stone bench as if nothing had happened, one leg crossed over the other, her hands folded neatly on her lap. She had put on a new dress, a sleek flowered one she had bought in Rocca Secca when some money had come from my father, and had combed out her hair. Di Lucci pulled up his brake.

'Vittorio said you'd been bitten by a snake,' he said, suddenly peevish.

The village women hung back, keeping the car between themselves and my mother.

'Yes,' my mother said simply, rising. She came around to the driver's side of the car, the women opening up a path for her.

'Well, aren't you going to let me in?'

Di Lucci, struggling to reassert some dignity after his excitement, collected himself slowly and heaved himself out of the car.

'You'd think you were just going to the market,' he said, pulling back his seat. Before letting my mother in he leaned inside. 'Vittorio, you get out and wait at home.'

'No,' my mother said behind him. 'I want him to

come with me.'

'*Ma* Andò,' my grandfather said, '*per l'amore di Dio*, just let her get in the car and let's go.'

'Anyhow it seems funny to me,' Di Lucci muttered, still put off by my mother's unexpected calm; but finally we ground into gear and moved up towards the high road, leaving the village women behind us. A few of my schoolmates ran alongside us before being discouraged by the dust. My grandfather and Di Lucci rolled up their windows, the car rattling wildly now from the ruts and gullies in the road; and finally my grandfather shifted in his seat and turned with a grimace to my mother.

'Where did it bite you?'

'On the ankle,' my mother said.

'Why didn't you tie something around your leg?'

'I didn't think of it.'

'Vittorio,' my grandfather said, 'take off your shirt.'

My mother helped me with the buttons, then peeled the shirt off my back and over my arms the way she did when she got me ready for bed.

'How long ago were you bitten?' my grandfather said.

'Ten minutes or so.'

'Tie it a little ways up from the bite.'

My mother twisted the shirt into a half-knot part way up her calf.

'Vittorio, help her to pull it tight. You take one end while she holds the other. Pull until it hurts.'

I pulled on my end with all my strength while my mother pulled on hers. The cloth sank into her leg and the skin around it turned white, but my mother did not wince or grimace. In the village, my mother was famous for her indifference to pain: everyone told the story about my own birth, how for three weeks I didn't want to come out, but my mother still went down to the river with the other women to do her washing, and how when the day finally came my mother didn't make a sound, and the midwife thought she had fallen asleep. At home, when she was baking bread, I'd seen my mother pull hot bricks from the fireplace with her bare hands, lifting them in one smooth motion into the oven.

'Pull harder,' my grandfather said.

We pulled on the shirt ends again, the cloth burning against my palm. My mother took up the loose ends and tied them neatly into a knot. The snake's poison hadn't changed the way she acted as I thought it would, wasn't making her groan or swoon, her eyes still bright and alert, and her lips stretched into what seemed the faintest hint of a smile, as if she was remembering something pleasant; but her ankle now had begun to swell visibly.

'You have to stop the blood,' Di Lucci said. We had pulled onto the main road, and Di Lucci was picking up speed. 'Remember when Giuseppe *lu forestier* was bitten down by the Valley of the Pigs? He was hoeing his vineyard, I remember it like yesterday—they had to cut his leg off because the poison had spread too far.'

'Don't be an idiot,' my grandfather said. 'They cut off his leg because some fool tried to get out the poison with a rusty knife. And slow down. These roads were made for mules, not cars.'

The main road was less pitted and scarred than the trail which led into Valle del Sole: work crews came through after the spring rains and smashed up rocks and stones from the countryside into coarse gravel which they used to fill in gullies and potholes. But the road had been carved straight out of the mountainside, and followed every one of the mountain's erratic curves, with little margin for error if you met a car or cart moving in the opposite direction, only a few feet of clearance between a solid rock wall on one side and a steep slope on the other. Di Lucci, though, was taking the curves wide and fast, my mother and I swaying against each other in the back seat.

'For God's sake, Andò, there's no need to kill us all,' my grandfather said, but Di Lucci did not let up on his speed, relying on his horn to warn in time whatever lay in wait around corners. He brushed off now a close call with a peasant and his hay-laden mule.

'Damn peasants,' he said. 'Most of them have never seen a car before.' Through the back window I saw the mule's wizened owner raise an angry fist after us.

Di Lucci took his eyes off the road now to shoot a quick sidelong glance into the back seat.

'What colour was the snake?' he asked, a little breathless.

'Green,' I said, without thinking.

'Green? You saw it too? Well, green is better than brown. Did it come from the right or the left?'

Di Lucci was up on his snake lore.

'Never mind about your superstitions,' my grandfather said. 'What do you know about snakes?'

'Giuseppe *lu forestier'*, like I was telling you—'

'We don't want to hear about Giuseppe *lu forestier'*.'

'*Beh, scusate*, I just thought—'

'Just think about your driving.'

Di Lucci remained silent for a moment, putting his energies into frightening a flock of approaching sheep to the side of the road, his hand leaning on his horn. We trundled past the sheep just as their shepherd, thrashing out wildly with his staff, beat the last of them into single file against the mountain face. But now Di Lucci was ready for another volley.

'Where did it bite you?'

My mother let out a sigh.

'Andò, you heard me say just a few minutes ago. On the ankle.'

'Yes, of course, on the ankle, but where were you when it bit you on the ankle?'

'Too close to a snake.'

'*Ma, scusate*, Cristina, I'm asking a simple question.'

'You ask too many questions,' my mother said. 'You're like an old woman. You've been sitting in that bar too long, listening to other people's nonsense.'

'Well maybe the doctor will want to know some of these things. What happens if you faint before we get to the hospital? Giuseppe *lu forestier*—'

'*Scusa*, Andò, what does the doctor care where I was when the snake bit me?' my mother said, her voice tinged with irritation. 'If it bit me in the church, or in the stable, what's the difference?'

Di Lucci paused for an instant, pensive, the way he did when he was adding up a total at his store.

'So you were in the stable then,' he said finally.

'*Beh*, fine, I was in the stable then! Are you happy now?'

Di Lucci did in fact seem suddenly calm and pleased, as if my mother's anger had given him the upper hand; and he paused for an instant to sweep his glance nonchalantly across the valley, as if to say that he could go on with his questions now or not, it made no difference to him. As we approached Rocca Secca he eased down on the clutch and downshifted, the gears catching the engine again with uncommon smoothness.

'And what were you doing in the stable?' he said finally.

'Oh, Andò, *basta*!' my mother said. 'What does anyone do in the stable? I was feeding the pigs!'

Now my grandfather, who seemed to have been paying much more attention to Di Lucci's driving than to this conversation, swivelled his head towards the back seat again.

'I thought you fed the animals this morning.'

'I was checking their water,' my mother said impatiently. She turned away towards her window. 'I didn't have time to fill the troughs this morning.'

Bumbling Di Lucci, man of light. Did he know something of what had gone on in our stable, of those blue eyes that had swooped down on me? Or was he just following the villagers' instinct that beneath every simple event there lurked some dark scandal? At any rate, he had succeeded now in causing a ripple to appear on the surface of my mother's calm; and if his small discovery made little difference in the long run, it gave him at least a claim to priority. No doubt a few weeks later he could have been seen leaning over the counter of his bar and whispering to one of his patrons: 'And then the old man turned to her and said, "But you fed the animals this morning." *You fed the animals this morning.* That's when I knew.'

~~~

III

The hospital in Rocca Secca was on the outskirts of town, a high-walled medieval building that had been an orphanage before the second war. We entered through massive front doors into a large reception room filled with whispers and moans, people everywhere, leaning against walls, sitting on the floor, shuffling around the room like ghosts— hard-featured peasants, mainly, some dressed awkwardly in Sunday suits but many still in their dirty working clothes, nursing bandaged limbs or internal ailments that showed themselves only in their low moans and pale skin. The only light in the room came from two tall narrow windows in one wall: a naked bulb hung down from the centre of the high ceiling, but it was not lit. A few babies were crying, but their wails seemed stifled by an atmosphere of almost religious reverence that hung over the room; and remembering that I was in my bare feet and undershirt I felt suddenly ashamed, like in dreams I had where I found myself inexplicably naked in school or in church.

A small desk was wedged in one corner of the room, and a woman in nurse's uniform and cap sat behind it painstakingly applying a coloured liquid to her fingernails with a tiny brush. Di Lucci, flushed with self-importance, stormed in ahead of us and went up to her, stepping over a man with a bandaged leg who lay stretched out on the floor with eyes closed, his hands propped behind his head as a pillow.

'This woman has been bitten by a snake,' Di Lucci said. 'Look at the way her ankle is swelling up.'

A silence descended on the room and a dozen heads turned in my mother's direction. An old woman in black made a sign of the cross and mumbled a few words to herself; and even the man with the bandaged leg opened his eyes and sat up suddenly, looking on with interest. My mother's ankle had swollen now to the size of a melon, and she dragged it the way my cousin Marta dragged her club foot, leaning on my shoulder as she walked.

'You'll have to fill out a form,' the receptionist said.

Now my grandfather had come up to the desk.

'How long before she can see the doctor?' he said, leaning heavily on his cane. 'It's been over an hour since she was bitten.' Though in fact Di Lucci had made good time: perhaps no more than ten minutes had passed since we'd left Valle del Sole.

The receptionist had the open, welcoming face of a child—dark eyes as large as chestnuts and a small nose that curved upwards at its peak; but my grandfather's sense of urgency did not seem to impress her.

'You can see the doctor is very busy today,' she said, tilting her chin towards the crowded room.

Di Lucci reached a hand into his pant pocket and pulled it out with a bank note crumpled in his fist. He set the note discreetly on the desk and pushed it with his fingers towards the receptionist. The receptionist opened a drawer, let Di Lucci's fingers push the bill into it, then closed the drawer again with her elbow. She shrugged.

'I'll see what I can do,' she said.

'Go find a place to sit with your mother,' my grandfather said to me. 'Help her to loosen the bandage, then count to thirty in your head and tie it up again.'

My mother had not spoken for some time. Her eyelids were drooping now, her eyes slightly glazed, and she was swaying on her feet the way Angelo the Red did after a bottle of wine. When I looked around the room for a place to sit, the man with the bandaged leg motioned me over to him. He squeezed his own thin body over so that there was space on the floor beside him. He made a show of wiping the floor with his hand, but the grime there seemed permanent, a layer of grey hiding the mottled green and brown of the marble underneath.

'What colour was the snake?' the man whispered when we had sat down beside him. My mother looked at him drowsily but didn't answer.

'Green,' I said. A murmur passed through the room.

'Green is good,' the man said. 'Maybe you'll have a good harvest.'

He helped me to loosen my mother's tourniquet while I kept time in my head. The swelling was spreading up her calf now, and when we tied the tourniquet again it sank into her flesh like a string into a sausage.

'You'll take care of me, eh Vittorio?' my mother said, stretching her lips into a sleepy smile; but her voice sounded dreamy and far-off.

'The poison is spreading,' the man whispered to me over my mother's outstretched legs, speaking as if my mother couldn't hear him. He put a finger to his head and screwed it back and forth. 'It starts to affect the brain.'

He spoke to me with the candour one would show to an adult, his voice low and confidential, his grizzled face leaning in close to mine.

'At least they have medicines now—in the old days, heh, *addio*! She'll be all right, once the doctor sees her. It's worse when they can't do anything for you, only say a prayer and send you home, like that one over there by the door.'

He gestured towards a man with jet black hair seated in one of the room's few chairs, his arm draped in bloody rags. The man was clutching the arm to his chest as if it were a child, rocking it gently back and forth, mumbling to himself.

'What can the doctor do for him now?' my friend said. 'The police brought him in here not an hour ago. He had a fight with his neighbour about a chicken. His neighbour came over with a shotgun, they started shouting and screaming, and, pom! the next thing you know his hand is gone, shot right off. Because of a chicken! And the boy beside him, with the patch on his eye—some of his schoolmates thought it was funny to tease him because one eye was green and one eye was brown. They said he had a devil in him. So what does he do? He takes a stick and plahck! that's the end of it. His own eye! God save us all!'

But now there was some commotion at the entrance. A young woman, led by a thin older woman in black, had come in doubled over from some pain in her stomach. As she crossed the threshold her body convulsed and a stream of bluish-green vomit shot from her mouth onto the floor, spattering onto people sitting or standing nearby. The nurse behind the reception desk looked up from the forms she was still filling in with my grandfather and Di Lucci and wrinkled her nose.

'Beatrice!' she bellowed out, mustering a surprising volume from her slender throat. 'Bring a bucket! And a mop!' And a moment later another nurse, somewhat heftier and plainer than the receptionist, her uniform stained and askew, came bustling out of a corridor to tend to the pool of vomit on the floor. The young woman's black-habited guide, meanwhile, had leaned her charge against a wall and joined my grandfather and Di Lucci at the reception desk, where she launched into a long plea in a cracked, high-pitched whine.

'I beg you, *signora*, I beg you, my daughter is dying. She's the only one left to me now, all dead—it's a curse, I tell you, the doctor must see her—'

'*Scusate, signora,*' Di Lucci interjected, 'but this man's daughter has been bitten by a snake—'

But the woman did not seem to hear him.

'*L'invidia!*' she cried out. 'A curse!' She broke into a long funereal wail that echoed through the room and made people shift uncomfortably in their places, though it seemed to liven them up, too, as if they were glad of the distraction. '*Poveretta,*' they whispered, and even the man with the bloody stump looked up for a moment from his mumbling, and shook his head sadly. My grandmother had wailed like that when *Tatone* Vittorio—my father's father, Vittorio Innocente, my namesake—had dropped stone dead in his kitchen on *la festa di San Giuseppe*, those same long shuddering groans that seemed to come from sources too deep to think about, all the misery of ages caught up in them. My grandfather had been a grim, unlikeable man, a constant rage seeming always to smoulder within him, waiting for some spark to suddenly ignite it; and though he had always been mean to my grandmother, had caged her like a frightened animal within his anger and violence, and though he had died with a fire poker raised up against her, ready to strike her, still she had wailed as if no greater humiliation could have befallen her than his death. To me my grandfather's death had seemed almost miraculous, an act of God—one moment he had been looming red-faced over my grandmother and the next he lay pale and still on the floor, his face frozen in a wide-eyed look of shock and his anger vanished suddenly from the room like smoke. His anger had always seemed to me something without limit, that could grow and grow until it somehow wrecked everything around it; and that afternoon it had burgeoned like a straw fire, when my uncle Pasquale had started to talk about my father.

'Mario was the only smart one,' my uncle had said, talking to Uncle Umberto about the crops. 'The rest of us will live like slaves the rest of our lives.'

And though my uncle had leaned back drowsily in his chair when he'd said this, nudging his plate away and folding his hands over his belly as if he didn't feel like a slave at all, and was only making a joke, my grandfather's eyes had gone suddenly bright with anger.

'Don't you have enough to eat?' he said. 'Didn't you always have enough to eat?'

And after that when my aunts and my grandmother tried to calm him it only seemed to fuel his rage, as if he felt the very force of it showed his rightness, and was determined that nothing should stand in the path of it.

'Mario this, Mario that—he can rot in America, and all of you after him! Do you think he did a good thing to go against his father? Do you think he's living like a king? I'll tell you where he's living—in a chicken coop! In a goddamned chicken coop, *per l'amore di Cristo*! Meanwhile he leaves his wife to run around like a whore!'

I had felt my mother's body go suddenly rigid beside me then. But that was when my grandmother had blurted out some reproof or exclamation and my grandfather had wheeled round on his chair to grab the poker; and a moment later his jaw dropped as if some invisible fist had slammed up hard against his chest, and he was dead. I had been glad to see him lying inert on the kitchen floor—glad at least until my grandmother had begun her wails and I'd realized that death must be a fearful thing, more fearful even than my grandfather's anger. I had never understood why this should be so: people died often, even in Valle del Sole, every month or so a funeral procession winding its way down via San Giuseppe to the cemetery, and nothing much seemed to change as a result. But now, as I sat on the cold hospital floor watching the woman in black plead with the receptionist, I felt suddenly as if I'd been hit by the same hard fist that had killed my grandfather, all the wind knocked out of me, for the thought had appeared in my head, surfacing there like a bubble in a pool, that even important people like my mother could die; and when I wheeled round to look at her I was certain that was what had happened, for her eyes were closed and her jaw had drooped open just as my grandfather's had at the moment of his death.

'*E' morta!*' I cried out. 'My mother's dead!'

Now all attention turned away from the woman in black and focused again on my mother. Di Lucci came pushing through the crowd that was forming around us.

'Stand back!' he shouted. 'Stand back! *Gesù Crist' e Maria!*' When he reached us he bent forward and slapped my mother hard across the cheek; but though her head jerked to one side her jaw did not close and her eyes did not open. Finally my grandfather came up behind Di Lucci and crouched with a grimace to take hold of my mother's wrist. The onlookers around us craned their necks for a better view, the room grown suddenly deathly silent. But finally my grandfather said: 'She's gone into shock. Everyone get back and let her have some air.' The crowd held its place for a moment, necks still craning forward; but finally, under my grandfather's urging, people slowly moved away, muttering and sighing their relief and mumbling benedictions.

Footsteps echoed now down the nearby corridor, and all heads turned again to witness the entrance of the doctor. From where I sat he seemed to stretch up almost to the ceiling, a tall, thin man with sharp features, black hair slicked neatly back, not a strand out of place. He had on a long white coat, which was spotless, and his shoes had been polished so brightly they showed a reflection. He looked out at the waiting room from behind small, wire-framed spectacles, then turned to the receptionist.

'Who's next?' he said, in a burnished Italian. But the man with the bandaged leg said, 'Take *la signora*,' and others in the room murmured their agreement.

'She's been bitten by a snake,' Di Lucci added,

assuming again a voice of authority. 'She's in shock.'

The doctor looked down at my mother and frowned.

'Very well,' he said, then called out down the corridor, 'Beatrice! Bring in a stretcher!'

Beatrice came hurrying down the corridor again. 'They're all being used, doctor,' she said.

'What about that one?' The doctor gestured towards a stretcher just visible, from where I was sitting, at the corridor's end. But the stretcher was occupied—a sheet draped over it formed the contours of nose, belly, knees, toes.

'Someone put him on the ground,' the doctor said. 'He won't be needing any more attention.'

There was some nervous shuffling in the room but no one moved forward to lift the body off the stretcher. Finally the man with the bandaged leg raised himself up and limped down the corridor.

'Well,' he called back, 'someone give me a hand.'

'Go help him,' my grandfather said to Di Lucci.

'*Ma scusate*,' Di Lucci said, 'that's a dead man!'

'If he's dead then he won't complain,' my grandfather said.

Grunting and cursing Di Lucci lifted one end of the body off the stretcher while the man with the bandaged leg lifted the other. It sagged for a moment as it came off the stretcher but then straightened again as the two men eased it onto the floor, where it sat wedged up against one wall like a plank. Di Lucci strained forward to bat with the tip of his fingers at a ripple that had formed in the sheet and left a pale hand exposed.

'*Dai*, Andò!' my grandfather said. 'Leave it!'

My mother sagged too when they lifted her, like a sack of grain, and Di Lucci, who had her feet, tried to prop them under one arm so he could reach a free hand under her backside; but when he thrust his hand out it slipped up inside her dress instead of beneath it, and red-faced he pulled it quickly away again.

'You might as well take advantage now,' the doctor said, smiling strangely, as if my mother wasn't sick at all, but only asleep. 'She won't let you get away with that later.'

When my mother was settled on the stretcher, Beatrice covered her with a blanket and wheeled her away. The doctor gave a last cursory glance at the waiting room and then followed Beatrice at a distance, the echo of his heels against the marble floor fading with him down the dim corridor.

~~~

IV

My mother survived her snake bite. Di Lucci took my
grandfather and me in to the hospital to see her the next
day; she had been placed in a large second-floor ward
containing about thirty beds, all of them filled with thin,
sickly women whose murmurs and quiet moans filled the
room like a wind. My mother, propped up against a
pillow, stood out like a flower in a bleak landscape, her
colour returned and her hair flowing long and sleek around
her shoulders.

'So you leave me to sleep with all these old women,'
she said, pulling me up beside her, 'while you run around
like a devil. Have you been studying your books?'

'When are you coming home?'

'If it were up to me I'd come home right now. They
make their tomato sauce here with water and old blood.
They take the blood out of your arm in the morning and in
the afternoon they feed it back to you in your food.'

Flanking my mother's bed on either side were two
old women with grey, wrinkled skin. One was lost in
prayers, her hand fingering the beads of a rosary; the other
lay with eyes closed and mouth half-open, a plastic tube
feeding into her arm from a glass bottle suspended near her

bed.

'Why does that woman have that thing in her arm?' I whispered.

'Because she's dying,' my mother said. 'Everyone in here is dying except me.'

That afternoon, while herding the sheep back into the stable after their grazing, I found a pair of tinted glasses that someone had dropped in the straw. When I had brought them up to my mother's room I bent their thin wire arms tightly around my ears and stared in my mother's wall mirror at the strange figure I cut. I looked like a small soldier: it was usually the soldiers, home on furlough from their army service, who wore tinted glasses, sometimes ones with a mirrored surface so you could see yourself reflected small and distorted in the lenses.

I had found another pair of tinted glasses about a year before, when my mother had taken me down to the river. It had been a spring day just after a rain, the slopes covered with a thick carpet of green and the air so clear that the world seemed encased in glass, trees and rocks and circling sparrows cut against a background of sky and slope like essences of themselves, so finely did the air etch them out. At the river, which was swollen from the rains, we waded for a while along the shore, the hem of my mother's skirt catching the water and clinging to her thighs, translucent; then we crossed on a bridge of large rocks to the other side, where my mother led me down a path wedged between the river and the wall of a cliff. Soon we came to a large opening that receded into darkness in the cliff wall, its mouth so evenly formed it might have been dug by human hands; a small stream flowed out of the darkness in the direction of the river, as if it had burrowed itself out of the mountain like a worm.

'It's a hot spring,' my mother said. 'Warm water coming up out of the ground. I used to come here when I was a girl.'

'How does the water get hot?'

'I don't know. Maybe the devil himself heats it up.'

Inside the air was stale and strange. A sandy ledge opened onto a large pool of water, the water bubbling in the centre as if boiling; but when I dipped my hand into it, it was only pleasantly warm, like the water my mother heated for my bath in winter. At the cave's back, wrapped in shadows, toothy shapes stretched down from the ceiling and up from the floor, some joining to form silvery pillars. My mother and I bathed together in the pool, my mother letting her dress fall casually to the cave floor and standing above me for a moment utterly naked, smooth and sleek, as if she had just peeled back an old layer of skin, before climbing into the water beside me.

My mother told me that no one knew of the cave except her; but when we were dressing I found the glasses, wedged between a rock and the cave wall, one lens in them broken.

'Can I keep them?' I said.

But my mother pulled them quickly away from me.

'Can't you see that they're broken? Anyway they're too big for you. And they're not good for your eyes.' And on the way home, she had tossed the glasses into the river.

The glasses I had found now were still intact, and showed a world, when I stared out through them from my mother's balcony, that was tinted a heady bluish-green; but instead of thinking to wear them in the village or to show them to my friend Fabrizio I hid them under the mattress like dangerous things, and in the morning I found that the lenses had shattered against the bed springs, shards of tinted glass littering the floor under the bed. I collected up the fragments in a handkerchief and took them along with the frame out to the pasture when I went to tend the sheep. Then, closing my eyes, I walked five hundred dizzying steps in a jagged line, knelt, eyes still closed, and bit blindly into the dirt with my fingers until I had dug what seemed to be a sufficiently large hole. I buried the remains of the glasses inside it, then walked another five hundred random, jagged paces, so that when I opened my eyes, finally, I could not say for certain where I had buried the glasses; that way, I felt sure, no one would ever discover them.

My mother remained in the hospital three days. When Di Lucci and my grandfather brought her home, there was a mattress strapped to the roof of Di Lucci's Cinquecento. From the bench in front of my grandfather's house I saw the small Fiat come barrelling down from the main road in a cloud of dust, the object on its roof tilting precariously to one side, straining against the ropes that had been used to secure it.

'*Il signor* Vittorio Innocente,' my mother said, coming to sit beside me after the car had lurched to a stop. There was no sign now of the trial she'd been through, though she looked more severe than usual, her hair uncharacteristically tied back in a bun. 'Pope Innocente, head of the Vatican and the Roman Catholic Church. *Come va?* Has the pope been studying his mathematics?'

'I don't want to be the pope anymore,' I said. 'I want to be Jesus Christ.'

My mother laughed.

'It's too late for that. When the angel came your mother was already in bed with St. Joseph.'

'That's how you speak to your son,' Di Lucci said, struggling to pull the mattress off his roof. But his tone was more than usually sententious, lacked the defensiveness it usually betrayed when he spoke to my mother. And my mother replied with more than the usual irritation: 'We know what you teach *your* children. How to cheat a peasant over 50 grams of salt.'

My grandfather, coming around the back of the car stooped over his cane, sat down beside me with a grunt and spat into the street, the spit glinting in the sun like tinted glass. He stared off towards the high road.

'Andò, see if you can get someone to give us a hand to bring the bed in.'

'*Mamma,*' I whispered, 'who is the bed for?'

My mother shrugged.

'Ask your grandfather. He bought it.'

'It's for you,' my grandfather said, his voice taut and dry. 'Next month you'll be seven. That's no age to be sleeping with your mother.'

A factory-made mattress was a rarity in Valle del Sole. Commonly mattresses were made at home, of burlap-covered straw; and even the wool mattress my mother and I slept on was home-made, stuffed full of shearings years before, my mother had told me, as a nuptial bed for her and my father. By village standards, though, we were well off—we had my father's remittances and my grandfather's pension and rents, and only the three of us to support; and it was a measure of our wealth now that my grandfather had bought me a mattress in Rocca Secca rather than having one made up in the village.

But I wanted nothing to do with this new bed; and all day long, while my mother prepared space for it in the dusty cobwebbed room next to hers that had sat unused till then, I brooded over the meaning of these changes being forced on me.

'If your father was home he wouldn't let you sleep with your mother,' Fabrizio had told me on one of our cigarette romps on the mountain. 'He'd want to do the thing to make babies. Like the goats.' And he'd made a circle with the thumb and index finger of one hand and passed a finger from the other hand through it, back and forth.

I decided finally it had been my father now who'd made me move out of my mother's bed, as if in some strange way he was able to control my life and see into it from whatever world he lived in across the sea, the way God could see into my thoughts. It did not surprise me that he had that power, because in my mind my father was like a phantom, some dim ghost or presence who could sometimes harden into the mute solid substance of a human form and then suddenly disperse again, spread out magically until he was invisible and omnipresent. My mother told me once how she had met him, at *la festa di San Giuseppe* in Castilucci—he'd been on furlough from his army service, dressed in his khakis and soldier's cap, and all the young women had been trying to catch his eye.

'But because I wasn't paying any attention to him, I was the first one he asked to dance. And there we were, dancing *la tarantella*, him turning me around like a devil and sweating like a pig, when I heard a zzzzzup, and your father turned as red as a tomato. He had split his pants, right down the middle.'

But whenever I tried to conjure up that image of my father, dancing *la tarantella* in his soldier's uniform and cap, it would shimmer in my mind the way objects did in the summer heat, refusing to take form; and because my mother told me little else about him, and we had no pictures of him in the house, I sometimes imagined that he had no face at all, merely a shadowy blank that hid him from the world like a veil.

The only solid link we had to my father now was the letters that came from him every month or so; but these my mother did not read to me, and when once I had retrieved one of them from the fireplace, where my mother had thrown it, and taken it out to the pasture, I'd been unable to make out anything in my father's erratic script. For a while I'd been able to gather scraps of information from the visits we made to his family in Castilucci; but we had not seen them now since my grandfather's death. At the funeral my aunt Teresa, my father's youngest sister, had winked at me from across the church aisle, and afterwards Uncle Pasquale had come forward cap in hand and said something to my mother that had made her smile; but my father's other siblings had turned away from us, straight-backed and cold, and we had gone back to Valle del Sole without staying for the burial.

Sometimes, though, an image of my father would surface from my memory, dredged up like the fragment of a dream, an image of a handsome, stocky man sitting at a table, his short black hair slicked back, and his face, clearly visible, strong-featured and hard, contorted in anger. We must have been living then at my grandparents' house in Castilucci, because I had an image of them too, sitting sullen and stoop-shouldered before a fire that was dying out, the room growing dark around them. I saw my father pick up something from the table, a dish or a bowl, and hurl it towards where my mother sat across from him, wrapped in shadows, saw my grandparents rise up suddenly from their chairs, saw my mother recoil, her lips forming into a scream or soundless horror as the object shattered against her cheek. The memory was so dim and insubstantial that I could not say if it had actually happened, or if the man I saw in it was really my father or merely a man I had imagined as him; but on one cheek, barely visible, my mother bore a tiny scar, a faint lightening of skin in the shape of a small disjointed cross.

My new mattress had replaced an old straw one, a remnant of my mother's childhood, bug-infested and smelling of mould, on a crooked wooden frame that held up planks of splintered wood for support in lieu of springs; but the frame was too big for the mattress and stuck out a foot on either side of it, making my sheets and blankets seem to stick out like wings. Apart from the bed the room held only a wicker chair I could drape my clothes over and a night table to set a candle or lamp on. Spider webs my mother had missed in her cleaning stretched silver and taut in the upper corners. No one had used this room in years, perhaps since the house had been built fifty years or so before, with money my great-grandfather had sent back from America—my grandfather's family had never grown large enough to fill it, my grandmother having lost her first two children to sickness before losing her own life giving birth to her third, my mother. It was a room without a history, and my first night there, lying stiff and awkward and alone in my new bed, its air of abandonment seemed to hang over me like a pall.

My mother's room, with its big metal-framed bed and tall armoire, its pictures on the wall, one of my mother in her First Communion dress, yellowed now with age, one of her and her classmates in front of the *media* school in Rocca Secca, had been warm and reassuring, rich with my mother's smells, the body smells that lingered on the bed sheets, the perfume my mother sometimes dabbed on her wrists and neck on Sundays or when she went to market, and rich with the memory of the years I had slept there with her, the hundred times I had felt her slip into bed beside me as I lay half-asleep.

But there were ghosts in my mother's room, too—during the war, two German soldiers had once spent the night there. My grandfather had shown me the chip in the bedroom wall where one of them had fired his rifle at a spider.

'You could hear the shot from here to Capracotta,' he said. 'But when I came up to see what had happened the two of them were rolling on the bed laughing like madmen. "I've just killed a spider!" one of them said, as if he'd just done the greatest thing in the world. After that, I made your mother lock herself in the stable.' Though later my mother had told me she'd had a nice walk with the soldiers in the pasture, when they'd come down behind the stable to pee.

Lying in bed at night in my mother's room, I had sometimes seen the ghosts of the soldiers through the gauze curtains of the balcony doors, cigarettes dangling from their lips, heard the wind nudging the muzzles of their rifles against the balcony rails, metal against metal. Now, shifting uncomfortably in my strange bed, trying to avoid my unlucky left side, I heard my mother's sandals slap on the stairs, heard her door open and close, the springs of her bed creak; and as I drifted into sleep I made out again the familiar scrape of metal against metal, fated to me this night because I had left my mother alone, prey to shadows. The wind nudged against my own balcony doors, slipped inside to sit in the chair beside my bed— '*Poveretto*,' it whispered, '*poveretto*'; but still the murmurs of the soldiers reached me as they conferred on my mother's balcony, as they slung their rifles over their shoulders finally, blue eyes glowing like flames in the darkness, and went into my mother's room.

'It's time to go,' they said, and my mother opened her eyes and gently set aside her covers. She was fully dressed: she had been waiting for them. Soundlessly she followed them out of her room and down the stairs. At the front door they stopped for a moment while one of the soldiers lit up a cigarette; then one by one they stepped through the doorway into the night. They moved in the direction of the main road, my mother walking between the soldiers in her slow, easy pace while I, borne up on my winged bed, watched from above. No one talked now, and for a long time, as they receded into the night, the only sound was that of jackboots trudging along the dry earth. Finally I could no longer make out their forms in the darkness, only the last glowing ember of a soldier's cigarette.

~~~

V

Sunday was the feast of San Camillo de Lellis, founder of the Ministers of the Sick, a local saint who some said had once cured a cripple at the top of Colle de' Santi, and in honour of whom a special collection was taken up at the village church for the hospital in Rocca Secca. *La maestra*, for whom the saints were not merely the ghosts of some mythical past but an ever-present possibility, the mundane and everyday verging always on the miraculous—'Who knows,' she'd said once, 'if there isn't a saint among us right now?'—had told us the story of San Camillo in school.

'When he was a young man he was a ruffian. He drank every night and then fought in the streets. He was as tall as a giant, but it doesn't matter how big you are because God will always make you pay for your sins.

'So one day San Camillo had to pay. He was drinking and gambling in a bar in the city with some thieves; but he didn't know that the Lord had sent the thieves to teach him a lesson. Each time he bet, he lost; and the next time he'd bet twice as much to try to get back what he'd lost the time before. But by the end of the night he had gambled away all the money he had in the world. The last thing he had was a gold crucifix his mother had given him for his First Communion, and when he lost that too, the thieves picked him up by the neck and threw him in the street.

'That night he started on foot for his parents' house in Bocchianico, hoping to beg a little money from them. But when he started to think of everything his parents had done for him, and how he had caused them only misery, and when he thought of how he had gambled away even his gold crucifix, he was filled with shame. He fell down on his knees and cried to God for mercy. And because God could see inside his heart, and could see that he had learned his lesson, He made a bright light appear in the sky, to let San Camillo know that he had been forgiven.'

Until I'd begun hearing these stories from *la maestra* I'd never thought very much about religion. My mother, certainly, had never made an issue of it—she attended church every Sunday with my grandfather and me, shared the front pew, a portion of which was always reserved for my grandfather because of his position in the town; but though I had quickly memorized all the Latin responses and spoke them out in *alta voce*, as the teacher had taught us, my mother did not even bother to move her lips.

'I say them in my head,' she told me. 'God can hear what you're thinking.'

My grandfather, at least, sang the hymns, his voice rising clearly above the rest, sounding like the wails of old women at funerals, though his face never lost its crusty composure. But towards the religion itself he was skeptical.

'My grandfather used to read the Bible,' he'd said, 'and it drove him crazy. Before he died he used to see angels coming down on the clouds to get him. All those old stories.'

But the teacher's tales of the saints worked on me like a potion. The teacher had me figured wrong—she thought I was a godless boy with a devil in me, because of the cigarettes and my truancy. But if the devil had claimed a hold on my soul, and I was sure he had, he had done so despite my best intentions; for even my truancy was born out of my battle with him, of a hard choice between the lesser of evils.

'You should tell the priest,' *la maestra* had told us when instructing us on sins suitable for confession, 'if you ever walk around in your underwear or naked in front of other people.'

And thereafter, whenever I passed *la maestra* on my way into school—she stood in the schoolhouse doorway each morning to welcome us into class, her face registering, as each of us passed before her, what place we held in her affections, smiles for the good children, stern frowns for the bad—I had a sudden vision of her standing *tutta nuda*, thick arms crossed against massive pink breasts, and a dark mound pulsing between her legs like a heart. This vision, which forced itself all the more surely into my head the more I tried to suppress it, filled me with excitement and horror, and I paid for it every week with ten Hail Marys, whispered surreptitiously as I sat beside my mother at Sunday mass. And whenever Fabrizio had filched a few cigarettes from his father and stood waiting to head me off before I got to the schoolhouse, I'd sneak off with him to the top of Colle di Papa, to be spared that day another vision of *la maestra*'s awful nakedness.

Valle del Sole's church, with its high stucco walls, bell tower, and spire, sat overlooking the village from the embankment that rose up behind Di Lucci's bar, the shadow of its tower inching daily across the square with the movement of the sun like the large slow hand of a clock. On the feast of San Camillo, my mother and my grandfather and I walked up to church together, circling as we always did up the path that cut in behind Di Lucci's from the square instead of taking the stairs, because of my grandfather's legs. Inside the church people nodded to my grandfather the way they usually did; but though the church filled to capacity before the service started, a few people even standing back in the porch, a long stretch of pew remained empty beside my mother. The priest, Father Nicola— *Zappa-la-vigna*, he was known as, hoer-of-the-vineyard, because that was what they'd called his grandfather— preached a sermon about San Camillo and about how we had to help the sick. Somehow from San Camillo he led into a story about a king and a man named Daniel, the only one who could read what God had written on the wall, and I couldn't understand what he meant; though the story made me think of my father, and the strange way he wrote in the letters he sent to my mother. Finally, as if to take full advantage of the large audience the feast day had brought in, he closed with a warning about the villagers' superstitions, which he said he would not name but which he assured us came from the devil. This last theme was by no means an uncommon one with Father Nick, and he never lost a chance to bring it up; but today as he spoke he seemed to cast a significant glance at my mother, as if pregnant with some secret meaning he wished to share with her.

Outside, though, my mother said: 'He was sweating like a pig today—and we like idiots still give him money for his wine and sausage, and eat stones all week. I'd like to see how much of what he took in today ever gets to the sick.'

My mother called Father Nick 'our fatted calf'— since he'd taken over the parish, she said, the church had gone to ruin, because all the money he collected went into his own pocket. Other people made fun of him too, behind his back; but if they saw him in the street they would still bow respectfully towards him and speak to him shyly, with their eyes averted downwards. At school we feared him because he would come to test us on our catechism, administering three thwacks to the buttocks with a short paddle for every incorrect answer, one for the Father, one for the Son, one for the Holy Ghost. Since the school sat just behind the church, only five paces from the back door of the rectory, Father Nick had only to slip on his shoes and retrieve his paddle from whatever dark place he kept it hidden whenever the whim took him to test us; and then suddenly he'd appear unannounced in the school doorway, like a dark angel, his black robes flowing to the floor, his collar tightly buttoned around his thick neck, and his paddle held discreetly behind his back. Immediately then all whispering, hair-pulling, note-passing, and paper-throwing would cease (*la maestra* was by no means as strict a disciplinarian as Father Nick) and the air would resound briefly with the scrape of chair legs against concrete; and finally, benches and chairs aligned in perfect columns, students standing beside them, evenly spaced, eyes forward, a burnished silence would descend on the room and a thin sour smile would stretch across Father Nicola's fat sour face.

'*Buongiorno, ragazzi.*'

'*Buon-gior-no, Don Ni-co-la.*'

When we had resumed our seats, Father Nick would circulate around the room and look into our eyes for signs of sin. When he'd chosen a victim, always a boy, he'd pass his desk and then slowly turn and call his name, so that he was always standing behind you, out of sight, when you stood to answer a question.

'Antonio Girasole, *alzati, per favore.*'

Antonio would rise and face forward, the priest standing only inches behind him, close enough for Antonio to feel his breath against his neck.

'Tell me, Antonio, *quante persone ci sono in Dio?*'

Always an easy question to begin.

'Three persons, Don Nicola.'

'*Tre persone, giusto.* And what are they called, these three persons?'

'*Il Padre, il Figlio, e lo Spirito Santo.*'

'*Bene, Antonio, molto bene.* You are truly a theologian, a Jesuit even.'

A titter would arise from the other students; Father Nick liked to play with his victims before going in for the kill, like a boy tearing the wings off flies.

'And now tell me, Antonio: how can it be that these three persons are one?'

A dead silence, broken finally by a shuffling of feet, a nervous cough; and then from Antonio a small 'I don't know, sir,' and Father Nick would have his first victim.

Father Nick never failed to crucify a scapegoat or two on his visits, allowing them to bear the burden of our collective guilt—for who among us could have answered those questions of his? But afterwards, our dues paid, he'd tell us stories about his days in the seminary; and somehow these stories would make me forget his paddle, so that it was always a shock when he next loomed up again in the school doorway, as if my mind could not understand how the Father Nick with the paddle and the Father Nick who told stories were one and the same person.

'I had a friend in the seminary named Dompietro,' he told us once, 'who I knew from Rocca Secca. When they gave us beds they put Dompietro in the dormitory across from mine. So on the first morning in the seminary I went to call Dompietro to come with me to breakfast—but when I came to where he slept I found him lying on the ground with his head under his bed.

'"Dompietro," I said, "what are you doing under your bed?"

'"I'm looking for my shoe," he said.

'After a few minutes he pulled himself out from under the bed and held up his shoe.

'"*Eccola!*" he said, with a big smile on his face, as if he was the happiest man in the world. Then he knelt down beside his bed, put his hands together, closed his eyes, and whispered a little prayer.

'What a strange fellow this Dompietro is, I thought

to myself. He's thanking God because he found his shoe!

'The next morning when I went to call Dompietro it was the same story all over again. There was Dompietro lying on the ground with his head under his bed.

'"Dompietro," I said, "what are you doing under your bed?"

'"I'm looking for my shoe," he said.

'And once again when he found the shoe he whispered a little prayer to the Lord.

'This went on every day for over a week—first the shoe, then the prayer. I was beginning to think that maybe Dompietro was a little crazy. But in everything else he did he seemed very wise—it was only this one thing with the shoe I couldn't understand. So finally I said to him one morning,

'"Dompietro, why is it that every day you have to look for your shoe under the bed? Don't you think the Lord would be much happier if you just put your shoes *beside* your bed, like everybody else, so you wouldn't have to bother him every morning about finding it?"

'"But it's not for my shoe that I speak to the Lord every morning," Dompietro said. "Every night I make sure I throw my shoe under the bed so that in the morning I have to get down on my knees to look for it. And once I'm on my knees I remember to thank the Lord for everything he has given me."'

My mother, though, did not think very much of Father Nick's stories.

'What are you doing under the bed?' she said, when I tried to follow Dompietro's example; but when I told her about Father Nick's story she laughed.

'What a thing! Don't believe those stories, silly, who knows where he takes them from.'

But I still couldn't keep myself from liking Father Nick's stories, though I guarded them from my mother now like secrets.

On Sundays Zia Lucia and her daughter Marta usually joined us for dinner; but when they came by on the feast of San Camillo our kitchen seemed oddly strained and tense. My mother burnt herself on the cooking pot while pulling the sauce from the fireplace, spilling some of the sauce onto the flagstones.

'*Stupida*,' my grandfather said sharply, 'can't you be more careful?'

Only my aunt Lucia seemed unchanged, in her almost vegetal calmness, sitting large and matronly in her usual place by the fireplace, wrapped in her usual thick skirts and apron and shawl despite the heat, her hair tied back in a kerchief. Before we gathered around the table to eat she called me to her and pulled a five *lire* coin from the pocket of her apron with a blue-veined hand.

'Something to spend on your girlfriends,' she said, the ghost of a smile on her lips. The skin of her palm was glossy with age, almost translucent.

But Marta seemed especially canny today, in her dark silence, as if some usually dormant receptor in her had been aroused, the way some people's limbs ached before a storm. Marta had always seemed ageless to me— she might have been fifteen or fifty, her large dark eyes wary and child-like but the skin around them wrinkled with age; and even in the village she was treated with a mixture of condescension and respect, as if she were both simple and yet possessed of mystical powers, a witch. Years of hiding her strangeness, perhaps, had taught her how to be invisible, for she moved through a room like a shadow, and when she sat it was as still as a stone, only her eyes moving, darting in their sockets as nervously as a bird's; but today I was always aware of her presence, and I felt suddenly as if I had crawled up inside her eyes, from where the world looked oddly warped and unstable, like something seen through a piece of curved glass.

I expected that other visitors would come in the

afternoon, to welcome my mother home after her stay in the hospital or at least to talk with my grandfather about some problem in the village, as usually happened on Sundays; but after Zia Lucia and Marta had gone my grandfather went up to Di Lucci's, and all afternoon the house remained quiet, my mother knitting in silence in a corner of the kitchen.

It was not till the next day that two visitors stopped by, finally, while my mother and I were making bread—Maria Maiale and Giuseppina Dagnello, childhood friends of my mother's, and distantly related to us, as was half the village, by blood. They appeared in our narrow doorway coming back from the fountain, laundry tubs perched on their hips, their knuckles chafed from scrubbing.

'Like dogs, that's how we live,' Maria said from the doorway, 'wash the clothes, haul the water, make the bread, feed the goats, *per l'amore di Crist'* let me rest my limbs for a minute.'

And so saying she moved into the stone coolness of the kitchen and set her tub on the floor, then dragged a chair away from the table half-way to the door and straddled it backwards, the way young men did at Di Lucci's bar. She rested her thick arms on the chair's back and extended her legs before her, her bulging veins leading like purple highways to the high lands of her hips. Her flesh, its tremors receding, came to uneasy rest, her breasts and belly pressing against the chair back like a cliff wall.

Giuseppina kept her place by the door, etched out there by the morning sunlight, her tub still perched on her hip.

'I don't think I can stay,' she said; but she did, just where she was.

Mothers in Valle del Sole—and these were mothers, as the clothes in their washtubs showed, the bleached diapers, the tiny knickers, the dollish socks—formed a class: ruddy, swollen hands, thick skirts of home-spun wool, hair short and tucked under a kerchief, round bellies protected with aprons of burlap or grey linen, like sacks of wheat. They moved with a slow, elephantine gait, arms akimbo, all the movement coming from the hips, a habit developed from carrying water-filled jugs on their heads, the bottom half of the body adjusting to all the undulations of the road while the top remained regal, exquisitely poised. They spoke the most flattened form of the local dialect, because unlike the men—who at the least would have improved their Italian during their army service, and who travelled more often to other districts—they were far from any edifying influence, whatever proper Italian they might have learned in their five years of schooling in Valle del Sole long forgotten (though my own mother had got as far as *la terza media* in Rocca Secca, and I'd sometimes heard her talking with merchants in an Italian more rounded and precise than *la maestra's*). Maria and Giuseppina had both married local farmers and borne several children, had long ago completed the rite of passage from the small freedoms of adolescence to the daily toils of peasant motherhood.

Maria was talking peasantries, gesticulating widely; when her chair let out a creak of protest she lifted a foot onto the crossbar to silence it, so that from where I stood against my mother, pouring water for her into the dough, I caught a sudden glimpse of the marbled fat of Maria's inner thigh. Maria was using metaphors I couldn't understand—something about Antonella, Alfreddo Catalone's daughter, down in the pasture with Antonio Girasole; something else about a priest in Tornamonde breaking a commandment, Maria didn't say which one. But here Giuseppina broke in.

'You're always making fun of the priests,' she said, her voice high and thin, like a mountain wind whistling around a cliff. 'It's not right.' In Giuseppina it was still possible to make out the curves of breasts, belly, hips; but it seemed only her clothes held her together, her flesh ready at any moment to burst its restraints and revert to formlessness. Her legs, though, tapered strangely to thinness.

'Why should you defend the priests?' my mother said, stretching out her dough and working her palms and knuckles into it. 'They're no better than the rest of us.' She wore a thin black sweater, its sleeves pushed up above her elbows, that caught her curves as she worked, now the roundness of her breasts as she reached up to brush a strand of hair away from her eyes with the back of her hand, now the feline curve of her back as she arched over the rolling board.

'You're too proud,' Giuseppina said, shifting her weight from peg-leg to peg-leg, like a sheep on rocky ground. 'Even when you were young. When's the last time you went to confession?'

'What does confession have to do with it?'

'Cristina doesn't need the priests,' Maria said, her voice wheezing, as if she was about to break into laughter. Despite the day's coolness, a line of sweat had collected on the dark down above her lip. 'She's going to get to heaven by climbing to the top of an olive tree.'

'When I climb an olive tree,' my mother said, banging the dough against the rolling board, 'it's to pick the olives.'

My mother kneaded now with increasing aggression, the dough thickening, retaining the impression of her fists. A bead of sweat formed on her brow and dropped into the dough.

'Giuseppí,' she said, 'why don't you come in and sit down? Whatever I have it's not contagious.'

But now for a moment a veil seemed to drop: Maria shifted suddenly in her chair to shoot a dark glance back to Giuseppina, and some secret message seemed to pass between them.

'I left a pot on the fire,' Giuseppina said, then mumbled her goodbyes and hurried away.

That afternoon, tending sheep on the slope beneath Colle di Papa, I overheard familiar voices coming from the fountain. My mother's name was mentioned. A steep slope led up to the road from where I was; when I got to the top, I peered across the road from the shadow of a bush to see Maria and Giuseppina filling their water jugs.

'You know what they're saying about her in Rocca Secca,' Maria said. 'As if everyone was blind. Walking around like a princess.'

'God will make his judgments,' said Giuseppina. 'It's not for nothing she was bitten by a snake.'

'What does the snake have to do with it?'

'*Beh*, you're one to talk. The way you pulled your chair away from her this morning, you might as well have been half-way across the road.'

Maria grunted.

'It's her father I feel sorry for,' she said, after a pause. 'And Vittorio. Growing up like a weed. Do you ever see him getting up at four to help with the harvest, like my Vincenzo? Never. He and his mother play like schoolchildren all day. Someone should write to the boy's father—I have a mind to do it myself.'

'Worry about your own troubles,' Giuseppina said.

The two women had begun to move back towards the town.

'*Beh*,' I heard Maria say as their voices faded, 'one way or another he'll find out. They always do.'

~~~

VI

Invidia, envy, had been the root of all the peasants' troubles according to my grandfather—the reason why brother did not get along with brother, son with father, neighbour with neighbour; why the lot of the *contadini* now was such a hard one, their plots of land scattered piecemeal across the countryside, often miles from the village; why the soil offered up yearly only the same closed fist, though the farmers cursed and cajoled it the way they did a stubborn mule.

Once, my grandfather had told me, long before the time of Christ, the land around Valle del Sole had all been flat, unpeopled jungle, rich and fertile, the trees a mile high and the river a mile wide. At last a giant named Gambelunghe had come down from the north and cleared the land with his two great oxen, then planted his crops—a thousand hectares of grain, a thousand hectares of vineyards, a thousand hectares of olives, a thousand hectares of vegetables, and a thousand hectares of pasture for his sheep. But in the winter, when Gambelunghe was asleep, wolves came and broke into his stores, then fell finally on Gambelunghe himself and tore him apart, his head dropped into the river, where it floated down to the sea, and his limbs scattered pell-mell across the countryside.

In the spring, a strange thing happened—the fingers on Gambelunghe's severed hands began to grow, those on the left growing into five women, those on the right into five men. When they were fully grown the men married the women and began to farm Gambelunghe's land, one couple for each field. But soon jealousy broke out among them: the one with the sheep was jealous of the one with the grain, for though he had meat and wool, he had no bread; the one with the grain was jealous of the one with the vineyards, for though he had bread he had no wine; and so it went. The wives, certain that the other women had an easier life, complained to their husbands, and encouraged them to steal from the other men's stores; and it was not long before fighting broke out amongst them, and the noise from their arguments—because they shouted very loudly— reached up to heaven.

'So that is what you do with your good fortune,' God said, and to punish them He caused mountains and rocks to grow up out of the ground, and made the soil tired and weak.

After that the farmers had to make a plan to avoid *invidia*. So they divided each of the thousand hectares into five equal portions and distributed the portions among themselves, making sure no one got a piece that was worse than anyone else's, that had more rocks or was too far from the river. And when they had children they divided the land again, a piece of vineyard here, a piece of pasture there, making sure everything was fair. Over the years the land became more and more divided—that was why a farmer might have a hectare of land on the slopes of Colle di Papa, another on the far side of Belmonte, a third all the way down by the Valley of the Pigs. It might take him a whole day of travelling just to visit all his pieces of land; and often, to save on walking, he'd have to spend the night out in the open, cooking up a little cornmeal over an open fire and sleeping in the scanty shelter of a lean-to.

Even in good years in Valle del Sole, the farmers

always complained of the meagreness of the harvest, afraid of calling *invidia* upon themselves by boasting; and mothers did not like to tell how many children they had borne, lest fate then take one away from them. It was not simply the envy of one person towards another that the villagers feared; it was the tremendous forces which envy stirred up, forces age-old and sacred, ones that found their incarnation in the evil eye. No less a man than Mussolini had feared the eye, it was said; and even the Pope himself had once banished a priest from the Vatican for possessing it. The eye was the locus of all the powers which could not be explained under the usual religion, the religion of the churches; and despite its name it stood outside the normal categories of good and evil, subsumed them, striking both the righteous and the depraved. It was drawn towards you merely by a certain lack of vigilance, a small flouting of fate, a crack in the door it might slither through, fangs bared, to catch you by surprise; and its fickleness made it deadly and all-powerful, like fate itself, a force which knew no masters, neither God nor the devil.

The villagers avoided anyone or anything that had been touched by the eye, as if there was a peril that the affliction might spread by contagion. When Girolamo Dagnello's best wheat field was burnt by lightning one fall, he let the field go fallow the next year, sprinkling it with a potion he bought from *la strega di Belmonte*; and when Fiorina Girasole gave birth to twins, both boys, and both dead within a week, the townspeople for a long time avoided her doorway when they passed, until finally the rumour spread that Fiorina, too, had been up to Belmonte. Belmonte, just off the high road on the way to Rocca Secca, had been destroyed by the Germans in the second war, and out of superstition the residents had refused to rebuild there, fleeing to Rome, to Argentina, to America, the toppled roofs and walls of the buildings of the town overgrown now with moss and weeds and wildflowers and overrun with lizards; and its sole inhabitant now was *la strega*, who wandered the countryside in summer and then holed up in one of Belmonte's ruined buildings in the fall and winter. Once, playing in the ruins there, I had caught a glimpse of her through the hollow of a window, an ancient woman with tough, darkened skin and long grey hair that hung in matted clumps down her back, though a grimace or grin she had flashed me before I had run had revealed two rows of brilliant white teeth.

At our own house now, no one stopped by anymore to speak to my grandfather, to ask his help in settling some dispute or have a word with him about village politics; and if the villagers passed my mother sitting in front of the house they did not look at her when they mumbled their greetings, and quickly moved towards the centre of the street. My mother began more and more to keep inside, spending her days knitting beside the fireplace, or sometimes simply shut up in her room; and she and my grandfather hardly spoke now, sometimes passing a whole meal together in heavy, awkward silence.

But one afternoon, my mother downstairs knitting while I lay upstairs studying my books, I heard footsteps echoing quickly along the street and then stopping abruptly in front of our house.

'Are you alone?' The voice was hardly louder than a whisper; but I recognized at once Giuseppina Dagnello's thin whine.

'What is it?' My mother's voice had taken on a hard edge in the past few days.

'Where's your father?'

'He's up at Di Lucci's. Where he always is.'

'And Vittorio?'

'What's the big secret, Giuseppí? What are you so nervous about? Come in and sit down and say what you have to say.'

'You know what I have to say,' Giuseppina started,

and I heard the kitchen door close behind her. 'How can you sit there sewing your socks?'

'They have holes in them.'

I crept out of my room to crouch at the head of the stairs. I could make out the shadows of my mother and Giuseppina etched against the kitchen floor by sunlight from the far window, my mother's seated in its chair, its hands still moving with its sewing, Giuseppina's stretching taller beside it at a distance.

'Cristina,' Giuseppina started again, 'you and I were like sisters when we were small. You know I wouldn't wish you any harm. But other people aren't so kind, they like to see a person destroyed. You can't afford to walk around like a princess. It turns people against you.'

'So what should I do? Should I lock myself in the stable, just to make other people happy?'

'You know what I'm talking about, Cristí. You have to make a gesture. You should make a confession. You should go and speak with Father Nicola—'

'Please, Giuseppina, you know I don't have any use for him.'

A brief silence; Giuseppina's shadow edged closer to my mother's.

'Look, Cristí,' she went on finally, dropping her voice low, 'if you won't see the priest you should at least make a cure.'

A chair creaked as my mother's shadow shifted, the hands abruptly ceasing their movement.

'What are you talking about?'

'It worked for my cousin in Rocca Secca,' Giuseppina continued, her voice still low and eerie. 'The old woman in Belmonte told her how to do it—you take a chicken or a goat and drain out the blood, then cut out the heart to put in your soup later, to give you strength. You have to wash your hands in the blood and then pour it into the ground and say three times, "This is my blood, which comes out of me like a river to the sea." Then in the same place where you poured the blood you make a fire for the offering—'

But my mother burst suddenly into laughter.

'Giuseppí, you're not serious! A good God-fearing woman like you talking to me about these *stupidaggini*! I thought you had more sense than that.'

But when Giuseppina spoke again a nagging severity had returned to her voice.

'I warn you, Cristí, you'll bring a curse on everyone around you. It's only for your father that people have kept quiet till now. But with the snake everyone has started to talk. I didn't want to say it but you force me to, you think that people are fools, that they don't see the way you carry on. But I don't have to tell you the name that everyone is calling you. You have to make a gesture.'

Later, when I came down for supper, my mother said nothing of Giuseppina's visit. A deep silence had descended on the house: the very walls, the floor, the splintered table seemed to have grown strangely distant and mute, as if guarding some secret about themselves. Over my grandfather's face a film had formed, tangible as stone, which he retreated behind like a snail into its shell, staring into space as if my mother and I were not there. My mother reached out suddenly once to fill his glass while we ate; in her movement there seemed some ghost of a hidden message, struggling at once to reveal and conceal itself, and I thought for a moment she was about to speak. But she turned quickly back to her plate and we ate on in silence. Later I lay awake in bed waiting for her footsteps on the stairs, wanting to go in to her in her room; but a long time passed and she did not come, and I drifted finally into sleep.

~~~

VII

On my seventh birthday my mother and I walked hand in hand up to the high road, in the cool damp of early morning, to catch the bus into Rocca Secca. The sun was just rising over Colle di Papa, round and scarlet, sucking in dawn's darkness like God's forgiveness, the mountain slopes slowly changing from a colourless grey to rich green and gold. The wheat in our region ripened in a slow wave which started in the valleys and gradually worked its way up the slopes through the summer, like sunlight emerging from behind a cloud, and of the highest villages it was sometimes said that they harvested in September and planted in August, sowing their new crop between the still uncut stocks of the old; and though down close to the river the fields had already been ploughed brown, around Valle del Sole the harvest was only just beginning, small bent figures dotting the countryside now, felling their wheat with short quick pulls of their scythes.

The bus into Rocca Secca was actually a small battered truck, the back fixed up on three sides with splintered planks for seats and covered with a dusty canvas. The truck, owned and operated by a small, swarthy entrepreneur called Cazzingulo (a nickname meaning 'balls in your ass'—what usually happened when you rode in his truck), plied the road between Capracotta and Rocca Secca, collecting and discharging passengers en route, rolling to the rhythm of the road. Cazzingulo didn't follow a schedule you could measure on a watch—he never left his point of departure until he had a full load, full by official standards, which didn't mean he couldn't fit in another eight or nine passengers after he'd passed the police checkpoint on the edge of town—but somehow the peasants always sensed when he would be passing, as if they could feel premonitory tremors in the earth. It was only a few minutes after my mother and I reached the main road that a cloud of dust rounded the curve of a slope, and Cazzingulo's truck appeared in the middle of it.

'Oh, Cristí!' Cazzingulo knew everyone in the region by name. 'Rocca Secca! Special today, the little boy rides for half price if he sits on your lap. And you ride for free if you sit on mine.'

About a dozen passengers had already been crammed into the back, their feet resting on the handbags and produce hampers and grain sacks that filled the small corridor between the seats, their knees jammed up against their faces. But after some jostling and muttered curses and a shout up to Cazzingulo about his greed and the suffering of peasants, a patch of bare wood appeared finally on one of the benches, and my mother eased herself onto it. I wedged myself between her legs, clutching her knees and crouching unsteadily on a sack of onions; then the all clear was sounded and the truck took off with a lurch, leaving a swirl of dust in its wake.

Rocca Secca claimed to be the site of ancient Aquilonia, a Samnitic fortress town from before the time of Christ. The Samnites, a fierce mountain people, had been the first to settle our region, riding down from the north along the ridge-line of the Apennines on the great ox the gods had given them. Their imposing cities, Aquilonia, Bovianum, Cominium, carved it was said right out of the bare rock of the mountains, had been levelled by the Romans, only a few odd ruins remaining now— roadside markers of forgotten import, the mossy foundations of a temple or shrine, the curved stone seats of an amphitheatre; though these were proudly tendered by local towns and villages as evidence of their ancient past. The church at Rocca Secca, just off the main square, was built above a huge corner-stone, accessible through a crypt, that was said to have formed part of Aquilonia's walls.

Rocca Secca itself had once been a great centre, renowned for its goldsmiths and bronzeworks, its schools, its convents, and the seat of the region's aristocracy. But in recent times its fortunes had declined: the politicians in Rome, the townspeople complained, thought only about collecting taxes and passing laws that no one could under-stand, and not about building roads or rail lines; and nowadays, at any rate, people wanted to buy things made in the city by machines rather than things made by hand. For many years now the people of Rocca Secca had been moving away, to Argentina mainly; whole sections of the town stood abandoned, the houses boarded up and crum-bling.

The last vestige of the town's former grandeur sat on a lonely hill on the outskirts of town—the Giardini estate, once the seat of the most powerful family in the region, who owned half the land from Rocca Secca to Capracotta. The last of the Giardini, Alberto, had died just after the war, and was still well-remembered in the town. In the 1890s he had served as an officer during the war in Abyssinia; but after the Italian defeat he had set off on a trek across Africa, more or less lost to the world for several years. Then one day a beggar had wound his way down the main street into Rocca Secca, his clothes in tatters, his face bearded and gaunt, and had done something which had caused the townspeople to stare in curiosity: he walked up to the *tomolo* in the center of the square, a hollowed-out stone of three compartments used to measure grain for rent and taxes, and dropped his pants to his knees to touch his bared buttocks to the stone. This gesture had a long tradition in Rocca Secca: it was the way in which a man who had exhausted all his resources might publicly declare bankruptcy. But it was only when the beggar pulled a latch key from around his neck and started up towards the estate on the edge of town that the townspeople realized he was Alberto de' Giardini, returned finally home after his mysterious absence.

Giardini never explained his long absence to anyone, living the next several years as a recluse, seeing no one; though sometimes at twilight he'd appear suddenly in the town in full regalia, his medals pinned in an even row to his chest, and wander the streets like a ghost. Then, just after the first war, he began the project which was to occupy the rest of his days, remaking the grounds of his estate in the image of a primal paradise, importing tropical trees, flowers, shrubs and building a great conservatory to house them in winter, beginning next on the fauna, monkeys, gazelles, strange tropical birds, until he had turned his hill into a small piece of Africa, the air at night resounding with strange jungle sounds. At his death, because he had no heirs, Giardini's estate reverted to the state, who kept it up briefly as a zoo; but there was little interest in our region for that sort of thing and the property soon fell into decay, the animals dying off, needed repairs neglected. The estate was abandoned now, the conservatory left to ruin, the lawns overgrown, the cages which had once housed the animals left to warp in the sun and rain and a great glass aviary which had been renowned once for its strange coloured birds now sprouting the limbs of trees which had been allowed to grow inside it unchecked. People in the town avoided the estate, as if a curse hung over it; and in the story of the *tomolo* and Giardini's gesture people saw now an oracle, the prediction of their own town's declining fortunes.

Compared to other towns in the area, Rocca Secca

was filled with life—mule carts and motor cars, men in suits and women in high-heeled shoes, coloured awnings over sidewalk restaurants, shop windows crowded with posters. But still a shadow seemed to loom over the town, as if all the pomp and display had been carted in only moments before your arrival, put on for your benefit, as if you had only to turn your back and the glitter would fade, the wind whistling through empty streets. In neighbouring towns Rocca Seccans had a reputation as people whose surface smiles hid a meanness of spirit. 'Ho, *signó*,' a friend from Rocca Secca would call out to you, 'have you eaten yet?' And if you had he'd say, 'That's too bad, I was just going to ask you over,' and if you hadn't, 'Then go home and eat.'

Only the market in Rocca Secca seemed real, at least honest in its transience: after all, it *had* been carted in, by peasants and traders who had hitched up their carts in the dead of night to be ready at their stalls by dawn, and by afternoon it would be faded and finished, the noise and colour gone, the stalls boarded up again until the following day. It was at the edge of the market that we disembarked on my birthday, at that hour still in full swing, the din of it, the shouts and laughter, the clatter of coins, reaching us under our canvas as Cazzingulo's truck pulled up to a stop on a small side-street. It had been many months since I had last been to the market with my mother; for a long time now she had preferred to make her trips into Rocca Secca alone. But as we threaded our way through the market street, jostling for space with goats and carts and thick-set town women come for the day's provisions, many of the traders called out to me by name, remembering me from my previous visits.

'Oh, Vittò! Look how big you've gotten! And handsome, too, like your mother.'

'It's his birthday today,' my mother told them. 'He's come to collect his gifts.' And this would be good for

five or ten *lire,* the coins collecting hard and tinny in my
pocket as we made our way through the market.

But the market seemed more than usually oppres-
sive today, the street too narrow, the crowds too thick, the
large-boned women of Rocca Secca jostling against me
without seeing me, caught up in their haggling. The
traders, after their moment of attention, would turn back
quickly to my mother, leaving me to stare up at great
pyramids of cabbages and tomatoes and onions piled
precariously atop sloping shelves. Beneath the shelves
chickens cackled wildly in wicker cages, poking their
beaks through the gaps to pick at scraps that had fallen to
the ground. Rivulets of grey water trickled between the
cracks in the cobblestones, giving off a strong sewer stench.

'*Mamma,* I want to go.' My mother was talking in
a low voice to an older man I didn't recognize. He towered
above me tall and husky, dressed oddly in Sunday clothes,
white shirt and tie, though his sleeves were rolled up over
his forearms and the upper buttons of his shirt were
undone, dark hair curling up thick and matted from his
chest.

'Here,' my mother said, turning to me, 'I'll get
Luciano to carry you piggyback. He can buy his vegetables
later. You don't open till noon, *vero?*'

'But by then all that's left here is what they feed to
the pigs,' the man said. 'My wife will break my balls if
there's as much as a bruise on an olive.' But he smiled and
gathered me up in his sinewed arms, then lifted me effort-
lessly onto his shoulders, his upper arms gripping my
calves.

'I'll bet you can see the whole world from up there,
eh Vittorio,' he said.

From above the market looked like a sea or a river,
waves of bobbing heads shored in by the sloping roofs of
corrugated tin that covered the market stalls.

'How do you know my name?'

'Oh, I know all about you,' the man said, turning to glance at my mother beside him. 'Your mother tells me everything.'

'You don't know what day it is today.'

'Of course I do. It's the feast of St. Bartholomew.'

'No it's not,' I said. 'It's my birthday.'

'*E' vero*? Why didn't you say so?'

We had reached the edge of the market. From here the street led towards the square; I could see the open brightness of it beckoning a few hundred yards on. But after walking a bit further, Luciano turned down a narrow, deserted side-street, the houses along it old and decrepit. From here the sound of the market reached us only as a distant hum, punctuated occasionally by a shout or a peal of laughter. Luciano slid his hands under my arms and lifted me onto the ground. My shoes had left two large smudges under the armpits of his shirt.

'Explain those to your wife,' my mother said. 'You shouldn't wear white if you can't keep clean.'

'You sound like a priest.'

My mother sat down on a step in front of a boarded-up doorway, drawing her knees up and wrapping her arms around them, like a young girl. Luciano sat down beside her, then dipped a hand into his pant pocket and pulled out a large silver coin.

'It's an old one *lira*,' he said, holding the coin towards me. 'From before the war, when you could still buy something with a *lira*.'

The date, printed in tiny numbers under the claw of an eagle, read 1927. Luciano pointed to a small indentation on the eagle's wing.

'I want to tell you about that mark,' he said, closing his fingers around the coin again like a magician. He motioned me up against his knee.

'I found this coin,' he said, 'in a field in Greece. During the war. It must have slipped through the pocket of one of the other soldiers, because I found it shining in the mud in somebody's footprint. Who knows what I was thinking—here we were marching against the enemy, bullets flying everywhere, and I stop to pick a one *lira* off the ground, like a schoolboy.'

Luciano glanced at my mother beside him.

'And then?' she said.

'Well, we had a hard time that day,' Luciano said, turning back to me. 'We lost the battle and many of my friends were killed. It was like a bad dream. But that night, when I was sitting in my tent, I found a little hole in my shirt pocket, like a bullet hole. Then I remembered the coin I had picked up, and when I took it out of my pocket I saw the mark on the wing. That's when I realized that the coin had saved my life—it must have stopped the bullet that had left the hole in my shirt. If I hadn't stopped to pick it up the bullet would have gone straight into my heart.'

My mother laughed.

'Is that true?' she said, tugging Luciano's hand toward her to look more closely at the coin.

'Every word of it, by Jesus, Joseph, and Mary. Ever since then I've carried this coin with me everywhere, for good luck. But now,' and he turned back to me with eyebrows raised, 'I'm going to give it to you.'

He set the coin in my palm. It weighed heavily there, not tinny like the five and ten *lire* coins I had been collecting but as thick and dense as a fifty or hundred *lire*. I rubbed the coin with my thumb, feeling its thickness and weight, the texture of its detailed surface. An intricate pattern of feathers stood out in relief on the eagle's outstretched wings.

'Look on the other side,' Luciano said. 'It even has your name on it.'

On the obverse side, in profile, was a bald-headed bust. Luciano pointed to the inscription etched around the coin's circumference, not the usual '*Repvbblica Italiana*' of newer coins but *'Vittorio Emanvele III Re e Imp.'*

It seemed strange to me that fortune could be as simple as Luciano made it out, that it could be passed along from one person to another or depend on something as slight as a hole in your pocket; but for the moment my time in the spotlight was over and I had become invisible, Luciano and my mother speaking together in low voices again.

'He came to the village?' Luciano had dropped his voice to whisper. 'Cristí, you're tempting the devil.'

'What could I do?' my mother said calmly. She stared down at her hands. 'A letter came in the morning, he came in the afternoon. How could I stop him?'

'Someone must have seen him,' Luciano said. 'I hear people are beginning to talk.'

'Let them talk.'

'I heard that someone from the German embassy had come looking for him. Did he tell you that?'

'Yes,' my mother said.

'All these years and they haven't forgotten. If it was the Italians they would have lost his file years ago. And it's not as if they won the war—if he went home now he'd be a hero, for what he'd done. Did he say where he was going?'

'What do I care where he goes? Milan, Switzerland—I haven't heard anything from him. Anyway I have my own troubles to worry about. I hope he didn't leave me a little gift—he got very excited when he saw that snake.'

'And the snake on top of everything. You know I'm not superstitious, Cristí, but a snake is a snake—'

'Don't be foolish. The snake was a stupid accident.'

Luciano shifted awkwardly on the stone step, bringing a hand up to rub the back of his neck.

'Still,' he said finally. 'The villagers. You know how they like to get hold of a scandal—for peasants like that everything is a sign. Things must be getting hard for you. What will you do if he comes back?'

My mother shrugged.

'Maybe we'll run off to America together.'

'Cristina, this is nothing to joke about.'

'Who's joking? America's a big place. No one would ever find us there.'

'Look,' Luciano said, 'I have to get my vegetables. Why don't you and Vittorio come around to the restaurant for lunch? On me. I have some good wine from last year. And a bowl of *tortellini alla bolognese* for Vittorio.'

He leaned over to kiss my mother on the cheek, then rose and put a hand on my shoulder.

'*Ciao*, Vittò,' he said, and then walking away he turned back to call out '*Auguri!*' before he rounded the corner and disappeared up the street, the echo of his footsteps quickly fading into the distant hum of the market.

~~~

VIII

Luciano's restaurant—the 'Hostaria del Cacciatore,' its name painted in red on the front window just above the small figure of a hunter with a rifle and a hunter's sack slung over his shoulder—sat just across from the main square, where Alberto de' Giardini had once bared himself to the hollowed-out *tomolo*; though the *tomolo* had recently been replaced by a stone obelisk, a memorial to the townspeople killed in the second war. After the market my mother and I had been up and down a dozen crooked streets—first into one of the shops to buy me a shirt; then into a cold dim office where my mother had filled out a form and talked in a low voice to a man behind a counter; then, strangely, into a photographer's studio, where a sleek-haired, spectacled man who reeked of perfume had taken our picture, my mother didn't say why—but it was still only late morning by the time we arrived at the restaurant, and most of the tables were empty. A single couple was seated inside, visible through the frilly curtains and plastic vines and leaves that decorated the front window, and outside only a thin old man in a suit and fedora who peered up from a newspaper to give a long narrow-eyed look at my mother as we sat down at the table next to his.

A heavy-set boy of about fifteen, dressed in black pants and white shirt, came out to serve us.

'Where's your father?' my mother said.

'He's gone out. He said I should take care of you

if you came.'

He took my mother's order and went inside, disappearing then through a door at the back of the restaurant. A moment later a large, rough-featured woman, heavy bosom straining against a black sweater, came bustling out of the same door wiping her hands on her apron. She stared hard towards our table for a moment before disappearing again.

'Do you like it here?' my mother said.

But despite the coins I'd collected in the market, the tinny fives and tens and the large one *lira*, despite the new shirt that lay wrapped in brown paper on the chair next to me, despite the photographs we'd had taken, a silent resentment had been building in me since my mother's conversation with Luciano, and I would not let go of it now until it had some issue.

'What's the matter with you?' my mother said. 'Do you have a bug in your pants?'

She reached under the table and poked me lightly in the ribs, but I pulled away from her sulkily.

'*Beh*, do what you want,' she said.

We sat silent. A bottle of wine appeared, set out and poured expertly by Luciano's son, then a bowl of *tortellini* and a plate of *trippa* in tomato sauce for my mother. We had begun to eat already when I felt the shadow of a large shape looming over us, and looked up to see the black-sweatered woman smiling down on us, her hands on her hips, a thin line of moustache overshadowing her smile. A dark wart stuck out prominently on one cheek, a few thin hairs spiralling up from it.

'*Buongiorno, signora*! And this must be your little son! How handsome he is! Are you going to tell me your name?'

She had reached down to run her fingers under my chin.

'His name is Vittorio,' my mother said, curt. 'He's

shy.'

'Isn't that sweet! And so many boys these days are little devils. *Diavoli!*'

My mother took another bite of her food.

'And your friend?' the woman said finally, her mouth remaining open around her last syllable.

My mother raised her eyebrows as if she had not understood.

'Yes, of course, he's gone out of town,' the woman said, forcing a laugh. 'A shame—do you like the way I've made up the tripe?'

'I've had worse,' my mother said.

'Yes, Luciano bought it in Tornamonde, you can't find good meat here in Rocca Secca anymore. But you should be careful how much you eat! A friend of mine ate tripe every day for a week, and she gave birth to triplets!'

My mother forced a smile. Pig tripe was what people in the region fed to grooms on their wedding nights, to help them have children.

'And did they have little tails, the children?' my mother said, still smiling.

The woman's face darkened for the briefest instant before she let out a long falsetto laugh.

'Oh, *signora*, always joking!' She laughed again, wiping her hands on her apron. 'Well, enjoy your meal, Luciano will be sorry he missed you. I'll give you a good price on the wine.'

'Eat your food,' my mother said when the woman had gone, returning to her own meal with a vengeance. My appetite, though, had died, the wet texture of the pasta in my mouth beginning to make my stomach turn. But when I set down my fork my mother looked at me in irritation.

'What's the matter with you? Oh! *Basta!*'

'It tastes like shit,' I said.

I had got it out now, spit out my resentment like something that had stuck in my throat. But an instant later my face was burning: my mother had slapped me, hard, against the cheek. A lump rose in my throat but I swallowed it, my lips sealed tight. There were a few people sitting at the tables around us now, but only the old thin man glanced over at us, peering up above the top of his newspaper for an instant before returning again to his reading; though almost at once I looked up through the restaurant window to see if the black-sweatered woman had been watching us. For some reason it was the thought of her having seen my mother's anger that made me burn more than anything now, the thought of the large false smile she would light for us then if she returned, like someone who had won an argument; and when I could not make her out anywhere I felt a great relief, as if my mother's slap had not been a punishment at all but part of some sin or crime we'd committed together, and which had gone undetected.

In silence I picked up my fork and began to eat my *tortellini*, my eyes trained now on the slowly emerging bottom of the bowl. When we had finished eating, Luciano's son came around to collect our dishes.

'How much is it?' my mother said tonelessly.

'But my father told me—'

'Never mind that,' my mother said. 'Just give me the regular price.'

~~~

IX

La festa della Madonna on the last weekend of September transformed Valle del Sole every year from a sleepy peasant village into a carnival town. Three days of festivities—music, dancing, processions, fireworks—to cap off the summer and to celebrate the harvest. People from neighbouring villages, from Rocca Secca, old residents from Rome and Naples, flocked into the village; day labourers working on distant farms took leaves of absence; migrants in the north, in Switzerland, in France, boarded crowded trains for the long journey home. Sometimes even a few *Americani* appeared, planning their return to their native village to coincide with *la festa*.

About a month before the festival, members of *lu comitato della Madonna* went around to each household in the village for *la questua*, the collection taken up to pay festival expenses, arriving in twos in their Sunday suits and summoning up their most proper Italian to make their plea. The poverty of many of the villagers sometimes made their job an uncomfortable one; but village loyalty assured that even the poorest families would reach into the pot or jug in which they kept their savings and separate out the expected number of notes with little hesitation. During the course of the year each village in the area had its own festival, in honour of its patron saint, and ancient rivalries ensured that the peasants would go hungry before they would allow their village to be outdone by one of its neighbours. *La festa della Madonna* was tied up in these rivalries in more ways than one: Valle del Sole's original patron was St. Michael, whose feast fell on the 28th of September, but once when a cholera epidemic had decimated the population of Valle del Sole but not claimed a single victim from Castilucci, the villagers, jealous that Castilucci's patron, St. Joseph, had been more powerful than their Michael, had applied to Rome for a change of saints. As their replacement they chose the Virgin, who had a long history of successful intercessions with a God who was sometimes distant and unapproachable; and though Rome had denied their request, they had finally made the change on their own authority, though they had kept the last weekend of September as their time of celebration.

These village rivalries, too, had led to a continual escalation in the lavishness of the festivities in the past few years, for though the peasants' fortunes had not improved much, *paesani* who had had good fortune overseas had begun pouring their own wealth into the festivals. This year, in Valle del Sole, rumours were being whispered of a celebration such as had never been seen before in the region, because Salvatore Mancini, who had left Valle del Sole before the war to make his fortune in America, had sent the *comitato* a sum that would have made the Pope himself suck in his breath.

But in my grandfather's house no sense of excitement had been building. Our kitchen had been strangely silent for that time of year; for though my grandfather seldom sat on the *comitato* himself, as mayor he presided over its selection in the spring and was usually kept well-informed of its activities as the festival approached and called upon to settle the committee's internal disputes, our kitchen often alive with heated debate well into the night. But this year no one had come to wrangle over the timing of the fireworks or the number of chairs that should be rented from Rocca Secca or the sum that should be paid to the band; and when the members of the *comitato* had come to our door for *la questua*, my grandfather, instead of inviting them in, as he usually did, for a glass of *amaretto*, had simply handed them the usual donation without fanfare, and they had come and gone without so much as seating themselves at our table. In fact my grandfather was seldom at home now, leaving the house early in the morning to go up to Di Lucci's and coming back only for meals, when he seldom spoke, retreating more and more each day into his grim silence. Once when I crossed town to buy some milk, I saw him sitting alone on Di Lucci's terrace, staring into space like an old man, as if he had been put there to be kept out of the way, like the ageing parents set out by their daughters or daughters-in-law on upper balconies during the day, left there to mumble to themselves in the sun and flies. Despite my grandfather's infirmities, his stooped gait, he had always seemed a man who had loomed large, who commanded respect; but now suddenly he seemed shrunken and small, as if some aura around him had faded or died.

My mother, too, had withdrawn into a shadowy silence. Since the day at the restaurant a veil seemed to have fallen between us, and for a while I had nursed this estrangement like a precious wound I could somehow turn to advantage; but the passing days brought only a growing awkwardness, as if my mother and I had suddenly become strangers, with no words now to bridge the silence between us. My mother had developed a sudden interest in our garden, staying out there sometimes from early morning till nightfall, hoeing, watering, coming in only to prepare our silent meals, smelling of dirt and sweat, her hands growing daily more calloused and rough. But though the garden, under her silent ministrations, grew daily more healthy and lush, watered carefully now and properly weeded, the lushness seemed more show than substance, the quick growth of leaves rather than the fattening of tomatoes and peppers and grapes which were already ripe or ripening by that late time in the season. The *sese di vacca*—Roman tomatoes, cow's teats, as we called them— had opened some new flowers, small throbs of yellow in the garden's green; but the fruit would have no time to ripen before the first frost.

I spent my time alone now, waiting for something to happen that would restore the normalcy of things, for the festival, for school to begin in October. At school, at least, I could see Fabrizio, who was busy now helping his father in the fields. Fabrizio was really my only regular friend in the village, though he was a year older than me and wasn't like me at all, wasn't shy and could make people laugh. He always walked with an exaggerated swagger, belly protruding, knees pointing outward, nose and chin upward, a faded brown corduroy cap which he took off only in school and church, when he stuffed it into his back pocket, worn well back on his head, with an odd sideways tilt; and he had only two pairs of knickers, one green and one blue, which underwent a bimonthly rotation, like phases of the moon, two weeks green, two weeks blue, even in winter, when he came to school with his bare calves white and goose-pimpled from the cold, though he didn't alter his swagger. His most prized possession was a jack-knife his uncle had brought him back from America, with a big blade at one end and a small one at the other; and sometimes, during our walks on the mountain, he would let me use it to whittle or to carve my name into a tree.

Fabrizio and I had been friends since the summer before I'd started school, when he'd come out one day to the pasture where I was tending sheep to show me the

welts on his back his father had given him for letting one of
his sheep fall over a bluff.

'Not bad, eh?' he'd said, lifting his shirt. 'He hit me
fifteen times with his belt. I counted in my head to keep
from crying. Then I said, "Now I'm just like Christ,"
because they hit him too, and my father started hitting me
again. If you don't cry it makes them angrier, so I started
crying to make him stop. Then my mother said, "*Basta*, Luí,
you're going to turn him into a cripple!"'

That was the day, too, that Fabrizio had taught me
to smoke, pulling two crumpled cigarettes from his shirt
pocket and guiding me through my first puffs until the
smoke began to pass down my throat with little resistance,
the world slowly starting to orbit around the rock I was
sitting on; and afterwards we'd spent an hour or so rolling
and wrestling in the grass, laughing because sheep fell off
cliffs, because fathers beat their sons, and because the
world, for all its seeming stability, was actually spinning
around at a tremendous speed, which only became appar-
ent when you'd had a smoke. After that whenever Fabrizio
saw me in the streets of Valle del Sole he'd call out 'Ho,
Vittò!' in a husky bass and pat his belly, mimicking the
bonhomie with which the men of the village often greeted
each other.

I was surprised at first that Fabrizio attached
himself to me—I had thought of him as someone who
belonged to the gangs, those coteries that seemed always to
form outside the world I lived in, as if they had secret
meetings in the night. But I had figured him wrong: in fact
he didn't belong to any gang at all, only insinuated himself
into this group or that, usually of younger kids, serving as
ringleader for a few hours but then saying to me suddenly,
in the middle of some game or exploit, 'Come on, let's go,'
and the two of us would wander out alone to lie in some
pasture or wade along the shore of the river. With older
boys he was cocky and defiant, and would get into fights,

fights he didn't win very often, since he wasn't very big; but he'd pick himself off the ground, wipe off his knickers, and then walk away as if nothing had happened, not caring finally whether he'd won or lost.

Now, though, with the harvest, Fabrizio was out in the fields from dawn to dusk. I'd been out a few times to look for him, had shown him the one *lira* coin I'd gotten from Luciano, which I carried with me always now. But Fabrizio's father, who was known in the village as Facciabrutta, Uglyface, would always find some reason to deliver a blow to the back of Fabrizio's head whenever I went around; so I stopped going around. I spent my time instead closed up in my room, pretending to look over my schoolbooks in the hope that my mother would come up to check on me. I'd watch her sometimes through my balcony doors as she hoed in the garden, her hair pulled back now in a scarf, her breasts straining against her blouse as she bent forward to pluck out some weed; but then I'd retreat again to my bed and the silence of the house would wash over me, filling my head like a scream, crowding out my private thoughts. The silence seemed to issue from every nook and cranny of the house, to dissolve furnishings and walls and leave me suspended in a pure, electric emptiness, so volatile that the crunch of my mother's hoe threatened to shatter the house to its foundations. Then at night, as I lay in the dark staring up at the cobwebs on the ceiling, I'd hear my mother's quiet sobbing mingling with the sigh of the wind like something inhuman, as if the air could no longer carry any human sounds, all of them smothered into the earth by the silence.

~~~

X

On the Saturday afternoon of *la festa*, while the church bells tolled, my grandfather and I made our way under a grey sky to the service that marked the festival's true beginning. We were dressed in our best Sunday clothes, my grandfather's war medals pinned in an even row to the breast pocket of his jacket. The streets were filled already with small crowds of men talking and joking in front of doorways and families hurrying up towards the church. Some former villagers had arrived from Rome and Naples, their Cinque- and Seicentos parked beyond the village on the path that led up to the high road.

'Oh, *lu podestà*!' one of them called out when my grandfather passed.

But then someone nearby whispered in his ear and he fell silent, and I knew he'd been told that my grandfather had resigned his position as mayor.

It had happened the night before, at the festival's official opening. The official opening had no entertainment or spectacle attached to it, but most of the villagers attended—not for the hour or so of speeches with which the various committee members opened the proceedings, but for the final tally of *la questua*, when the villagers learned whether anyone in the village had shamed them by giving an outrageously large sum, or they themselves had called envy upon their household by giving more than their neighbours. My grandfather had sat up on the festival bandstand along with the committee members, rising to speak in his turn, his voice dry as winter.

'It's not for an old cripple like me to be involved in politics,' he'd said. 'There are plenty of young men anxious to take my place. Let one of them step forward.'

The bells had stopped tolling by the time my grandfather and I arrived at the church, the last pews filled and newcomers spilling into the porch, no longer able to reach the stoup to anoint themselves; but a small path was cleared for my grandfather and me, and I was surprised to see that a few spaces had still been left open for us in the front pew. The crowd kept swelling, reaching out finally into the church square, the doors propped open and a cool wind breathing into the church like a sigh, cutting wet and fresh through a heavy must of sweat and old wood and crumbling plaster.

The church had no organ, the cue for the beginning of the service always the first quivering note of the Introit from Father Nicola as he entered from the rectory door at the back of the church and made his way to the altar. His voice announced him now, and we stood in our pews, though he came not from the rectory but from the church square, the crowd in the portico parting to let him pass. But today Father Nick, dressed simply in his usual black robe and white mantle, a small skull cap on his head, had been sent ahead merely to prepare the way; for behind him, dressed all in white, a short brocaded mantelet draped over his shoulders and a stole of white silk shimmering so richly around his neck and down the front of his vestments it seemed on the verge of bursting into colour, came Monsignor Felano from Rocca Secca, four cherub-faced altar boys flanking him and supporting a tasselled canopy of ornate purple brocade above his head. I had seen Monsignor Felano in Castilucci once, at *la festa di San Giuseppe*, but he never attended our festival, because the church in Rome had not forgiven us for our change of saints, people said; but today he had come, and in full regalia. Everyone had turned to watch his entry, and for an instant a chorus of murmurs and whispers cut beneath the trill of the Introit. There was a brief pause in the procession as the Monsignor's canopy caught on the door frame coming in from the square; but in a moment he moved on again unperturbed, up the short aisle towards the altar, his altar boys, singing in honeyed sopranos, moving in synchrony with him, their small fists wrapped tightly around the metal poles that held up the canopy. At the foot of the altar the altar boys withdrew and collapsed the canopy in a corner, and Monsignor Felano took a seat modestly in one of the chancel pews.

Father Nicola took us through the first part of the service, Monsignor Felano remaining seated in his pew, hands folded neatly on his robed lap, raising his baritone only to join in plainsong with the congregation. Father Nick preached with an unusual fluency, each word rolling off his tongue with a flourish, as if frilled with elaborate swirls and curlicues; though the Monsignor's presence at his side seemed to pull on him like an invisible thread, slowly inclining him in the direction of the chancel pews, so that a dozen times he swung suddenly in the opposite direction in compensation, preaching briefly above the heads of the congregation to the stations of the cross that hung on the far wall, until slowly he drifted back again in the direction of the Monsignor. Finally, at the homily, Monsignor Felano rose and Father Nick retreated to a chancel pew with a small bow, pulling a handkerchief from a pocket of his robe and patting discreetly at the small beads of sweat on his forehead.

Monsignor Felano loomed over the church's small

lectern like a great mountain bird, his quiet presence seeming to force itself out over the pews, the church for a moment poised in an absolute stillness. He began quietly and calmly, in a polished Italian stripped clean of dialect, hard to follow at first but taking on more and more a clarity like glass, as if the words themselves had disappeared and only their meanings remained, hanging in the air like the wind.

'Mary was a woman,' he said, his long-fingered hands folded on the lectern, 'inscribed with the grace of God. A woman for whom a virgin birth was merely the outward sign of an inner purity. But she was also a woman of flesh and blood, the wife of a simple labourer, such a woman'—and now he brought one hand up, two fingers extended, and gestured broadly across the church—'as you might see walking down the streets of this village with a child on her arm or a jug of water on her head. The gospels tell us of a woman filled with goodness and grace. But there is a story that they don't tell us. They don't tell us'—stepping away from the lectern now, coming down towards the congregation—'of the *shame* she must have endured from skeptics who did not believe in a virgin birth. They don't tell us'—tempo and volume slowly building—'of the *hardships* she and Joseph underwent to feed a family and raise it, the same hardships we all face, the hardships of the poor. They don't tell us'—and now he was beating words out singly like bullets, one hand striking the palm of the other in time—'of the mother's *pain* she must have felt when her *first born son* was spit on by the crowds and nailed to a cross like a common criminal.' Then a pause, like stormy waters grown suddenly calm, and a voice that was almost a whisper saying, 'This, too, is the story of Mary.'

As soon as the service had finished, four husky members of the *comitato* squeezed their way through the crowd at the back of the church and made their way up the aisle, bearing a wooden rack that was normally used to carry coffins from the church to the cemetery. They set the rack before the arched niche to the right of the chancel that held the Madonna, a large smiling figure in starry halo and robes of bright blue, the infant Jesus cradled in her lap. We remained in our seats while she was being set down onto the rack, Father Nick waiting patiently on the chancel steps to begin the procession, aspergillum in hand. The Monsignor had sat down again in one of the chancel pews—he would not, it seemed, be taking part in the procession, but was lending it the use of his *baldacchino* and his altar boys, who were struggling now to re-erect the canopy in the church aisle while the committee members waited to squeeze under it with their load.

The head of that year's committee, Alfreddo Mastroantonio, had come up a side aisle to greet the Monsignor. Alfreddo, an uncle of Father Nick's, was respected in the town because he didn't work, living off the rent from land he'd inherited; and though he wasn't rich, didn't own a car or a big house, he always walked around the village in a suit, and he spoke to everyone in a careful, florid Italian, because he'd been to *la scuola superiore* in Rocca Secca. He approached the Monsignor now on bended knee, bringing his lips to the back of the Monsignor's proffered hand and then loudly thanking him for his presence, so that heads in the church turned towards him. When he rose his eyes shot briefly towards my grandfather a few feet away in the front pew; he seemed about to call him to the attention of the Monsignor, his hand gesturing out in our direction, but at the last instant he checked the gesture and suddenly clasped his hands together as if closing us out, then shifted position, still speaking brightly to the Monsignor, until his back was to us.

The procession was under way now, Father Nick in front, walking solemnly towards the exit and sprinkling the aisle with his aspergillum, his voice rising up in song, and the Madonna, seated atop her litter like an ancient queen, the purple canopy above her, falling in behind him. Soon the aisles were crowded with people sliding out of their pews, the air filled with song:

> Your eyes are more beautiful than the sea
> Your skin is as white as ocean pearls
> And Your cheeks, kissed by the Saviour, your Son
> Are two roses, and Your lips are flowers.

My grandfather and I brought up the rear, he grim and silent beside me as we made our way down the aisle and out the door. The procession was stretched out now along the path that sloped down behind Di Lucci's in a switchback that opened onto the main square; it moved slowly, and even at my grandfather's pace we were able to keep up with it. But the grey mass which had been hanging in the air before the service had thickened, the wind grown wet and cold; and by the time my grandfather and I had brought the tail end of the procession into the square, a light drizzle had begun to fall.

~~~

XI

From the square the procession moved down the S that cut towards the lower edge of town. The column had begun to swell as people who had missed the service came out of their homes to join it, lifting sweaters and jackets above their heads to shield themselves from the drizzle. In front of some houses sat tables covered with white cloth like altars and laid out with fruit and eggs and garlands of dried figs; here the procession would stop for a moment and women would come forward with their offerings, some placing fruits and eggs at the Madonna's feet or hanging garlands around her neck, others thrusting bank notes into the plaster folds of her lap. From second-floor balconies old black-cowled women tossed handfuls of grain or rice in the Madonna's path as they did at weddings. One old woman threw out a fistful of coins, and a flurry of boys raced out suddenly from the line of the procession to gather them up. But I did not join them, too shy to leave my grandfather's side; instead I reached instinctively into my pocket to palm my lucky one *lira*, passing it between my fingers to test again its texture and weight.

People had crowded in behind my grandfather and me now, though a small sphere of open space seemed to circle us, room enough for my grandfather to swing his cane freely. I had begun to sing, but beside me my grandfather's lips remained sealed in stony silence, his cane swinging with a stiff, determined rhythm over the mud-slicked cobblestones. Finally the procession branched off via San Giuseppe onto Giovanni Battista, the poorer section of town, where Fabrizio lived, the street here unpaved, turned now into a thick imprinted paste under the rain and the marchers' feet. The houses in this part of the village were built of the same thick stone as in the rest of the village, but were single-storied and more ramshackle, paint on door frames peeling, the wood underneath crumbled and rotting, windows covered in some houses only with yellowed oil-paper. Some of the houses were deserted, their owners gone to America, the shutters nailed closed and the doors boarded up, walls beginning to crumble, roofs caved in from rot and termites. We passed Fabrizio's house, ramshackle like the rest, its tiled roof slanting in a single slope from back to front. I had never been inside it, because Fabrizio's mother, a gaunt dark-eyed woman with a limp, always eyed me with suspicion and made me wait outside when I came to call; but from the doorway I'd made out a single dim room split down the centre by a soiled curtain, a few spare furnishings, a floor of plain hardened dirt, a fireplace that seemed simply a hollow in the wall. At night, Fabrizio had told me, he and his family slept on one side of the curtain, the goats and sheep on the other. The house seemed deserted now, no one standing before the doorway to make an offering; the family was likely out working in the fields, Fabrizio's father one of the few in the village who seldom made a contribution for the festival.

But as we came to the end of the street, where it sloped down in a sharp switchback to join up again with via San Giuseppe, someone whispered to me from an alleyway.

'Oh, Vittò.'

It was Fabrizio, motioning me towards him from the shadow of the alley, his cap drooping from the rain, his naked shins glistening with wet.

'I had the sheep out,' he said, grinning, 'but I left them in the pasture to come and see the procession. I don't have to cut wheat any more because I cut myself.' He showed me a long black-scabbed scar across his calf where he had caught himself with his scythe.

'Won't the sheep get lost?'

'*Beh*, whenever I want to go for a walk I make them jump in that hole near the cemetery where people used to hide during the war. But *madonna*! when I have to get them out later. They're as fat as cows.'

On the street behind us the last stragglers of the procession were still filing by, their voices echoing briefly in the alley as they passed. Fabrizio, looking out towards them, ducked down suddenly and pulled me deeper into the alley.

'Christ,' he said, crouching in the shadows, 'I think my aunt Carmella saw me. If she tells my father I was talking to you he'll break my balls.'

Instinctively I crouched down now too and glanced behind me into the street, feeling suddenly fugitive.

'It's not because of you,' Fabrizio said, whispering now, our voices seeming suddenly loud with the fading of the procession's song. 'It's because of your mother and the snake. *Lu malocchiu*.' He twisted his face into a scowl and brought two fingers up to his head as horns, to mimic the evil eye.

I crouched silently for a moment.

'Can't we play together tonight?' I said finally.

'It's not safe,' Fabrizio said. 'We have to wait till school starts. Then we'll have some laughs. My father's smoking cigarettes with filters on them now.'

He reached into his pocket and pulled out a cigarette grown damp and soft with the rain.

'Keep this for later,' he whispered. 'I have to go back to the sheep.'

The rain had stopped now, small patches of limpid blue appearing in the canopy of grey overhead. The procession had made its way back up via San Giuseppe and through the square again, Father Nicola still in front, shaking his aspergillum, holy water mingling with the mud underfoot, Mother Mary still riding dry and purple-canopied above the crowd, bobbing with the movement of her bearers, though her canopy sagged now from the wet and from the rice and grain that had collected in it. A small crowd of watchers, Romans, mainly, stood waving at the procession from under the awning of Di Lucci's terrace, not wanting to dirty their clothes in the mud and rain.

I took my place again next to my grandfather, who still plodded stiff and silent over the mud-slicked street, his heavy shoes clacking like hooves against the cobblestones. The wind had stiffened, but overhead the sky was clearing quickly, the patches of blue widening as the clouds flitted like ghosts towards the east, torn now into a thousand ragged shreds. As we approached the edge of town a cold sun appeared suddenly, reflecting gold and silver from the droplets of rain falling from the eaves of houses. As we approached our own house, I looked out from the line of the procession to see if my mother would appear at the door as the Madonna passed; but the house seemed deserted, even the curtains on the upper-storey balcony drawn.

The procession ended about a half mile out of town, at the rusted iron gates that led down to the cemetery. The cemetery itself, which filled only a small plot of hedged-in land—the newly dead were usually buried in old grave sites, to save on land, a heap of anonymous bones unearthed each time a new grave was dug—lay on a grassy plateau at the bottom of a steeply sloping dirt path; but at the cemetery gates, before the path sloped downward, stood a small, ancient chapel, its roof and walls overgrown with moss and creeping vines. The chapel would serve as the Madonna's home until Easter, when another procession would bring her back to the church. Inside, the chapel was unadorned, to avoid temptation for thieves, the only spots of colour the small circular window of stained glass at the peak of the back wall and the mottled greens and browns of the slab of serpentine marble that formed the chapel's tiny altar. Every year the Madonna was set in a fireplace-sized niche in the chapel's back wall, from where she would have a clear view of the valley through the fans of clear glass in the upper half of the chapel door, and could watch over the greening of the slopes in the spring.

I had left my grandfather's side and wormed my way up to the chapel doorway to watch the men setting the Madonna in her grotto. The canopy had been collapsed and two of the Madonna's bearers had lifted the statue off the rack and were squeezing it now through the narrow chapel door, a small gasp coming up from the crowd as one of them stumbled on the chapel's threshold and almost lost his grip.

'Gently now,' Father Nick said from inside, standing by officiously as the men squeezed past him. 'The material is very fragile. Perhaps some day we will have a real Madonna, made of marble.' He smiled at his joke.

'With all due respect,' one of the men said, gently forcing the statue into its niche, 'this one is real too, if I can believe my shoulders. If you get a marble one you'll have to leave it here the whole year, because no one will be able to carry it.'

'If you get a marble one,' someone beside me said, 'you'll have to make sure she isn't pregnant yet, to cut down on the weight.'

'Or she'll have to leave the baby at home, like everyone else.'

But now an ear-splitting explosion echoed through the valley, and all eyes turned skyward, to where a wisp of white smoke was still lingering against the sky's now almost solid blue. In a moment another small burst of white appeared, blossoming in the air like a flower, followed a split second later by its accompanying bang, and then at short intervals a third and a fourth; and finally a long series of bursts and blasts in quick succession, again, again, and again, the echoes accumulating one on top of the other until the air rang with them. These were the first of the fireworks, testaments to the power of loud noises, and announcing to all the valley that tonight there would be feasting and song in Valle del Sole.

~~~

XII

It was approaching nightfall by the time my grandfather and I returned home, the sun setting red and cold behind Castilucci, my bones chilled from the afternoon rain. Our kitchen, though, was warm, my mother sitting in front of a small fire, her body slouched forward to take in the heat. Two plates had been set on the table, a platter between them holding bread and a few thick slices of cheese, a decanter of wine at my grandfather's place.

'You couldn't have made some soup?' my grandfather said, but my mother did not turn away from the fire. My grandfather draped his jacket over the back of a chair and set it before the fire, then moved towards his room.

'It's all right to waste firewood to keep your feet warm, but not to feed your family.'

When we had changed from our damp clothes my grandfather and I sat down at the table to eat, my mother keeping her place by the fire. My grandfather downed his wine now the way *Tatone* Vittorio used to, in short quick gulps that emptied a glass in a few draughts; though the wine did not unleash his anger the way it had with my grandfather Vittorio, only seemed to wind it up more tightly inside him.

'*Mamma*,' I whispered, going up to her when I had

finished eating, 'aren't you coming to listen to the music tonight?'

'I'm not feeling very well,' she said tonelessly. 'I think I'll just go to bed.'

'Fool!' my grandfather said suddenly, wheeling around in his chair. 'You might as well make an announcement!'

My mother shifted in her chair, but did not turn towards him.

'Like you did last night?' she said finally.

'What I do is my own business.'

'And what I do,' my mother said softly, staring into the fire as if sharing a secret with it, 'is my business.'

'Not while you're living in this house, *porca madonna*! Not while you want to remain my daughter!'

His face flushed, my grandfather took up his cane and rose from his chair, leaving a plate of unfinished food. When he had gone into his room and closed the door my mother rose and cleared the table, tossing the remains of my grandfather's food into the fire—something she never did: even the bread might have been saved for the pigs— and then going upstairs. I sat in front of the fire, prodding the embers; the piece of cheese my mother had thrown there sizzled richly for a moment before it burst finally into flames. At last my grandfather came out of his room, wearing a heavy sweater of dark wool, his suit jacket with its row of medals still drying before the fire.

'Put on your coat,' he said gruffly. 'It'll be cold.' But now the door of my mother's room opened and she came downstairs with my coat in hand, a thick shawl draped around her shoulders. My grandfather glanced up at her briefly as she came down the stairs and then stepped out into the darkening street, my mother and I following him, melting soon into the file of other villagers and visitors making their way to the square.

The street was lined now with cars and carts that

had squeezed up along the gutter, mules snorting and braying in the chill, tugging against reins that had been tied to car fenders or to rings embedded in the fronts of houses. The square itself was already alive with people, small crowds of men in thick sweaters and women in shawls gathered around dim lanterns, children racing in and out of the shadows. Many of the chairs that had been set out in the square were filled, the older women sitting in front, to have a good view of the dance area: by the end of the evening they would be able to predict with accuracy the marriages of the coming spring. There was a bustle of activity around Di Lucci's terrace, a steady flow of people moving in and out through the door with glasses of beer or wine in hand, dark-haired young men leaning up against the railing, a crowd gathered around a table where a card game was in progress.

To the side of the terrace, wedged between a corner of the bandstand and the bar, was a large bus that had somehow managed to squeeze its way up via San Giuseppe. Inscribed in large black capitals on its back door were the words *'Capo di Molise,'* *'Gruppo Folkloristico'* in smaller capitals beneath. This was the band that would be playing tonight, its presence a coup for the *comitato*, made possible by money from America: it was said the band was known all over Italy, its songs often played on the radio. Usually Valle del Sole hired a band from Rocca Secca or Capracotta, motley assortments of singers, sometimes of a single family, who arranged themselves in a semi-circle on stage as if for a wedding photograph and followed the lead of a sole accordion player, with occasionally a drum and a horn or trombone for accompaniment. But 'Capo di Molise' had come up all the way from Campobasso, a trip that would have taken the better part of a day; and the band's equipment, already arranged under the stage's canopy, gleaming silver and black and blood red under the light of a few lanterns, looked strange and unreal, like something that had no connection to the square or the people gathered there, that might have descended suddenly from the sky to impose itself among us.

Valle del Sole did not have any electrical service; but a web of wires led away from the band's equipment, connecting finally to a large black cable that snaked along the ground towards the band's bus. And around the bandstand, suspended from post to post, hung a string of white and orange bulbs, with two other strings stretching out from the stage over the dance area, one ending at Di Lucci's terrace, the other at the eaves of the house across the square, the bulbs swaying like tiny balloons in the evening chill. For years now the people of Valle del Sole had anxiously awaited *la luce*, light, pressing my grandfather to lobby the government representative in Rocca Secca; and though a project had actually got under way once, the Communists from Castilucci, when they had learned that the line would not be extended as far as their town, had gone out in the night and set fire to the machinery doing the work, and all that remained of the effort now was a half mile of wireless poles that stretched like dead trees from the edge of Rocca Secca down the high road towards Valle del Sole. But tonight, it seemed, we were to have light, the white and amber bulbs hanging patiently above us, as if some miracle was shortly to fire them. The members of the *comitato*, for their part, rebuffed the questions that were put to them with indifferent authority.

'You'll see,' they said. 'Like magic. Poof!'

But my grandfather led the way through the crowd without glancing right or left, mindless of the buzz of curiosity the lights seemed to have sparked. Towards the far side of the square, I caught sight of Fabrizio's older brother Fulvio smoking a cigarette amidst a group of older boys. Fulvio was five or six years older than I was; he had been pulled out of school early to help his father in the fields, his body grown as tawny and muscled as a young man's.

'Looking for Fabrizio, eh?' he said, catching my glance as I passed. 'He's sick at home. He's got a broken ass.' The boys around him laughed.

My grandfather led us to the very back row of seats. For a long time the seats beside us remained empty; but finally someone emerged from the chatter of familiar voices behind us, a slim, dark-eyed man in a fedora and well-tailored blue suit who nodded respectfully to my grandfather before sitting down beside my mother.

'Alfreddo!' my mother said. 'No one told me you were back.'

'I got in last night,' the man said, speaking with the recognizable twang of Castilucci's dialect. He took off his hat and stared into it, avoiding my mother's gaze. 'I came back to sell my land.'

'Sell your land? Why, to pay for that suit? You look like someone from the camorra.'

'I'm bringing my family back to Canada,' he said. 'Five years is long enough to be separated.'

'It doesn't look like you mind being separated tonight. I don't see your wife with you.'

But the man didn't smile.

'I brought you something from your husband,' he said after a pause. He reached into an inside pocket and handed my mother an envelope. When she unfolded the letter inside a bank note fell into her lap, the number 50 inscribed in each of its corners.

'What's this?'

The man shrugged.

'Something to get you through the winter.'

'He sends me money through the bank,' my mother said. 'He probably needs this more than I do—I hear he's living in a chicken coop.'

'It's a room attached to Umberto Di Menna's barn,' Alfreddo said. 'He must have told you in his letters. They fixed it up so he has water and electricity.'

'He doesn't tell me anything in his letters,' my mother said. 'He only complains. Here, look for yourself.' She scanned quickly the letter the man had given her. 'Ah, *perfetto*, here—"Make sure Vittorio has some warm clothes for the winter." And I should feel lucky he reminds me, because otherwise the poor boy would run around naked.'

Alfreddo fingered the rim of his hat.

'He's going to buy a farm,' he said. 'He wants to bring you over.'

'He knows I won't leave my father,' my mother said, a little quickly. 'Anyway if he thinks I'll go there to live in a barn he's wrong. We have some fine stables right here in Valle del Sole.'

My grandfather, through this conversation, had been staring up towards the stage as if wrapped in his own thoughts; but now he rose up suddenly on his cane.

'*Brava*,' he muttered, spitting the word out with such restrained force and contempt it seemed to hang in the air like ice. 'God forgive me for raising you to talk like an idiot.'

He started back across the square, the crowd opening to let him pass and then swallowing him up again. Alfreddo's eyes caught my mother's for a moment, and she looked away from him awkwardly, her cheeks flushed. When Alfreddo spoke again a peremptory note had crept into his voice.

'It hasn't been easy for Mario these last months. He lost his job at the factory, but still he sends you money, even if he has to borrow it.'

'He lost his job because he can't get along with anyone. I hear things too, even if he doesn't tell me. And I know Mario—he's always right, there's no way to talk to him. The only way he knows how to talk is with the back of his hand. Now he sends me money because he's too proud to admit he was fired.'

'That's right, you hear things,' Alfreddo said, in a low voice, almost menacing. 'And how long do you think it takes people there to hear things? Then you'll see if he still sends you money.'

'Ah, so that's it, isn't it? *Che cretino*! You think it's the money I want, don't you? Here, take it back to him, *stronzo*, tell him I don't need his money.' My mother crumpled the bill she still held in one hand and stuffed it in Alfreddo's side pocket. 'Or tell him whatever you like, I don't care.'

Alfreddo pulled the bill out of his pocket and slowly smoothed it, then folded it into a tight wad and wedged it into the wicker of his chair seat.

'I won't be the one to tell him anything,' he said, rising. 'But it's for his sake, not for yours.'

When he had gone my mother pulled the bill free from the chair and unfurled it.

'Idiot,' she muttered, tearing the bill down the centre with a quick jerk, then tearing the halves again. She glanced to her side and behind her as if looking for a place to discard the shreds; but finally she stuffed them into the pocket of her skirt.

The show was beginning now. After a long speech praising the accomplishments of that year's committee, the chairman introduced the first act, Silvio the postman, who every year opened the Saturday night festivities with some of his poems. Silvio's father had made a small fortune in America before the first war, and had sent his son to university; but there Silvio had gotten in with some young men who had taken advantage of him and had begun to drink and gamble, and finally his father had had to leave the village to fetch his son home, and to pay the debts Silvio had accumulated from his gambling. They said that when his father found him he was huddled in rags in front of a small fire in his room, burning pages from Dante to keep the fire going. Now he worked as the village postman, delivering mail in the morning and drinking alone for the rest of the day in the large house his father had built with American money. His parents were both dead, much of the father's fortune lost on Silvio's failed education and debts; and Silvio's yearly recitations had become a kind of joke the villagers indulged in, as if to remind themselves of the dangers of high aspirations. Silvio stood now centre stage in the light of a few lamps, his checkered suit too tight over his plumpish body, a missing button on his shirt revealing a patch of pink, hairless belly. His collar, adorned with a small black bow tie, was buttoned tight, his head seeming squeezed out of it like a balloon, his ruddy cheeks showing the effects of too much wine; though his eyes, dark pools that brimmed with moisture, seemed to belong to a different person, as if his body was a mask or costume that had trapped some stranger inside it.

'*Signor' e signori*,' he started, in meticulous Italian, 'it is a great honour to be asked again to share my little poems with you—'

'Bravo, Silvio!' someone shouted.

'Never mind the speech! Give us a poem!'

Other people took up the shout.

'Oh, Silvó, a poem! A poem from the gods!'

'Every year it's the same *stupidaggini*,' my mother said. '*E quel cretino*, smiling through it all like a child. As if these people knew anything more than sheep and goats.'

Silvio turned his eyes skyward and began to recite, mingling poems about love and the countryside with ballads that told the stories of the bandit-heroes who had fought against Garibaldi, his fist coming up often to strike his breast or pound the air with emphasis. With each poem the crowd applauded and cheered, goading Silvio on to greater animation. He ended with a paean to the Madonna, hands clasped against his breast like a Roman orator's:

Signora, we think of you
In the time of pregnant fields

When the olives fall like tears from heaven
And the grapes hang heavy as milky breasts.
Signora, we think of you
In the time of barren fields
When the trees stand deserted like women
without love
And the wine cellars are as dry as the wind.
Signora, we come like lovers
Offering kisses and caresses
You bless us in fall, you comfort us in winter
Signora, we think of you.

Catcalls and cries for an encore followed Silvio as he bowed
away, his face beaming, from centre stage; but when he
seemed about to return the chairman of the *comitato*, waiting in the shadows on the other side of the stage, frowned
at him and shook his head disapprovingly. After a last
round of fitful applause, the chairman came up to centre
stage.

'*Per favore*,' he said, 'the band has asked that we
turn out all the lamps before they come out.'

Hesitantly at first, but more surely under the
chairman's remonstrances, the lamps went out and darkness slowly swallowed the square. The audience sat for a
moment in utter silence; but when nothing happened
people began to fidget in their seats, wondering aloud
whether it would be all right to light the lamps again. Then
everything happened very quickly: an engine sputtered
into life from the direction of the band's bus, the sound
growing to a high hum and then dropping again to a groan,
and finally a gasp came up from the audience as the bulbs
above us burst into light, the square suddenly bright as
day. There was hardly time to adjust to the shock before an
explosion of sound rolled out from the stage like thunder,
the band members, already behind their instruments, starting in on a vigorous overture. In a moment the chorus
members had filed up and arranged themselves on stage,

three women on the left, three men on the right, all dressed in bright costumes of green, white, and black and keeping up a synchronized marching movement in time with the music as a final couple emerged into the stage's halo of lights and sashayed hand in hand up to centre stage, a young dark-skinned woman whose arms were adorned with a dozen golden bangles, like a gypsy's, and a man in wide sequined sleeves, his hair groomed to a silver sheen.

'*Buonasera, signor' e signori.* We are "Capo di Molise".'

The crowd, it seemed, was still in a trance from the sudden rush of light and sound, Valle del Sole's medieval square transformed in an instant into a pocket of rich modernity, as bright and alive as any street in Rome or Naples; but on stage the singers, picking up the tune of the overture, embarked at once on a singing duel:

I think you do me wrong if you lose your head
Because you found a soldier hiding under my bed.
Your first romance is wonderful
Your second one is better still.

Only slowly now did people begin to recover from their shock, shaking their heads and moving slowly towards the stage as towards an oracle. It seemed as if we had been transported into one of *la maestra*'s stories of the saints, the world suddenly filled with light, and all possibilities open again; but beside me my mother sat unmoved, still as a sentry, her arms folded tight over her chest against the cold, though around us the seats soon emptied, only the older villagers staying behind, everyone else pressing up closer to the lights of the stage for a better view. Gradually couples began to filter into the dance area.

'As if no one had ever seen a light bulb before,' my mother said.

All through the first set my mother sat still and silent beside me, staring up towards the stage as if still expecting some secret to be revealed there. Behind us the square lay dark and empty now, a cold wind biting at our backs; a small group of men hung back at the terrace of Di Lucci's bar, but the rest of the crowd had moved up to the warmth and light of the stage. The band's songs seemed strange and foreign to me, even the few local ones it played rendered unfamiliar by the twang and blare of its equipment, which filled the air so totally that in the hush at the end of each song it seemed the square had suddenly been sucked free of all sound, despite the continued hum of the crowd and of the engine in the band's bus; but the peasants by now seemed to have taken to the blare as if born to it, the dance area always filled, the couples adapting their *saltarelli* and *tarantelle* to the band's strident rhythms. In between songs the lead singers—Mario and Maria, they introduced themselves—joked with the audience.

'Tell me, Maria, honestly, how many times have you been unfaithful to me?'

'Look up at the sky. How many stars do you see?'

'Ah, Maria, that many! You should be careful, you know—a wronged man can turn into a devil.'

'Not everything with horns is a devil. Goats have horns too.'

During one of these pauses Di Lucci appeared suddenly beside us, emerging like a ghost from the shadows to squat next to my mother's chair.

'*Crist' e Maria*, have you ever seen such a festival? The lights! I knew all about it, of course, because they wanted to hang them from my terrace, so it was only right that I should know, but still I was just as surprised as everyone else. Like a miracle! What happened to your father, didn't he see it?'

'He went home,' my mother said tonelessly.

'Home? Yes, yes, now that you mention it I saw him going that way before, I thought maybe he was sick— he looks thin these days.'

'We can't all be fat.'

'Eh? Ah, *sí*, it's true, it's true,' Di Lucci said, patting his belly and forcing a laugh, 'maybe some of us have to be thin to make up for the ones that are fat, eh? So I see Alfreddo Pannunzio is back, maybe he had some news from your husband, no?'

'He told me he's living in a stable.'

'Ha, *sí*, in a stable, I know how they live in America, just look at that suit Pannunzio was wearing. Though maybe your husband is saving his money to bring you over, no? Just old men like me and your father,' shaking his head now, 'that's all there'll be left in Valle del Sole. And no one to take care of us in our old age.'

The band stopped now for an intermission, and the crowd around the stage began to disperse, small groups moving in the direction of Di Lucci's bar. With a sudden bound Di Lucci rose up off his haunches, surprisingly agile.

'Well, back to my place,' he said. 'For you a festival means enjoyment. For me it means work.'

'What a jackass,' my mother said, when he had gone.

The band's second set started out on the same high pitch as the first, but as the evening wore on the tempo seemed gradually to slow, modern songs giving way more and more to local ones, the band's accordion beginning to take centre stage, its melancholy notes seeming all in a minor key, riding out over the sound of the other instruments to hang on the wind like the threat of a frost. Eventually I drifted into sleep, the glitter and noise of the square receding: I had a sudden image of what the square looked like in winter, after a snowfall, silent, the cobblestones covered in a thin blanket of white, icicles hanging from the eaves of houses and from the branches of the crooked trees that rose up from the embankment. But a hand reached out suddenly to pull me back into the light and noise, and I opened my eyes to see my mother standing over me. The band was announcing the last song of the evening.

'Come on, Vittorio,' my mother said. 'We're going to dance.'

She took me by the hand and led me up towards the stage, heads turning as we passed, couples in the dance area edging away as we approached, clearing a small circle as if to cordon us off. But as soon as the band had begun to play we seemed to be forgotten, the crowd of other dancers slowly closing in around us, as if the music had made us suddenly anonymous, invisible. The singers had arranged themselves now in the familiar semi-circle, the musicians abandoning their instruments to join them, leaving only the accordion player to pick out the tune; though Mario and Maria still held centre stage, singing alternately the verses of a familiar local song, no longer the duelling lovers of the evening's first set but a happy couple remembering their days of courtship:

> *Vorrei far ritornare un'ora sola*
> *Il tempo bello della contentezza*
> *Quando che noi giocando a vola vola*
> *Di baci i' ti coprivo e di carezze.*

But the energy of the crowd seemed to have reached some strange peak now, many of the men drunk with beer and wine, whirling their partners around the dance area at a speed that was out of all time with the music, with a kind of joyless intensity that bordered on violence, as if they were anxious to spend before the end of the evening some anger or resentment that had been bottled up inside them. One couple stumbled out onto the circle of old women who had pulled their chairs up close to the perimeter of the dance area; but the man righted himself with a stagger and a laugh, ignoring the shrieks and curses of the old women, and quickly pulled his partner back into the crowd of other dancers. A crush of bodies churned around my mother and me like the wheels of some great machine, jostling us to the centre of the dance area; but my mother too seemed suddenly infected by the crowd's strange energy, twirling with me at a breathless pace, faster and faster, the crowd around me fading to a dizzy blur. The audience had begun to sing along with the band, and a thousand voices started in now on the final refrain:

> Ehhhhhhh—vola vola vola vola
> E vola lu pavone
> Lu cuore tuo è buono
> E famme lu provar.

Then suddenly the song was over, and a great clamour of shouts and applause and catcalls came up from the crowd, caps flying up into the air; but in the clamour there were only a few scattered cries for an encore, as if most of the dancers had forgotten already about the band and were merely crying out to the air, or as if they had grown irritated now with the band's novelty, Mario and Maria seeming to bow away from the stage with their wide forced smiles as if retreating from a threat. A moment later, the chorus still filing off the stage to the last applause, the engine in the band's bus died and the square went black, the noise of the crowd suddenly disembodied. My mother and I still stood at the centre of the dance area; but in the sudden darkness the crowd seemed to have faded away, as if we had been left alone, the voices around us only so many ghosts. Then a small explosion sounded and the sky above the valley was suddenly filled with coloured light, small fading speckles of green, white, and red. It was midnight, and the final fireworks had begun. The Madonna, too, cloistered in her little chapel, would be watching.

~~~

XIII

The week after the festival I was tending the sheep by the cemetery when Fabrizio called out to me from the shadow of the chapel. His father, he told me, had locked him in the house with the goats the night of the fireworks.

'Pom!' he said, grinning, making a quick arc through the air with his hand to mimic his father's blows. But I didn't want to hear about his beating, wanted only to get back to the quiet of the sheep. When he offered me a cigarette I didn't take it.

'What's the matter with you?' he said. 'It's not your fault, it's your mother. Because she was screwing in the stable.'

But my head started pounding then and suddenly I couldn't bear Fabrizio anymore and his stupid grinning. I wanted to make him stop talking, make him disappear, and I picked up a rock beside my foot and flung it squarely at his chest. He deflected the rock with an arm but I threw myself on him, arms flailing, and the two of us fell to the ground, Fabrizio holding out his elbows to ward me off.

'Oh, *scimunit'*, have you gone crazy?'

'It was the snake's fault, you stupid! You're just a stupid like your stupid father!'

'*Sí, sí*, stop, it was only the snake, you're right, it was only the snake.'

The first day of school Fabrizio did not show up in class, nor the second or third; I thought he was staying away because of our fight, but then I overheard one of the older boys say that his father was keeping him out of school to work in the fields. I was alone now, without friends, and it quickly became clear what my status was with the other boys. For the first few days I was merely shunned, and could not make out the insults which they whispered to each other in class while they smirked at me from their desks; but by the end of the first week I had had another fight. It was Vincenzo Maiale, Maria's son, who provoked me, as we were coming out of class on our way home, with some veiled comment about my mother which I didn't understand; but suddenly we were on the ground, rolling in the dirt in the square in front of the church. I did not have any experience fighting, but somehow my body seemed to know instinctively how to do it, how to fling a fist, what areas to strike to cause the greatest harm; but in the midst of my attack I suddenly felt my rage ebbing, giving way to a vague fear, not simply the fear of being beaten up but a fear of my own violence, of the strange thing which was not me that had just flung itself with such dangerous force on Vincenzo Maiale.

Vincenzo was about two years older than me, and taller and stronger; and in an instant he sensed the sudden lag in my resolution and moved from surprised defense to attack, throwing me off his chest and pinning me to ground, his fist beating my head against the dirt while the other children stood round watching or urging him on. I struggled to free myself but Vincenzo pinned my arms with his knees. Another wave of violence took hold of me like a possession, and I flailed my legs and let out a long stream of curses. But Vincenzo only laughed, to show what an easy victory I had been.

'Oh, *la maestra*!' someone called out, and suddenly everyone scattered, Vincenzo leaping off me to disappear down the church steps with his friends. In a moment *la maestra* was standing over me, her large breasts quivering. She had heard my cursing, I thought in horror; but she only pursed her lips and shook her head, then reached out a hand to pull me off the ground.

'Look at you,' she said. She pulled a handkerchief out of her skirt pocket and wiped at my nose; it came away wet with blood. 'It's that woman's fault, all of this, she thinks she's as free as a bird, she doesn't think about other people. Who did this to you?'

But I only stared down at the ground, watching the blood that dripped from my nose splatter against the dirt.

'Well, you're probably right not to say, it would only make things worse for you. Go home and let your mother see you now.' She handed her handkerchief to me. 'Here, hold this under your nose, and when you get home lie down with your head hanging over the side of your bed and tell your mother to put a bit of garlic in each nostril. Make sure you drink at least three glasses of water before you go to sleep. Look, even your lip is bleeding. In the morning it'll be as big as a melon.'

It was only when I had begun my descent down the church steps that I allowed myself finally to begin whimpering, the whimper growing into a low drone as I started down the street past the village women knitting or shelling beans on their stoops and the classmates waiting in alleyways to see what had become of me. When I opened the door of our kitchen I broke out at last into full-fledged sobs. My mother was at the kitchen table kneading dough.

'*Per l'amore di Cristo*, what happened?' In an instant she was at my side, wiping at the blood under my nose. 'Who did this to you?'

She went to the sideboard and poured some water into a basin, coming back to wipe the dried blood from my face and daub my swelling lip with a wet cloth, the water in the pan turning a pale crimson.

'Who did this to you, Vittorio, tell me! *Dio mio, che figura!*'

'It was Vincenzo,' I blurted out finally.

'Vincenzo? Maria's son?'

'*Sí.*'

'*Quella cagna! Quella strega!* She's the one who put him up to this!' My nose had stopped dripping now. My mother passed her cloth over my scraped elbows, then brushed at the dirt on my clothes with her hand and tucked my shirt back into my pants. She stood back from me a moment to survey me, then suddenly crouched forward to take me in her arms, rocking me gently back and forth.

'I'll make her pay for this, Vittorio, you'll see, by the blood of Christ I'll make her pay.' Then, wiping at some tears in her own eyes, she took me suddenly by the hand and marched me out the door into the street. We walked up via San Giuseppe at a quick pace, some of my classmates still lurking in the shadows and a line of women still on their stoops, staring after us as we marched. Finally we reached Maria Maiale's door, just before the square, my mother letting go of my hand to pound on the door with both fists.

'Open the door, Maria, or I swear I'll break it down!'

Behind us, at a distance, some of the women had come off their stoops to watch us from the centre of the street, a few children dodging behind their skirts.

'Open this door!'

At last the door opened, Maria's large form looming for a moment in the doorway; but she had time for only a surprised 'Cristina!' before my mother lunged at her with arms outstretched. Maria stumbled backwards open-mouthed and fell with a cry to the stone floor of her kitchen, and in a moment my mother had straddled her mountainous hips, Maria struggling wildly to keep my mother's hands from closing around her throat, writhing on the floor like a great beached fish.

'*Gesù bambino!*' someone behind me said. A small circle of women had moved up close to the door now for a better view. 'She's going to kill her!'

And someone else whispered: 'Remember what she did to her father-in-law, everyone says it was her that killed him, for what he said.'

Maria had kicked up her legs now, trying to get them up around my mother's head, her skirt hiked up high over her thighs so that her underwear showed.

'Vincenzo, help me!' she screamed, and only now I noticed Vincenzo and his small brother and sister cowering in a corner of the kitchen. 'Cristina, what's got into you? Have you gone mad?'

My mother had worked her knees onto Maria's elbows, leaving Maria's forearms to claw helplessly at the air, and finally her hands closed around Maria's throat. Maria grunted and gasped, her face reddening, but then with a last desperate burst of energy she pulled an arm free and lightning quick grabbed a clump of my mother's hair and yanked sharply. My mother cried out and released her hold on Maria's throat to free herself; but Maria, suddenly agile, pulled her other arm free and shot both fists into my mother's stomach, sending her rolling doubled up onto the floor. In a flash Maria had scrambled up, heaving but quick, and lurched through a nearby doorway. She slammed the door shut just as my mother was lunging towards her again.

'Get out of my house!' Maria shouted, ramming a bolt into place. 'You've got some devil in you! You and your proud talk, you see what it's come to? God help us, she wants to kill me!'

My mother glanced wildly about the room. Finally she threw open a cupboard and flung a bowl from it against the door Maria had barricaded herself behind, bits of pottery scattering across the room like spray.

'You tell your Vincenzo,' she said, flinging another bowl, 'that if he lays another finger on my son I'll tear out your eyes and feed them to the dogs! To the dogs!'

My mother turned to the corner where Vincenzo still stood cowering with his brother and sister.

'Do you hear that, Vincenzo? I swear I'll kill her, even if I have to rot in hell for it!'

More than a dozen women had gathered outside Maria's door now, standing in a hushed semi-circle, a few of my classmates lurking among them; but they parted now like a sea as my mother stepped through the door.

'And you can tell all your children the same thing,' she said, looking around at the women. 'If you have anything to say you can say it to my face.'

But the women only stared on silently; and I realized with a shock that they were frightened, as if they believed my mother was as good as her threat, or that she could cast some curse against them if they crossed her. My mother held her ground but none of the women would look her squarely in the eye. Finally, under my mother's hard stare, they began awkwardly to disperse, one by one returning like wraiths towards the safety of their kitchens.

~~~

XIV

Not long after my mother's fight, some new demon took possession of her. I found her in the stable, leaning against the low wall of the pig's stall, the pigs squealing wildly and a pool of vomit, a pale unearthly blue, sitting viscous on the stall floor. She was moaning lowly when I came up to her; then her body whipped forward and another stream of vomit splattered onto the floor. Her hands, I saw now, were covered in blood: in a moment I was up the stairs and running, up via San Giuseppe and back again to Di Lucci's bar.

Things went more smoothly this time. My grandfather was sitting alone in the back room; within a few minutes he and Di Lucci and I had climbed into Di Lucci's Fiat and were back at the house. Di Lucci and I found my mother crumpled against the wall of the pig pen, moaning softly, arms clasped around her belly; but now the mystery of the blood on my mother's hands explained itself, for on a wooden block in front of the chicken run lay the limp headless body of a chicken, a bloodstained cleaver beside it and a pan of blood resting on the ground nearby.

Di Lucci lifted my mother up by the armpits and leaned her against the stable wall.

'*Dai*, Cristina, what happened?'

But she only moaned softly again, her eyes drooping, and finally Di Lucci draped one of her arms around his
shoulder and lurched with her out the stable door and up
the side steps. My grandfather was waiting outside Di
Lucci's car.

'Go tend the sheep,' he said to me. 'Your mother
isn't going to die yet.'

Di Lucci lumped my mother into the back seat, and
in a moment the car was off, a cloud of dust following it
until it veered onto the main road and disappeared around
the hump of Colle di Papa.

I had already decided by then what needed to be
done, had begun to go over in my mind the visit that
Giuseppina had paid my mother just after her snake bite.
There was a chance that when Di Lucci had been in the
stable he'd seen the chicken that my mother had slaugh-
tered there, so that at some point it would have to be
accounted for; and my grandfather, though he seldom
went down to the stable, still kept very close count of his
livestock, as if every winter brought with it the prospect of
famine. But I had already accepted the risk, my mind
straining now to remember Giuseppina's instructions. It
was important in these things to be very precise—wasn't it
possible that my mother herself had been preparing to
follow Giuseppina's advice (after all why had she saved
the blood? or was she merely planning to use it to thicken
some sauce or soup?) when some slight error had angered
the very spirit she was trying to appease? But now all the
lore I had ever collected, from schoolmates, from overheard conversations, from my grandfather's stories, from
the random horde of facts Fabrizio shared with me, seemed
tangled in my head in a great muddled heap. There were
the ways of hurting an enemy, by putting glass in his
footprints or by roasting his coat over a fire; there were the
birds that shouldn't be killed except at certain times of the

year, pheasants and wrens, because the killer would break a bone or his cows would give bloody milk; there were the places it was forbidden to spin or carry a spindle, along the high road or in front of a freshly seeded field, because the crops would grow up crooked and dwarfed. Then, already in the stable stuffing the chicken and its severed head into a burlap bag, I remembered my mother's bloodied hands and the whole sequence came back to me with a sudden clarity, from the draining of the blood to the final fire; and more confident now I glanced outside the stable door to be sure no one was watching, then stole down to the ravine with the burlap bag slung over my shoulder.

A small path led through the ravine to the pasture beyond it; I followed it to a place where the dead growth and gnarled vines and thorny bushes formed an almost solid wall, then forced myself up through the thorns and brambles to a small clearing at the base of an old chestnut tree that had long been left to the wild, the ravine grown up around it, because it was said that one of the villagers had once hanged himself from it. The sun barely penetrated here, shut out by the surrounding growth and by the thick mantle of gold and yellow leaves overhead. Hundreds of chestnuts spotted the spongy layer of rotting leaves that covered the ground, looking in their spiny husks like small furry animals.

I cleared a patch of bare earth, my fingers catching on worms and millipedes which I shook away with a shiver, then built up a pile of dead weeds and twigs and branches nearby. Next I retrieved the pan of blood from the stable and hid it along with the burlap sack underneath the pile of branches, covering the pile with a curtain of dead leaves to camouflage it. As a last preparation I took a box of matches from the fireplace mantle up to my room, where I stuffed it under my pillow. Now I had only to wait for night, when I could carry out the burning undetected.

When I came in from tending the sheep, a cold

wind by then creeping along the fringes of nightfall, my grandfather was sitting sullen and distracted at the kitchen table, a half glass of wine in front of him.

'Did my mother come back?' I asked.

'Make yourself something to eat,' he said. 'Your mother's staying in the hospital a few days.'

Later, in my room, I pulled on a heavy sweater in readiness and tried to study my books; but I returned again and again to my balcony to stare into the ravine as if expecting a sign from there, some sure proof that the spirits would be willing to accept my offering. Finally I turned out my lamp and watched from the balcony for the lamp in my grandfather's room to go out as well, a dozen times nodding against the railing before a blast of cold wind would make me wake with a shiver; and at last the light died, only a scattering of stars and a thin crescent moon, cold wisps of cloud flitting across it, giving any shape now to the darkness beyond the balcony. I counted to a thousand in my head, to give my grandfather time to fall asleep, then counted to a thousand again, rolling the numbers off in my mind, seeing them take shape there as if cut out of stone; then, matches and darkened lamp in one hand, I picked my way quietly down the stairs, inched open the door, and slipped into the street.

Outside, not a single light shone along via San Giuseppe, not even up at Di Lucci's, where card games often went on long into the night. It was strange to think of the other villagers asleep in their beds while I stood alone and unwatched in the street, all the village stilled and quiet, as if God himself had gone to sleep; some secret village seemed to be lurking there in the darkness, one that could not be seen in the light of day, as if it huddled itself away then against the noise and light. Under the light of the moon I crept down the steps next to our house and through the garden into the bramble-choked darkness of the ravine, making my way by touch now, like a blind person, feeling for the break in the bushes I had made earlier in the day. Finally I stumbled into empty space, so black and void it might have been limitless; though when I lit my lamp, keeping the flame low and squat, bright enough merely to light a small private circle of clarity around me, I found myself safely in the clearing under the chestnut tree, everything as I had left it, the pile of leaves and branches, the circle of cleared earth.

A few dead leaves had fallen into the basin of blood; I plucked them out, one by one, then pushed up my sleeves and set my hands palm down into the blood. It was thick and cold now, oozing like mud between my fingers. I rubbed my hands together until a thin layer of it was spread evenly over them up to my wrists, then poured what remained into the centre of the bare patch of earth, where it sat for a moment in a viscous puddle before seeping finally into the dirt. Then I spoke the words, three times, 'This is my blood, which comes out of me like a river to the sea'; all that remained now was the burning.

I pushed the pile of leaves and branches over the spot where I had poured the blood, then dumped the chicken and its severed head out of the burlap bag onto the ground. The body was still flaccid, not yet stiff with death, though a black clot had hardened around its neck. I prepared a small hollow at the top of the pyre and set the body inside, draping the burlap bag over it like a shroud.

Beside the pyre, though, the chicken's head stared up at me through lidless eyes, its mouth agape like a question. I could recall nothing about the head from Giuseppina's instructions; but it seemed there was something I had forgotten, some crucial part of the chicken that should be spared, to guarantee the ritual's success. I decided to devise a test. I forced a sturdy stick into the earth and impaled the chicken's head on the end of it; then, stretched out on my belly, eyes closed, I twisted the stick between my bloodied palms, three full turns to the right, three to the left, then a few random turns in each direction to let fate do its work. I made up a charm as I went along:

Head of a chicken, red and white
Turn to the left and turn to the right
If you face to the front then I keep you out
If you face to the back then I burn you up.

When I opened my eyes I was staring directly into the chicken's gaping beak—the spirits had sent a clear message.

'*Grazie, signor Gallino*,' I whispered, then turned the head back towards the pyre so it could watch the sacrifice of its nether part.

I had only four matches, but on the third the small pile of leaves and dead grass I'd set at the pyre's base as kindling began to smoulder and burst finally into flames. Though the fire spread slowly at first, hissing and sizzling with moisture and sending up clouds of grey smoke, at last it had spread in a triangle up the pyre's side and was burning in earnest, my face flushed now with heat. Finally the flames began to lick at the burlap sack at the top of the pyre. They teased it for a moment before the sack finally took fire; but then it burned with such a quickness and force that in an instant tall shafts of flame were leaping up suddenly as high as the overhanging branches of the chestnut tree, the leaves there cracking and shrivelling with the heat and popping into flame. The sudden blast of heat sent me scampering backwards; but even up against the bushes at the clearing's edge the heat reached me, pressing against me like a wall. It seemed that in a moment the great chestnut tree itself would go up like a giant torch and the fire would spill across the ravine; it would be only a matter of time then before the whole village would be up in flames, all the stables along via San Giuseppe chock-full of dry hay and straw now from the harvest.

I had taken my lucky coin from my pocket now and was rubbing it furiously, hoping to calm the spirits.

But then as quickly as it had erupted in fury the fire gave up a few last tongues of tall flame and died down again—the burlap bag and the outer shell of leaves and branches had burnt themselves out. Gradually the pyre settled into a low comfortable burning, the fire retreating inward, muffled by a cloak of dying ashes. Atop the sinking heap of burning wood I could make out now the outlines of the chicken, the black stump of its neck, the charred feathers, the hooked claws. But it seemed to have lost little bulk from its ordeal: I had expected it to burn up like a log, crumble finally into a heap of glowing ashes, yet there it still lay in its solid mass, refusing to give itself up to the fire.

I added a few more faggots of wood, cautiously, then a few handfuls of dead leaves, watched the flames leap up in momentary fervour and dwindle again; then finally I sat to wait the fire out, hoping that its now slow, patient flames would eat away at the corpse more surely than the wilder ones had. A deep exhaustion had come over me suddenly, as if my body had only just remembered that it was the middle of the night, and lulled by the fire I drifted finally into a fitful sleep. Strange images troubled me: my mother squatting in a field as if taking a pee, but getting up to reveal a large blue egg; Father Nick standing solemnly before a coffin in the church, reciting a mass for a Mr. Mario Gallino; some great black jaw stretching open in front of me, ready to swallow me like the whale that swallowed Jonah.

I woke stiff and numb, my bones chilled and my bladder aching; beside me my lamp sat dead and cold, its fuel used up. The fire had died down now to glowing embers; but the chicken had held its ground, the feathers burnt to blackened stubs but the body still intact, merely slightly shrunken. Then an image from one of my dreams surfaced suddenly, of a large bloody mass pulsing ominously in my outstretched hands: I had forgotten to cut out the chicken's heart. Somewhere inside the chicken's shrivelled corpse the heart still lay sheltered, protecting the corpse from the fire spirits, while the head, mistakenly spared, gaped at me in mockery from atop its observation post.

Through a small gap in the underbrush I could see that the eastern sky was already tinged with the deep blue of pre-dawn; soon many of the villagers would be rising to go out to the fields to harvest their grapes. I unbuttoned my fly and emptied my bladder onto the remnants of the fire, my urine steaming against the embers, then dragged away the chicken's corpse and covered the fire's ashes with dirt, stamping the dirt down before spreading a new blanket of leaves over it. Then, with the chicken head in my pocket, the charred corpse in the basin, and my lamp over one arm, I made my way through the ravine towards the steep slope that led up to the fountain. The corpse I tossed into the clay pipe that came under the road from the fountain, stuffing it down as far as I could with a long stick; then I shimmied up to the road, checked to make sure it was still deserted, and crept across to the fountain to wash my hands and the basin free of blood. The valley was already filled with grey light by the time I had slipped back into the house and up to my room, where I stuffed the chicken head into a sock and hid it under my mattress.

That morning I failed to get up when my grandfather called me to feed the animals—normally my mother's job—and he had to do it himself.

'What happened to the chicken your mother was cleaning when she got sick?' he said irritably when at last I had come downstairs.

I shrugged.

'Idiot,' he said. 'You should have known enough to bring it upstairs. Some dog probably walked off with it.'

At school that day I kept nodding off at my desk.

'Vi-ttoh-rio!' the teacher called out once, in a sing-song. She had been being strangely nice to me since my fight with Vincenzo. 'Don't tell me you're sleeping? You must be upset. I heard your mother was in the hospital again.'

'Yes,' I said, coming out of a dream. 'But she's going to get better.'

'Of course!' the teacher said. 'Of course she is.'

~~~

XV

Since my fight with Vincenzo, I had taken to coming to school early in the morning to avoid being headed off en route by any of the village boys. *La maestra* seemed to guess the reason for my early arrivals, and now when school let out she kept me behind to help her in the classroom.

'Vittorio, *per favore*,' she'd say with forced sternness, as if meting out a punishment, 'you'll stay behind today to sweep.'

There was no use, of course, in the teacher's adopting this tone—my classmates saw through it, knew that the status I'd held the previous year as a troublemaker, a status which though misplaced had at least given me a certain notoriety, was giving way to a new position as teacher's favourite. But so far the system had worked, all the boys gone home by the time I finished my sweeping, though the price I paid for this amnesty was a heavy one—the cloying *'Grazie*, Vittorio' that the teacher offered up to me every day when I left the classroom; and the looks of saint-like pity I'd catch her directing towards me sometimes when I was sweeping, looks that made me squirm and twitch, that filled me with revulsion and self-hatred, hatred for that part of myself which was grateful for the teacher's kindness. And I knew, from the whispered insults I suffered through each day in the classroom—*citro di mamma*, the boys called me, mama's boy—that the amnesty was only a temporary one, great forces gathering against me, preparing a day of reckoning; and no one would be there to protect me when some rough hand dragged me behind a bush and paid me with a fist for the immunity I'd enjoyed.

A few days after my midnight vigil in the ravine, my mother then still in the hospital, I came out of the classroom after my sweeping to find Guido Mastroangelo sitting on the wide stone steps in front of the church. Guido was a gangly, stoop-shouldered boy whose body didn't seem to have any support to it, as if he were made of straw; the other boys called him *buffone*, because he could not open his mouth without something peculiar coming out of it, as if he wasn't able to make sense of the world in the way other people did.

'Guido Mastroangelo,' the teacher would ask, 'why did Joseph and Mary have to stay in a stable when they were in Bethlehem?'

'Well,' Guido would start, rising up slowly and lifting a spidery arm to scratch the back of his head, 'in those days all the hotels were owned by the Fascists'—but already the class would be in stitches, and even the teacher's reproving face would crack into a smile.

Guido had never shown me any ill will; but he hung around with Alfreddo Girasole, the leader of Vincenzo Maiale's gang. He did not seem to notice me now as I walked past the church, too intent on removing a fleck of snot from his nose, his face screwed up in concentration; but just as I reached the stairwell that led down to the square he said, 'Do you have any matches?'

When I stopped to look back at him he was staring intently at a small dark spot at the end of his finger.

'It doesn't really matter if you don't have any,' he said, talking to his finger, then looking up finally with a

serious, almost sad expression, 'because Alfreddo probably does. But he told me to ask you, just in case.'

What would Alfreddo want with my matches?
Guido was just talking; or he had made some kind of
mistake.

'I have to go take the sheep out,' I said.

Guido wiped his finger slowly and meticulously
on his pants.

'You don't have to worry about the sheep,' he said.
'Alfreddo talked to Fabrizio and he's going to take them
out for you. Your grandfather said it would be all right.
Didn't the teacher tell you?'

Guido was looking at me so matter-of-factly that I
flushed with embarrassment. Surely he wouldn't lie, with
the teacher so close? I had only to walk the few hundred
paces to the classroom to ask her—

'I have to go,' I said, but very uncertain now where
I had to go, or why.

'I thought you were coming up on the mountain to
smoke,' Guido said. 'That's why I was waiting for you.
Alfreddo was at the hospital yesterday to see his aunt from
Tornamonde and he asked your mother if you could be
part of our gang. She said that was all right. When
someone's in the hospital it's good to smoke some cigarettes, to keep the spirits away.'

Guido had my head spinning with all these com-
plicities. Nothing he said made sense—it was as if the
world had abruptly changed into its opposite, been completely overturned. But suddenly everything came clear:
the chicken had started to take effect. Every morning now
I had been singing a little charm to its head to help the spell:

Head of a chicken, white and red
Watching me from under my bed
Keep us safe from harm and hurt
Or I'll stick you in the dirt.

And because I had persisted, the spirits had finally listened to me. That was how it was with these things—sometimes the spirits had to be cajoled, urged on. But then once they had decided, that was that. Things changed.

Guido had stood up and was waiting for me to join him.

'We'd better go,' he said, as if there had never been any doubt about my coming. 'They're all waiting for you.' And when I came up to him he put a long gangly arm around my shoulders.

Fabrizio and I had wandered along the paths of Colle di Papa a hundred times together; but the path Guido led me by, winding and twisting in all directions, through thick patches of bush, over steep rocky slopes, across half-familiar streams, left me disoriented and lost, the landscape seeming to repeat itself endlessly, as if we were going in circles.

'We're almost there,' Guido kept saying. 'You've probably never been to this part of the mountain before. We had to make a special map so people would remember how to get there.'

But the sheltered clearing we finally arrived at looked very much like the one where Fabrizio and I often smoked our cigarettes. Now about a dozen boys were gathered there in a rough circle, leaning against trees or seated on rocks, passing a lit cigarette from hand to hand.

'Oh, *finalmente!*' someone said as Guido and I broke through the bushes into the clearing. A chorus of cheers went up.

'Ho, Vittò! It's about time!'

And now all the boys had come up to gather around me, some of them clapping a friendly hand on my shoulder. It was Vincenzo himself, a thumb cocked in his belt, his ruddy face all smiles and good will, who passed me the cigarette.

'Friends, eh?'

He gestured for me to take a puff of the cigarette;

but when I did, sucking in too quickly, the smoke burned at my throat and set me coughing. Vincenzo, though, was all concern, patting my back gently to help me clear my lungs. When I had recovered another chorus of cheers went up.

'Hey Vittorio.' It was Alfreddo. He was the only one who had not come up to greet me, seated in a rocky hollow like a king on his throne, his brown corduroy cap cocked to one side, his legs stretched out on the ground with a studied casualness. Alfreddo had a long, lank body that did not look as if it would stand up well in a fight; but his air of calm confidence seemed to work like a charm or potion over the other boys, and his control over his group was absolute.

'We hope you're not angry about those names we called you,' he said, smiling warmly. Alfreddo always spoke in a low drawl that was almost a whisper, as if anything louder or faster might disturb his own inner calm. 'We were just having a joke. Here, come over and sit beside me.' He patted the ground beside him. When I had settled there he put a warm arm around me, and as if on cue the other boys re-formed their circle in front of him. For a moment nobody spoke.

'Guido said you saw my mother at the hospital,' I said finally.

'Did he?' Alfreddo lifted his head with the slowness of a great bird to look over at Guido. 'At the hospital. That's right, isn't it, Guido?'

'That's right,' Guido said. 'You saw her yesterday, when you went to visit your sick aunt from Tornamonde. She said it was all right if Vittorio joined our group.'

The other boys murmured in agreement.

'Your mother told me to ask you,' Alfreddo said, with an encouraging smile, 'what happened that day in the stable when the snake bit her. She said you saw the whole thing.'

But now my thoughts began suddenly to clot.

'I only saw the snake,' I said, flushing. 'It was coming out of the stable from the door.'

'From the door,' Alfreddo said, pursing his lips and nodding. 'And what colour was the snake?'

'Green,' I said.

'Green,' Alfreddo said. *'Na bella serpe verde.'* He smiled, and around the circle the other boys smiled too. 'And how long was this green snake?'

But though I tried to think, the image of the snake would not come to me.

'I don't know,' I said.

'Three feet long? Four? Five?'

'Five feet long,' I said. 'I think it was five.'

'Five feet long! *Gesù e Maria*, a beautiful green snake five feet long!' Alfreddo had begun to laugh, but a low, friendly laugh. The other boys started to laugh too.

'Imagine that,' Vincenzo said. 'Five feet long!'

'I saw the tongue too,' I added.

'The tongue too!' Alfreddo said. 'The tongue on top of everything!'

But now suddenly Alfreddo drew up close to me again, as if to tell me a secret.

'You know, you're lucky your mother didn't go with another man,' he said in a whisper. 'Then there'd be trouble, eh? They say that if a woman goes with another man and gets bitten by a snake, then the next baby she has will have the head of a snake. And then the only thing you can do'—he made a sudden jabbing motion with a clenched fist, and I started back—'is to kill the baby the minute it's born, and cut out its eyes, so the evil eye won't follow you.'

For an instant then I wished I hadn't come up to the mountain at all, wanted to bolt into the woods and be away, my mind filled suddenly with the vision of the two eyes that had lunged at me from the stable the day of the snake, and with the fear that I had been party to some unspeakable crime which Alfreddo would slowly unmask now; but Alfreddo had already sat back and begun cleaning his fingernails with a jack-knife, as if he had suddenly lost all interest in me. When he spoke again, though, it was in a new tone, distant and slightly ominous.

'Did Guido tell you what you have to do to become a member?' he said.

'I didn't want to tell him,' Guido said, 'because *la maestra* was following us.'

I hadn't noticed *la maestra* at all, could not imagine her scrambling furtively up Colle di Papa's rocky slopes to keep up to us or lying in wait for us behind bushes; but Alfreddo nodded knowingly, as if he was well-acquainted with *la maestra*'s ways.

'That old whore,' he said, and the other boys laughed. 'Good. Vincenzo can tell him, he knows how we do it, eh Vincenzo?'

'Sure, we all had to do it, it's easy,' Vincenzo said, and the other boys murmured in agreement. 'First you have to show us your bird, to prove you're a man, and then if it's big enough you can join. It has to be at least half as long as a cigarette.'

So there was still a test. A sick feeling began to build in the pit of my stomach. The Fascists, my mother had told me, used to test people sometimes by making them drink cod liver oil—that was how I felt now, as if I was being forced to swallow something I didn't like, the bile already beginning to collect in my throat at the thought.

Vincenzo was pointing to a small hole in the ground in front of Alfreddo.

'After you show everyone,' he was saying, 'you have to put it in the hole and move it up and down fifty times. Make sure you go as deep as you can. The rest of us will count out loud. When you reach fifty, then you're a member.'

Everything happened quickly now. On a nod

from Alfreddo, Vincenzo and one of the other boys lifted me by the armpits, and before I had had time to think or object I was already pinned face up on the ground, one boy on each arm and Alfreddo sitting on my ankles, the other boys peering down at me like a flock of strange birds. Alfreddo unbuckled my pants with a ritual slowness, pulling the belt free with a low hiss of leather, then undoing the buttons at my waist and down my fly. His nails brushed against my skin as he pulled down my pants, and I shivered; but even if I had wanted to bolt now I could not have, my body held to the ground as if nailed there. The boys were looking down on me, eyes wide.

'Look at the size of that,' Vincenzo said. 'It must be five feet long.' But no one laughed.

'It's a big one, all right,' Alfreddo said, leaning back so the other boys could have a better look.

'It's almost as big as a mule's,' one of them said, and then Guido reached down and grabbed the wrinkled end of it between thumb and forefinger, moving it back and forth to inspect it.

'It's not the regular kind,' he said finally, and the other boys fell silent. But then, after a pause: 'This is the kind they used to have before the war. You can tell because it has more meat on it.'

Some of the other boys agreed that Guido was right. But one of them said that it was more like the kind the Africans had, and that maybe one of my great-grandfathers had been an African; and someone else said it was in America that you found birds like that, which meant that one day I would go to America. Now each of the boys took sides, arguing about the colour and the length and the thickness; but they couldn't reach a conclusion.

'Give me a cigarette,' Alfreddo said finally. 'We'll do the test.'

Vincenzo reached into his pocket and handed Alfreddo a wrinkled cigarette. But just as Alfreddo was reaching forward to apply the measure, the eyes of all the other boys fixed on my groin, he lurched forward suddenly and let out a powerful grunt, his hand shooting up to the back of his head. Suddenly the clearing was filled with shouts and confusion: in an instant the boys around me had scattered, shouting curses and running towards some distraction at the edge of the clearing. Alfreddo himself quickly recovered from whatever blow had felled him, leaping up in one quick motion and raising his voice for the first time that afternoon: '*Ammazzatelo!*'

Kill him. There at the far edge of the clearing, backed up against a cliff wall and wielding a long thick stick which he whirled back and forth in a mad semi-circle, striking anyone who came in his path, was Fabrizio, answering curse for curse the abuse which the other boys were hurling at him.

'I'll break the heads of all of you!'

And for a moment it seemed that he would: time and again his stick found its mark, striking elbows and heads and ribs with a dull thud, holding the boys back. But what had gotten into him? He had ruined my chances now, that was certain, and as I struggled up, still buckling my pants, I felt myself flush with anger and hate, hate for Fabrizio, my only friend, who seemed suddenly stupid and useless beyond all bearing. I hated him in that moment more than I had ever hated Vincenzo or Alfreddo or any of the boys who tortured me at school, hated him as if he were something shackled to me that I must cut away at all costs, the way animals gnawed off their own limbs when caught in a hunter's trap. And I hated him even though an awful truth was already forcing itself on me, all the events of the afternoon beginning to distort and skew like objects in a curved mirror.

Alfreddo had stepped into the fray now, and as Fabrizio's stick arched towards him he reached out a swift hand and caught it in his open palm, then quickly closed his other hand around the first and yanked mightily. Fabrizio, still holding the other end of the stick, lurched forward suddenly and fell to the ground. In a moment the other boys were on him, and Fabrizio was shouting, 'Oh, Vittò, get the stick!' But I was already running, wildly, tumbling down the slopes of the mountain until I emerged finally breathless and bleeding behind the church, running still until I had slammed myself at last into my own bedroom, where I dragged out the sock that held the chicken's head and flung it from my balcony out towards the ravine, as far as I could manage, before breaking into sobs on my bed. And I did not have to wait until the following morning, when Alfreddo whispered 'Five feet long!' as he passed my desk, to a chorus of laughter, to know that I had betrayed Fabrizio, as surely as if I had wished him dead, and to know also that I had sunk so low in shame now that no magic or miracle could ever reclaim me.

~~~

XVI

My mother had come home from the hospital with little
fanfare, in Cazzingulo's truck, after being away more than
a week. She had begun to wear long, loose dresses now,
ones that fell straight at the waist, and that hid for a while
the slow swelling going on underneath them; but she did
not go into the village anymore, not even for Sunday mass,
and if she stepped out of the house at all it was only to feed
the animals or to pick the olives at the back of the garden.
If there were other errands to be done, water to be fetched
or something to be bought at Di Lucci's, she would send me
off early in the morning before I left for school, or wait till
I had returned in the afternoon. It was only to send me on
these errands that she spoke to me now; other times she
hardly seemed to notice my presence, her face expression-
less as a ghost's, as if the swelling in her stomach had
sucked all the life out of her. Not a word passed between
her and my grandfather: it was as if they simply did not see
each other, moving through the same house, the same
room, as if they only sensed each other's alien presence
lurking like a shadow nearby, and kept clear of it. For a few
days after my mother's return, my grandfather kept to his
room; but then he began to go up to Di Lucci's again, sitting

not on the terrace any more but in the back room where Di Lucci sometimes served meals, and where people like Angelo the Red or Silvio the postman would sit sometimes for a night of drinking. In the evening when my grandfather returned home the wine would be heavy on his breath.

Meal times were the worst. Sometimes my grandfather would not come home at all, though I'd gone up to Di Lucci's to call him, and my mother and I would wait in silence for half an hour or more, the table set, before sitting down to eat without him. When he did come he remained walled up in his stony silence, his head bowed over his plate, while my mother sat turned away from him crosswise, her legs never under the table, as if she expected at any moment to have to rise up suddenly on some errand. All our meals now had this provisory quality about them, as if there were something more important that they were standing in the way of; but at the same time they seemed to stretch out interminably, as if we were mired in the strange torpor of an afternoon dream, some force retarding our movements to a painful, maddening slowness. In the charged silence each sound, a fork against a plate, the muffled clenching of teeth, seemed unnatural, a violation.

On Sundays, Aunt Lucia and Marta still came to eat with us, even when my grandfather was out. For a while I was comforted by this one sign of constancy and by Zia Lucia's continued dignified calm, which seemed the mark of a rare wisdom, as if a few words from her could suddenly set right all the troubles of our house; but the Sundays passed and only the same commonplaces crossed her lips whenever she spoke, as if she were merely blind, had not noticed our household's agitation, and a resentment began to build in me for her stupidity or obstinacy, for the five *lire* coins she still gave me with the same ghost of a smile, as if nothing had changed. It was Marta, instead, in whom knowledge seemed to be growing, burgeoning in her crooked and strange, like a plant in rocky soil. Marta seldom spoke, and when she did she seemed to waver between nonsense and sudden lucidity: sometimes without warning she'd break into a conversation to say how she'd hurt her foot that day when she'd gone to the fountain, or how she'd seen a rat behind her house; but a few minutes later she might make some remark that seemed suddenly to the point, as if she'd been following all along what others had been saying. Sometimes she'd begin clearly and then slowly twist away into her strange logic, her comments like riddles or oracles that refused to give up their meaning, that slipped away as soon as you tried to grab hold of them. But mainly she sat silent, watching over us with her nervous bird-eyes, drinking in every gesture, her glance darting sometimes to my mother's belly with what seemed like sharp understanding.

Fabrizio had not come back to school. From his brother Fulvio I found out he'd been hired out to a farmer near Rocca Secca.

'Oh, *stronzo*,' he called out to me once in the street. 'Five feet long, eh? You fixed my brother all right, that's for sure. My father threw him out of the house—he left the sheep alone on the mountain, we had to look for them halfway to Capracotta. He's out at the Valley of the Bones now, with Rompacazzo, that old bastard, he'll be lucky if he lasts the winter!'

But at school the other boys seemed to have grown suddenly bored with their teasing; either that or, understanding the meaning of my mother's loose dresses, they had begun to fear the truth of Alfreddo Girasole's prediction, his whispered warning to me about a snake-headed child. *La maestra*, though, continued unabated in her attentions. 'Vittorio!' she'd call out as I hurried past her in the morning. 'Look, your shirt is coming out of your pants.' And she'd bend with a smile to tuck it in, while a dozen other untucked shirts slipped past us unnoticed. Some part of me encouraged her in her new attitude—in the space of a few weeks I had become a model student, took my books home every night and studied them diligently, my tests coming back to me now only with large red swirls of approval. When the teacher assigned seat work now she always let me work in peace while she went around to the other students scolding and rapping heads; and then finally when I had set down my pencil she'd lean over me, with her garlic and perfume smell, and rest a heavy hand on my shoulder.

'*Bene*, Vittorio, *bravo!*' she'd say, picking up my exercise book and holding it open to the class. 'Vittorio has got every question right!'

After class I still stayed behind to sweep the room and clean the chalkboard, and though the threat of violence seemed to have abated I was grateful nonetheless to be spared for half an hour or so from returning home; but sometimes I'd look up from my corn broom and catch the teacher staring at me with her wet-eyed look of pity, and something inside me would grow cold and I'd begin to sweep more furiously, raising great clouds of dust that hung in the windows' shafts of light like fog. Then one day as I was scooping up the last of the day's dirt, dawdling, I noticed her glancing pregnantly at me several times, some new devilment surging in her.

'That's fine, Vittorio,' she said finally. 'Now come over here, I have something to show you.'

I went up to the front of her desk but she motioned me to come around beside her.

'*Più vicino.* Don't be shy.'

She reached down between her legs and from a chafed leather handbag under her desk drew a large cloth-bound book. *Lives of the Saints*, the title read, *adapted by Giambattista del Fiore from the tales of The Golden Legend.* Underneath was a glossy colour plate, glued to the book's cover, showing a cassocked man in a garden or courtyard, two white birds perched on his outstretched hand. A golden halo hovered above his head.

'San Francesco,' the teacher said. 'He was so gentle that even the birds came to eat from his hands.'

'In Rocca Secca I saw someone feeding the pigeons like that in front of the church,' I said.

'It's not the same thing,' *la maestra* said firmly. 'San Francesco was a saint. The birds came to him because he was a man of God. Those pigeons in Rocca Secca are like rats, they only come for the food.'

The teacher cracked open the book and leafed through its thumb-worn pages, stopping finally at the saint for that day's date. Here was another colour plate, covered by a sheet of fine white tissue which the teacher lifted gingerly aside: another haloed man, this one in a forest, his hair long and golden, his right hand holding a wooden staff and one foot resting atop the head of a large snake whose body lay coiled and inert in the foreground.

'San Leonardo,' the teacher said, and then she began to read me his tale. San Leonardo had the strength of a lion, and wrought many miracles; he was the patron saint of prisoners, and broke their chains whenever they invoked his name in prayer. As the teacher read I inched up closer to her, caught up by the sound of her voice; and finally she had reached out an arm and circled it around my shoulder.

'And once when San Leonardo lay on the ground in prayer,' she read, 'a huge serpent came out of the woods and slid up inside his shirt. But the saint did not even get up from his prayer. He waited until he had finished, and then he said to the serpent: "I know that ever since the day you were created you have made as much trouble for men as you could; but now, if God has given you power over me, then do to me whatever I have deserved!" And at these words the serpent jumped out of San Leonardo's shirt and fell at his feet dead.'

So began what became almost a daily ritual over

the next weeks: every day after my sweeping the teacher would call me up gently to her desk, and read to me the deeds of the saints. At first I kept up my grudging resistance; but finally I could no longer hide from myself the vague longing that focused each day now on the teacher's afternoon readings, when I seemed to drift briefly out of the world as into a dream, or deny the disappointment I felt when the reading was finished, and I had to return again to the thickening gloom of my grandfather's house. Sometimes, still, when I was sweeping, my hate for the teacher would well up inside me until I could not bear it, until I could feel the muscles in my jaws begin to tense with it, as if someone was interminably scratching a nail against the chalkboard; but during the readings the hate slowly drained away from me. When she read the teacher seemed suddenly to lose her flesh and blood presence, to become merely a voice, disembodied and pure; and it was always a shock at the end of a reading when I became aware again of her strange mountain of flesh, with all its swells and summits, sitting real and solid beside me.

La maestra more or less followed the order of the calendar in these readings; though sometimes she'd make digressions to pick out saints that would be special to me. There were my name saints—San Victorinus, known for his great fortitude in suffering, martyred by being pounded to death in a great marble mortar; San Vittorio the First, a pope, who underwent constant persecutions for his energy and zeal; San Innocente, also a pope and zealot, who was spared by his absence from the sack of Rome just as Lot had been spared from Sodom. Then my birthday saint, San Bartolomeo, one of the Twelve Apostles: after Christ's Resurrection he preached the Gospel in India, and when he had worked many miracles and converted many sinners he was skinned alive by barbarians and then beheaded, thus fulfilling his martyrdom.

When school let out for Christmas *la maestra* had a

treat for me: I was to be allowed to take her book home for the holidays. I smuggled it home with me under my other books, anxious that my classmates and my mother not see it; but when I had got it up to my room and begun to leaf through it I saw that the stories were full of long words whose meanings I didn't know, and which the teacher must have been leaving out during her readings. Still, over the next few days, with the help of a *vocabolario* I found in my grandfather's room, I made my way through the story of Santa Cristina, on July twenty-fourth, a virgin and martyr famous for the wonders she had worked through the power of Christ.

Santa Cristina had been born into the house of a rich Roman nobleman, but at a young age she became a Christian and broke up all of the gold and silver images of the pagan gods in her father's house, selling the pieces to help the poor. When her father discovered her crime he beat her without mercy and brought her before the magistrate for final judgment, and thus began a long series of chastisements. First the judge ordered that Santa Cristina be thrown into a pit with a hundred venomous serpents; but these Santa Cristina overcame, through the strength of Christ, and she was brought once again before the court. Now her flesh was torn away with large iron hooks; but Santa Cristina picked up a chunk of her own flesh and threw it into the magistrate's face. Finally the judge had her tied to a stake to be burnt as a witch; but when a fire was lit beneath her it spread to burn down a whole block of the city, killing hundreds but leaving Santa Cristina untouched. That night, while Santa Cristina waited in a cell, the magistrate suffered a seizure and died.

In the morning Santa Cristina was brought before a second magistrate. He ordered her put into a large tub of boiling oil; but Santa Cristina emerged from it as if she had merely taken a warm bath. Next her head was shaved and she was led naked through the city to the temple of Jupiter;

but when she reached the temple the image of the god fell headlong into the street and shattered into a thousand pieces. And now the second judge, too, suffered a seizure and died.

On the third morning, her hair grown back, her flesh healed, Santa Cristina was brought before the third magistrate. Two guards shackled her to a wall and cut off her breasts; but milk, not blood, flowed from the wounds, and Santa Cristina, slipping from her shackles, warned the judge not to go on, because the power of Christ was surely greater than his own. The judge ordered her tongue cut out; but Santa Cristina, still talking freely, threw the tongue at the judge's eye, which immediately went blind. Finally the judge ordered Santa Cristina to be cast into the sea. A battalion of a hundred men marched her, naked and shackled, to the port, where she was tied to the prow of a ship and rowed out several miles from the harbour, to the deep water. A great slab of stone was strapped to her body with chains—it took a dozen men to lift her to the ship's rail and thrust her towards the sea. But just as Santa Cristina was about to strike the water, the stone and chains slipped mysteriously from her: for an instant she hovered above the surface of the sea like a shade, dressed now in flowing white, while the sky, a moment before a clear blue, was eclipsed suddenly by a mass of purple clouds, a sole shaft of light trained on Santa Cristina. Then the archangel Michael was standing beside her; and while the soldiers watched, Michael cupped a palmful of sea-water and brought it to Santa Cristina's forehead. At last he reached out his hand to her and he led her up into the heavens, while on the earth a great storm was finally unleashed, and the Roman ship and all aboard it were swallowed into the sea.

~~~

XVII

By Christmas my mother's loose dresses had begun to swell around her waist, hanging like tents above her shins; and with each day the tension in our house seemed to thicken, as if the swelling itself had become the measure of it, was responding to it like a gauge or meter. Then on Christmas morning, my grandfather broke a silence that had lasted more than two months.

'Get dressed,' he said to my mother. 'You're coming to church.'

My mother was standing at the side counter scrubbing a pot with fistfuls of dirt.

'He's crazy,' she muttered, when my grandfather had gone into his room to dress; but after a moment she abruptly ceased her scrubbing, wiped her hands on her apron, and went up to her room.

I was the first to be dressed, and stood waiting at the kitchen door in my Sunday suit and blackened shoes, staring out into the street. The morning was cold and clear and brilliant, the village coated with a thin crust of snow that had fallen in the night; the coldness crept up at my ankles and wrists, my suit grown too small, almost two years old now, not replaced that year as I'd hoped it would by a new one from Rocca Secca. Finally the bell began to toll, with all the unbridled violence and clarity of a crisp winter morning, cracking the air with its peals. The bell was coated with a layer of pure silver: during the war, it was said, Father Nick's predecessor had smeared it with soot to protect it from the Germans, and my mother said that Father Nick had not cleaned it since; but this morning it was polished to a sheen, glinting brightly from its tower as it swung to and fro and caught the sun, seeming to silver the air with its fine hollow ringing.

My grandfather emerged finally from his room in his fedora and baggy corduroy suit, his medals pinned in a line to his breast pocket, the silver and bronze medallions of them freshly polished. He came up to the door and stared into the street, grimacing at the light.

'Let's go,' he said finally.

But the door to my mother's room creaked open now and my mother appeared at the top of the stairs, dressed not in one of her loose dresses but in a white blouse and a black skirt which fit tight around her waist, the swell there rising up like a hill. She had wrapped a blue shawl around her shoulders, her hair flowing over it in loose waves, and her face was composed in a look of stern resoluteness, her eyes suddenly alive again for the first time in months, as if they had caught a glint of light and scattered it back like cut glass.

Outside, the sun had already begun to melt the night's snow, crystal drops falling from the eaves of houses, small icicles forming on the goat horns posted above doorways to protect against the evil eye. The bells had stopped tolling now, but up ahead some of the villagers were still passing through the square. Then behind us a door creaked open and a babble of family noises filled the street, curses and babies' cries—the Mastronardis, late for mass. But as they came up behind us, overtaking us because of my grandfather's slow pace, their voices went suddenly quiet. They made a small arc around us, eyes averted, mumbling holiday greetings which my grandfather returned with a stiff formality.

We would be the last to arrive. The church would be full today, congregants spilling out into the porch; but a few places would still have been left free for my grandfather in the front pew, no one having thought yet to strip that privilege from him. In a moment the Mastronardis, too, had disappeared up the church steps, and when we came finally into the square, our shoes crunching strangely loud against the snow underfoot, it was deserted and still, the barren trees on the embankment leaning towards us like silent magi, offering down their crystal drops of melting snow.

~~~

XVIII

If the cock was in the fields, the men of Valle del Sole said, the hen would lay her eggs in someone else's nest. Yet that was what the men had always done, left their wives behind while they travelled out to farm their own fields or to earn a wage, away for days or months at a time, or now, if they worked in France or Switzerland, or across the sea, sometimes for years. Their fears had given birth to a wealth of proverbs: 'Guard your women like your chickens,' they said, 'or they'll make food for the neighbour's table'; or 'A woman is like a goat: she'll eat anything she sees in front of her.' Yet it was the women of the village who had been harshest towards my mother, and who watched hawk-eyed from their stoops for the slow progress of her disease, as if they had taken it upon themselves to keep the disease from spreading; and even at mass now, and afterwards as we filed back into the village, the men seemed merely awkward and put out by my mother's presence, passing by us stoop-shouldered, their eyes averted almost guiltily, as if they had been forced into a posture that did not sit well with them, while the women avoided my mother still with a cold-eyed rectitude, hurrying their children around us with their backs straight and their eyes forward.

But later, after we'd finished a sullen meal with Zia Lucia and Marta, my mother just clearing away the dishes, there was a knock at our door. Marta's eyes darted to the door with a look of wild-eyed curiosity, but for a moment no one moved to answer it, as if we could not make sense of the sound we'd heard there.

'Go on, Vittorio, open it,' Zia Lucia said finally.

A moment later Giuseppina and her husband and children were huddled in a close group inside the doorway, reeking of winter and looking stiff and formal in their Christmas clothing. Almost in unison they uttered a forced *'buon natale,'* Giuseppina moving awkwardly towards the centre of the room, offering a tray she'd held in the crook of an arm towards my mother as she pulled a white cloth from it.

'I brought you some pastries,' she said. 'You probably didn't have time to make any yourself.'

She'd brought a tray of *ostie,* paper-thin wafers like large Communion hosts sandwiching a thick layer of honey and chopped almonds. Every family in the village had irons for making their *ostie* and their *cancelle,* crusty diamond-shaped waffles, at holiday times, the irons made up by the blacksmith in Rocca Secca and bearing the family name or initial on the plates, so it came out in relief on each pastry; but this Christmas our own irons had sat in their corner of the kitchen untouched.

'*Grazie,*' my mother said, but she didn't reach out to take the tray. 'Why don't you offer some to the children?'

Giuseppina's husband still hovered near the doorway, cap in hand, his children grouped around him awkwardly, as if for a photograph.

'Come in and sit down,' my grandfather said gruffly. 'Cristina, get a glass for Alberto.'

'It's so nice what Father Nicola did with the church this year,' Giuseppina was saying. 'The wise men and the little animals and the baby. I went up after and even the diapers were made of silk. Silk diapers! The whole thing must have cost a fortune.'

'You paid for it,' my mother said.

But now there was another knock at the door and Di Lucci burst into the room, his wife and one of his sons (he always left the other at home on Christmas, to tend the shop) hanging back behind him.

'Oh, *buon natale!*' he called out, plunking a bottle of brandy on the table. '*Bicchieri*, Cristina, glasses for everyone! A Christmas toast!' And he immediately helped himself to one of the *ostie*.

'Sit down, Andò,' my grandfather said. 'Cristí, bring us some more glasses.'

And so our home, which for months had known only a lenten silence, was once again filled with a little life and conversation. Some consensus had been reached, it seemed, at dozens of houses across the village, my mother's presence at church, debated and discussed over Christmas dinner, finally taken perhaps as some kind of a sign, the sign of the repentance and guilt which the villagers had no doubt long been waiting for; and now they felt free to flock to the sinner like comforters to Job, for the matter had passed out of their hands and into the hands of God. If anyone had noticed the cold defiance with which my mother had walked down the aisle of the church and taken her place at her pew, they had chosen to ignore it; what my mother thought, after all, was her own business, but the people had to have a sign. It was as if my mother had simply written a character in the air, a cipher, and those who looked on it were happy enough to give it the meaning that suited them.

As the afternoon passed our house began to fill. Alfreddo Mastroantonio came by, former head of the *comitato* and, it was rumoured, a candidate to fill the position of mayor my grandfather had vacated; though he stopped in only to offer an overly hearty *buon natale*, straining to force

a little gaiety into his usual stiff formality, and to drop off
a bottle of *amaretto* for my grandfather. But several of the
neighbours stopped in too, as well as my grandfather's
nephews and nieces; and soon the tray of *ostie* was empty,
everyone taking a ritual one as they entered the house, to
be replaced by platesful of *cancelle* and other pastries,
children flitting between the grown-ups like ghosts to dart
a quick arm towards the kitchen table and then retreat to a
corner with their catch. A dozen conversations buzzed at
once, swelling to a peak and then lulling suddenly to build
again, borne along by some secret rhythm; babies in their
mother's arms cried just loud enough to be heard above the
din, until a mother interrupted herself suddenly to cry 'Oh,
basta!' and her baby retreated into a brief whimpering
silence.

        The room had gradually divided in two, the women
standing near the side counter, where my mother was
constantly pouring drinks and washing glasses, the men
grouping around the kitchen table, straddled backwards
over chairs. But a strange shift seemed to have happened
since that morning: the women had dropped their straight-
backed rectitude, as if they had suddenly remembered
some sin or crime for which they themselves had gone
unpunished, now openly solicitous towards my mother,
offering to help pass out drinks and pastries, to wash
glasses, even though my mother refused them each time
with the same tired smile; but the men, when my mother
came round to serve them, made way for her with a casual
indifference, as if she were invisible, and wrapped up in
their own conversations they did not bother so much as to
glance up at her as they took a drink or pastry from her
proffered tray. It was as if something in my mother's
misfortune had made them suddenly feel invulnerable
and strong, and they joked with each other in a way that
seemed strangely candid and coarse, all their timidness
gone. My grandfather, though, sat by saying little, down-

ing glasses of brandy in quick gulps. He reached an arm
out feebly once to draw Giuseppina's little girl Rosina to
him as she reached out to the table for a pastry; but Rosina
shied away from him, and he quickly withdrew. From a
corner of the room Marta watched over us all like a fate,
nibbling on a host, and when I followed her eyes they
seemed always to light away from the centre of things—on
my mother scrubbing glasses at the sideboard, her back to
the room, her shoulders working with a restrained violence; on my grandfather turning suddenly to spit into the
fire.

But as twilight descended, the light from the fire
casting long flickering shadows across the room, the guests
began to take their leave. Soon the last of them had gone,
leaving the same air of desolation as the village square had
after the festival, the kitchen quickly reverting to its familiar heavy silence. My grandfather sat staring silently into
the fire while my mother lit the lamp that hung above the
table and set out some bread and cheese. She poured out
a glass of wine and my grandfather reached back to take it
up, his hand trembling.

'They came here,' he said, still staring into the fire,
'to laugh at us.'

My mother sat down at the table and took up a slice
of bread, tearing it in half with a quick pull.

'They're idiots,' she said finally. 'It was only for
your sake that I didn't chase them out of here with a whip.'

But my grandfather wheeled round suddenly and
slammed his glass onto the table.

'For *my* sake! Was it for my sake you behaved like
a common whore? Do you think you're better than those
people? *They* are my people, not you, not someone who
could do what you've done. I've suffered every day of my
life, *per l'amore di Cristo*, but I've never had to walk through
this town and hang my head in shame. Now people come
to my house like they go to the circus, to laugh at the

clowns! You've killed me, Cristina, you killed your mother when you were born and now you've killed me, as surely as if you'd pulled a knife across my throat. In all my days I've never raised a hand against you but now I wish to God I'd locked you in the stable and raised you with the pigs, that you'd died and rotted in the womb, that you hadn't lived long enough to bring this disgrace on my name!'

My grandfather had taken up his cane and risen from his chair, his face flushed. My mother flinched, as if she expected him to raise up his cane against her; but without looking back at her he crossed the room to his bedroom and slammed the door shut behind him. But the silence was broken again now by muddled sounds from his room—a crash, a thud, a cry of pain. In an instant my mother was at the door; but when she had opened it a crack it wedged up against some obstacle.

'My leg,' my grandfather said, his voice tight with pain. He had fallen, his bedroom table toppled onto him and one leg stretching up at an awkward angle towards the door, blocking it. My mother knelt and reached a hand into the room to move the leg aside; but my grandfather let out another cry of pain.

'Don't move it.'

My mother rose and stood a moment undecided, her eyes wildly searching the room till they alighted finally on the axe by the wood pile.

'Stand back, Vittorio.'

She had the axe now. She clicked the bedroom door shut again and swung the axe hard against the door frame near the bottom hinge, the wood there splintering with a sharp crack.

'Go get Di Lucci,' she said. 'And tell him to bring the rack from the church. We'll need it to carry him.'

But I stood for a moment frozen, awed by the force of my mother's swings—she nearly had the bottom hinge free—until finally she turned to me and shouted, 'Hurry, *per l'amore di Cristo!'* and in a flash I was out the door and running once again up to Di Lucci's bar.

~~~

XIX

By the time I returned, Di Lucci and Father Nicola hurrying
behind me with the rack from the church, my mother had
axed the door off its hinges. We had picked up a small
crowd en route, and all along the street now the word was
going round that *lu podestà* had been hurt; within minutes
half the village had gathered, crowding into the kitchen
and around the front doors, craning for a better view.
Father Nick, in his black cassock and wide-brimmed cleric's
hat, stood next to my mother and me at the doorway to my
grandfather's room, rubbing his hands against the cold,
while inside Di Lucci issued instructions to two of my
mother's cousins, Virginio Catalone and his brother Pastore, who had elbowed their way through the crowd and
were struggling now to wedge the rack into the tight space
between the bed and my grandfather's prone form. Virginio and Pastore, identical twins, sullen and thick-set, had
kept clear of our house since my mother's troubles had
started; but they had not hesitated to push their way to the
front of the crowd when the word had gone out that my
grandfather was hurt.

'Try to slide it under him, like a spoon,' Di Lucci
was saying. But finally the two men, ignoring Di Lucci,

tilted the bed up against the wall with a single thrust and laid the rack flat on the floor. My grandfather let out a grunt as they lifted him onto it, his jaw clenched with the pain.

'Careful,' my mother said sharply. 'Can't you see you're hurting him?'

'He's broken his leg,' Father Nick said.

'*Grazie, dottore.*'

We stood aside as Virginio and Pastore carried the rack through the crowded kitchen and into the street, where a few thick flakes of snow had begun to fall. But now it was suddenly obvious that there would be no way of getting my grandfather into Di Lucci's cramped Fiat in his present state. Someone suggested that the front and back windshields be smashed away, and the rack slid through them.

'Don't be crazy,' Di Lucci said, paling. 'And anyhow, how would I drive, tell me, squashed under that rack like a worm?'

'Vittorio,' Father Nick said, standing by with a look of forced calmness, 'go inside and get a blanket to cover your grandfather.'

When I had come out again with a blanket, my mother was coming down the street trailing Mastronardi's mule and cart, a lantern swinging from one hand.

'At this rate you'll be here all night,' she said, pulling up in front of the house. 'Load him into the cart, there's no other way. Has anyone thought to cover him?' Then, seeing me standing with the blanket still in my hands, she took it from me and bent to drape it over my grandfather, brushing away the snow that had already begun to collect on his clothes.

'*Ma,* Cristina,' Di Lucci said, 'it'll take you half the night to get him to Rocca Secca on that cart. In this weather.' It had begun to snow in earnest now.

'Do you have any other ideas?'

'At least I could drive to Rocca Secca and see if they'll send out the ambulance.'

'You know as well as I do that ambulance hasn't left the garage since the war. And on Christmas night? They wouldn't come out here for Christ himself. But go on, if you want to, see what you can do. In the meantime I'll start out on my own. Someone bring some more blankets, *per l'amore di Cristo.*'

Di Lucci stood by hesitantly for a moment.

'*Dai*, Andò, smash out the windows,' someone suggested again. 'They'll freeze to death before they get to the hospital in that thing.'

'*Sí*, smash the windows,' Di Lucci said, already moving to the door of his car. 'You and your foolish ideas.' And in a moment he had heaved himself into the driver's seat, gunned up the engine, and sped off into the snow.

My mother had already motioned Virginio and Pastore to lift my grandfather onto the cart. His eyes were closed now, but he was muttering softly to himself, as if in troubled sleep, his face beaded with droplets that may have been sweat or melted snow. With a single discreet finger Father Nick made a quick sign of the cross over him as the two men slid the rack onto the cart. Several women had come forward now with blankets; my mother covered my grandfather with a thick layer of them, then draped one around her own shoulders and moved up to the head of the cart.

'Go back to your suppers,' she said to her cousins, 'I can manage on my own from here. There'll be someone at the hospital to help me carry him in.'

'Don't be an idiot,' Virginio said, moving up to take the reins from her. 'Pastore and I will take him in.'

'No. This is my affair.'

'Let Virginio take him in,' Mastronardi said, eyeing his cart proprietorially. 'The woods are full of thieves. And in your condition—'

'I can take care of myself,' my mother said quickly. And while Virginio and Pastore still hovered uncertainly near the cart my mother heaved herself onto the bench and gave the reins a quick jerk, the cart lurching suddenly forward as the mule raised up his head and thrust himself against his bridle.

'Wait, Cristina.'

It was Father Nick. My mother pulled back on the reins.

'What is it?'

'I'll come with you,' Father Nick said. 'Thieves won't harm a priest.'

'You?' My mother stared at him hard a moment. 'All right, then, let's go,' she said finally. 'Put a blanket around yourself, that padding on your belly won't be enough to keep you warm.'

There were a few muffled laughs, quickly suppressed. Father Nick blushed and hesitated a moment, but finally he took a blanket that was offered to him and draped it over his shoulders. He hiked up his skirts and walked briskly up to the cart, pulling himself onto the bench with surprising nimbleness.

'I'll take the reins,' he said, suddenly stern. 'You can get back in the cart and keep the snow off your father.'

'Suit yourself.'

Father Nick jerked the reins and the mule set off with a snort, the cart wheels creaking, flattening the snow beneath them with a soft crunch. The snow was falling heavy and thick now, and shortly the cart had been swallowed into its white hush; but for a long while we could still make out the haloed haze of my mother's lantern. Finally this too faded into the snow and night, and the villagers still gathered in front of our house brushed the snow off their shoulders and moved quietly back towards their unfinished suppers, and home.

~~~

XX

My grandfather had fractured his hip and broken a leg, the same one a horse had shattered in the war. He was in the hospital almost a month, my mother and I riding into Rocca Secca in Cazzingulo's truck once or twice a week to visit him. A metal frame enclosed his bed like a cage, his broken leg, wrapped in thick plaster up to his thigh, suspended from an upper bar of it by a cable, as if he were a strange sculpture that had been set out to dry and harden. His skin had taken on the same pallor as the white plaster of his cast, and when we came to see him he'd mumble to us as if talking out of a dream, hardly aware of our presence, his face limp with fatigue. Once the doctor came in with a nurse to give him an injection, the same doctor who had tended to my mother's snake bite, his eye going down to my mother's belly now with a gleam, as if he shared some secret with her about the bulge there.

'You've been well, I hope?' he said, in his burnished Italian, taking a needle from a tray the nurse held out to him and sucking a clear liquid into it from a tiny bottle.

But my mother took him quickly aside.

'Is it necessary to keep feeding him all those drugs?

Look at him, he hardly recognizes us. You'd never know I was his daughter.'

But the doctor moved aside my grandfather's blanket and jabbed the needle with a quick thrust into the soft flesh of his thigh.

'The bone in his leg shattered like glass,' he said when he had finished. 'We got out what we could, but there are still some splinters floating around there now, moving every time he breathes. Do you know what it feels like when one of those splinters brushes up against a nerve?' He set his needle back onto the nurse's tray. 'Like a knife.'

'He's had to deal with pain all his life,' my mother said. 'I'd rather see him in pain than like this.'

'Maybe that's a little selfish of you,' the doctor said.

Once when we visited, my grandfather called out to me by name, and my mother motioned me to stand beside him.

'Vittorio,' he whispered, taking my hand in his own and squeezing it feebly; but his hand was moist and clammy, and I pulled my own away as soon as I felt his fingers loosening.

While my grandfather was still in the hospital, letters began to arrive at our house from America. Only a few came at first, but soon they were coming almost daily, Silvio the postman handing them to my mother each day with the same sheepish shrug, each of them bearing the unmistakable scrawl of my father's hand. The inevitable had happened—someone had poured some poison in my father's ear. Some word from a friend or a family member or from one of the messengers who departed regularly from Castilucci and Valle del Sole for America (and from Valle del Sole itself there had been already three departures since *la festa*) had finally pierced the veil that shrouded my father's mysterious life across the sea; and now he let forth a fury of letters, my mother reading each with the same wild-eyed impatience before crumpling them and flinging them into the fireplace. 'He's crazy,' she'd mutter, and for the rest of the day a silent rage would seem to simmer inside her, and I'd know not to cross her. I thought that she would sit down soon at the kitchen table and write some response to him, the way she used to, then send me off to Di Lucci's to buy stamps for it and to post it at the mailbox there; but the days passed and still she had no letter for me to post. Late at night, though, I sometimes heard the scratch of her pen from her room, and the next morning she would be up early and gone to Rocca Secca, on what missions I did not know.

When my grandfather returned home, ferried to the village in the back of the mail truck, his leg still in a cast and his hip wound round with wide bandages, the fog that had clouded his mind during his stay in the hospital seemed to have lifted.

'I'll rot in this bed!' he'd shout out from his room. 'I'll die and rot here, you might just as well have put me straight into the grave!'

The muscles of his face never relaxed now, screwed into a perpetual grimace, and his eyes were ringed round with the pink of an infection he'd gotten at the hospital, as if the skin there were raw from crying. My mother served him his meals on a wooden stand the carpenter had made up to fit over the bed, and every night she emptied out the sack at his bedside fed by a long plastic tube that came down from his groin. Then once every two days or so my grandfather would call out to my mother with an embarrassed, angry shout, and she would close the door of his room and come out several minutes later with a pile of linen in a basin.

'Like a baby,' my grandfather would rumble. 'Sixty-six years old and my daughter has to change my diapers.'

But after months of silence my grandfather's curses seemed almost comforting, as if a storm had broken less disastrously than it had threatened; and my mother, too, had refound her voice, an almost ceaseless banter going on now between her and my grandfather, the subject of which was the letters which continued to stream into our house from my father. Long arguments were carried on daily between kitchen and bedroom, tensions hovering around a critical point but never seeming to move beyond it, the arguments finally petering out to a resigned silence that was more the calm after a storm than the one before it.

'He doesn't know what he wants!' my mother would say. 'One day he says he's coming back to wring my neck, the next that I can go to the dogs, the next that he wants me over there on the next boat. Last week he sent me a letter to give to the embassy in Rome, to get a visa. As if I'm going to travel half-way around the world in my condition. And then to put up with the same idiocy there that I put up with here!

'*Sei scimunita*, Cristí! Idiocy? Who's the idiot? You're lucky if he doesn't crack your skull and throw you in the streets!'

'Then to hell with all of you! I'll go to Rome, Naples, anywhere—'

'Ah, *bello*! Like a gypsy. And what will you live on, the few thousand *lire* you've saved from what he sends you? Because you'll not see a cent of my money, I swear on my grave. And with two children to take care of, you can work in the streets. *Disgraziata*.'

'Ah, *sí*, he's probably slept with every whore in America by now, but for me it's a disgrace. Women have had their faces up their asses for too long, they let their men run around like goats and then they're happy if they don't come home and beat them!'

'*Brava*. And you, *communista*, are going to change all that. With your Communist boyfriend, a foreigner no less, who's just a coward and a beggar. Yes, you think I'm blind, but I know all about him. Where is he now, your Communist boyfriend? Go, go, to Rome, to America, to the devil for all I care! Get out of my sight and let me die in peace. I'll sell the house to some rich Roman for a summer house, or I'll burn it to the ground and feed the fire with my own bones, and all the bones of my fathers who worked to build it!'

The arguments and curses left me with troubling images. I had a vision of my dark-haired father looming suddenly large and angry in our doorway one day, bringing with him some unspeakable doom; of my mother and me left to wander the streets of Rome or Naples like beggars, or packed suddenly onto a ship and sent off to a dark future across the sea. But a few weeks after my grandfather had returned home a final letter arrived from my father which seemed somehow to carry more weight than the rest.

'He thinks we're still in the dark ages,' my mother said the day it arrived, 'when women used to dump their babies at the back door of the convent in the middle of the night and leave them there to die from the cold. Let him carry a baby for nine months and see if he feels that way.'

'You'll do as he tells you,' my grandfather said. 'The orphanage is full of babies just like yours, don't think yours will be special. I'll not have that bastard child living under my roof.'

An uneasy truce settled over our house now, and it seemed that despite my mother's objections the matter was settled: whatever my mother was carrying in her belly—'that bastard child,' as my grandfather called it, which I thought might be a reference to the snake-headed baby Alfreddo had warned of—could be got rid of at the orphanage in Rocca Secca, so that for the time being we would be troubled by neither arrivals nor departures. Gradually an air of normalcy began to assert itself again in our household. My mother still kept up a tight-lipped aloofness around the other villagers; but she went about the town freely now, and the villagers did not skirt her as they used to, only nodded in greeting and continued on their way. And with the last day of March set now by the town's election committee as the date for the election of a new mayor, a hand-painted sign announcing the decision posted prominently on the front wall of Di Lucci's bar, some of the older men in the village had begun to visit my grandfather in his room, talking strategy and politics long into the night.

But I had learned by now that Valle del Sole had more than a single face.

'Still holding her nose up like a queen,' I overheard Maria Maiale say at Di Lucci's. '*Quella Maria!* Maybe it's a virgin birth.'

'Maybe it's the other Mary, *Magdalena*, you're thinking about,' Di Lucci said.

'We'll see what happens when her husband gets his hands on her. He'll crack her skull, you remember what he was like, just like his father. Then she'll see how good she's had it here.'

But there were other scandals too, more cryptic, which seemed about to surface. The election, it seemed, had stirred up much emotion in the village. My grandfather's party had chosen Alfreddo Mastroantonio, the former chairman of *il comitato della festa*, to replace my grandfather; but this time the election was not to be decided by acclamation, as it always had been during my grandfather's reign. The Communists, too, had fielded a candidate—Pio Dagnello, son of Angelo the Red, who every night now rose up on a crate in the square, his face flushed with emotion, and told the villagers how the government in Rome had ignored them since the war because no one among them had had the courage to raise an angry voice. At first the villagers paid him little atten-

tion, as if they took for granted that the government in
Rome would ignore them, and it was useless to think it
would ever be otherwise; but night by night the crowds
around Pio began to grow. Alfreddo Mastroantonio, who
did not make speeches in the square but held small private
meetings in the back room of Di Lucci's bar, seemed
alarmed: one day all the walls along via San Giuseppe
were suddenly covered with large posters that had been
printed up in Rocca Secca, an unheard-of expense, Alfreddo Mastroantonio's plump-cheeked face beaming its
strained smile from every one of them. But still the villagers continued to flock every night around Pio, and every
night Pio grew bolder in his denunciations, until there was
no mistaking who he blamed for the village's ills.

'You see how he paid for it in the end? He was the
first one to take them in when they came. Roads, he said!
Lights! *Viva il Duce*! The Communists will eat us alive! But
where are the roads now? Where are the lights? He sold
us to the devil for fifty *lire*, and because the people are like
sheep it's taken them twenty years to open their eyes. You
don't see Alfreddo Mastroantonio knocking on his door
now. Alfreddo may be a horse's ass, but he's no idiot. He
knows the old man sold us out.'

As election time grew nearer the visits to my
grandfather became more and more sporadic, only a few
old loyalists still coming by, mumbling consolations in
response to my grandfather's increasingly bitter invec-
tives.

'The village will go to the dogs, I tell you. Dagnello
is a liar and a coward. Where was he during the war? I'll
tell you where he was, gone out to some hole in the
mountains the very day the letter came calling him up for
service. If I'd had half a mind then I would have turned him
in. Now he makes it seem like he was a hero, when half his
cousins died in the same war, just so he could come back to
his house in one piece at the end of it. And Mastroantonio

is no better, the fool—you could buy him with the change in your pocket.'

Towards the end of February, another letter arrived for my mother; but this one bore a small neat script of bright blue, not at all my father's violent hand. My mother whisked the letter up to her room, closing the door behind her; and when I went up later I found her packing some clothes into a hamper.

'I'm going to Rome for a few days in the morning,' she said. 'I'll get Marta to come by to look after you and your grandfather.'

She drew open the drawer of her writing table, rifling through some papers there and sliding a few into her hamper.

'I don't want Marta to come,' I said.

'Please, Vittorio, don't start. I have some very important business to look after.'

When my mother brought in my grandfather's supper that night, I caught snippets of subdued conversation between them.

'If you ask me he's as foolish as you are,' my grandfather said. 'You should have waited till after, the way you'd decided. He won't have that child in his house.'

'We'll settle that,' my mother said. But her words were curiously empty and dead, as if they were not her own. 'I spoke to Zia Lucia, everything is arranged. But I don't want you to say anything to anyone until I get back.'

'What difference will it make? Now you think about keeping secrets. You should have thought of that months ago. I should have sent you away.'

'It would have been the same,' my mother said. 'Everyone would have known.'

'No. That's where you're stupid, Cristina. You carry your shame in the streets, you force people to point a finger at you. What you've done you've done, and may God forgive you for it; but that's not the way to be with people.'

'Please, don't start.'

Later, in bed, I heard the scratch of my mother's pen again. But when I went to her door she quickly slid the piece of paper she'd been writing on into her drawer.

'What is it?' she said, annoyed. 'You should be in bed.'

'Why do you have to go to Rome?'

She took in a breath in irritation; but after a moment her anger seemed to melt, and she drew me towards her and nestled me against her knees.

'Poor Vittorio. No one ever tells him anything.' She wrapped her arms around me, and I saw that she'd begun to cry. 'Do you promise to keep it a secret, if I tell you?'

'Yes.'

She pulled me closer, putting her cheek against mine.

'We're going to leave the village, Vittorio,' she whispered finally. 'In a few weeks, we're going to America.'

~~~

XXI

America. How many dreams and fears and contradictions were tied up in that single word, a word which conjured up a world, like a name uttered at the dawn of creation, even while it broke another, the one of village and home and family. In Valle del Sole the men had long been migrants, to the north, to Buenos Aires, to New York, every year weighing their options, whether the drought would ruin the year's crops, or a patch of land bring a sufficient price to buy a passage, whether to strike out for Torino or Switzerland, with the promise at least of a yearly return, or to reckon on an absence of years or a lifetime, and cross the sea.

Tales of America had been filtering into Valle del Sole for many years already. My grandfather's own father, who in the 1890s, just after my grandfather's birth, had left his family to fight in Abyssinia, had been among the first to reach there: when the war was over he had begun to wander, first along the coast of Africa—my grandfather used to joke that he had taken an African bride, and that somewhere now I had a brood of creamy-brown cousins who prayed in African but swore in Italian—then on to Argentina and finally New York. For several years he had sent money back, in increasingly large sums, enough to build the house we now lived in; but suddenly the money stopped, and nothing more was heard of him. After a year my grandfather's oldest brother had gone in search of him, but had returned in despair.

'Vanished,' my grandfather had told me. 'He might have died, or he might still be there now, a hundred years old, living like a king with some American wife.'

Others, too, had been swallowed up by America, never to be heard from again, a few like my great-grandfather leaving behind wives and children; but most, after an absence of years, had returned to the village, using their savings to build a house and to live out their years in relative ease. There were several houses in Valle del Sole that had been built with foreign earnings; though only an extra storey or room or a tarnished brass knocker on the door distinguished them from the rest, their owners perhaps fearing the envy that greater ostentation might have brought.

But since the war the village had known mainly one-way departures. The men left, and a few years later wives and children and sometimes ageing parents followed, land and livestock sold off, clothes and old pots packed up in wooden trunks made by the village carpenter, houses left abandoned, their doors and windows boarded up.

'Only babies and old people left behind,' my grandfather would grumble. 'No one left to work the land.'

But no one went to New York or Buenos Aires now, or to Abyssinia; they went instead to a place called the Sun Parlour. Before the war two men from our region, Salvatore Mancini of Valle del Sole and Umberto Longo of Castilucci, had smuggled themselves across the ocean and settled there—and it was the first time in history, people said, that a man from Valle del Sole and one from Castilucci had been able to work together without slitting each other's throats—and now one by one their relatives had begun to join them, every year the tide increasing. The Sun Parlour was in a new part of America called Canada, which some said was a vast cold place with rickety wooden houses and great expanses of bush and snow, others a land of flat green fields that stretched for miles and of lakes as wide as the sea, an unfallen world without mountains or rocky earth.

But for the many of us who had never been much beyond the small world circumscribed by the ring of mountains that cut off Valle del Sole's horizon in each direction, who had never passed out of hearing range of the village church bells, America was still all one, New York and Buenos Aires and the Sun Parlour all part of some vast village where slums and tall buildings and motor cars mingled with forests and green fields and great lakes, as if all the wide world were no larger than Valle del Sole itself and the hollow of stony mountains that cradled it. And for all the stories of America that had been filtering into the village for a hundred years now from those who had returned, stories of sooty factories and back-breaking work and poor wages and tiny bug-infested shacks, America had remained a mythical place, as if there were two Americas, one which continued merely the mundane life which the peasants accepted as their lot, their fate, the daily grind of toil without respite, the other more a state of mind than a place, a paradise that shimmered just beneath the surface of the seen, one which even those who had been there, working their long hours, shoring up their meagre earnings, had never entered into, though it had loomed around them always as a possibility. And these two natures co-existed together without contradiction, just as goats were at once common animals and yet the locus of strange spirits, just as *la strega* of Belmonte was both a decrepit old woman and a witch, a sorceress. When occasionally, now, a young man returned from overseas to choose a bride, the young women of the village primped and preened themselves, made potions, promenaded daily through the square, caught up in a dream of freedom, their every second word then a wistful 'Ah-merr-ica'; but when the young man had chosen, those left behind said *'Tutt' lu mond' è paes'*,' life was the same all over the world, sorry now for the one who had had to leave behind the familiar comfort of family and village for an uncertain destiny across the sea.

My mother, though, never spoke about America, as if the place did not exist for her, and what images I had of it I'd had to gather from my grandfather's stories and from the talk of the town. 'In America,' I'd heard Giuseppina Dagnello say once, 'the bread sticks in your mouth like glue. They have to put sugar in it or it wouldn't taste like anything.' Giuseppina, though, lived with her ageing parents, who had no one else to look after them, and had little prospect of crossing the sea. But Maria Maiale, who had a brother in America, told a different story. The houses there were so warm, she said, you could walk around in your socks even in the middle of winter. 'And telephones in every room, *per l'amore di Cristo*, it's the law there, you have to have a telephone. And when will we see a telephone in Valle del Sole? When our children's children are dead and buried in the grave!'

Fabrizio, ready with facts on any subject, had told me once that in America everyone lived in houses of glass.

'When you're taking a bath anyone can come by and look at you. You can see all the women in their underwear. People look at each other all the time, over there, because nobody believes in God.'

My mother was away in Rome for a week. She returned with passport in hand, one of its thick parchment pages stamped with a box of foreign script where numbers and dates and signatures had been filled in in pen, 'Canada' printed in capitals at the top beneath a blue crown. On the passport's signature page, layered over with stamps and seals, was a photograph of me and my mother that I had never seen before.

'Don't you remember?' my mother said, when I asked about it. 'We took it in Rocca Secca on your birthday.'

'Did you know we were going to go to America?'

'Of course not, *stupido*. I found out last week, just like you. I didn't have time to get another picture.'

Inside a blue plastic folder was the ticket that would get us from Naples to a place called Halifax, a tiny ship etched across the top of it.

'But where is *quest' Alifax*?' I asked. 'I thought we were going to America.'

'America is a big place,' my mother said.

Departures for America were common enough in Valle del Sole; Maria Mancini had left not a month before, with her parents and three children, to join her husband in the Sun Parlour, and one of the Mastroangelos had left around Christmas. But proper time was always allowed for the rituals of separation to be played out, for each relation to prepare a final meal, for belongings to be sold off or bequeathed, for trunks to be built and packed, for dozens of small parcels to be wrapped in brown paper and string by those being left behind to be delivered to some relative across the sea, as little packets of food were sometimes dropped into graves to be carried to the spirits on the other side. But my mother and I, it seemed, were being ripped untimely from our womb, without gestation: our own trunk was built in a day, and packed in a matter of hours; and our house, which had once seemed, even through the months of silence and anger, like a solid constant, unchangeable, infested as it was with our lives and smells, our histories, became almost overnight an empty shell, all the serviceable furniture carted up to Zia Lucia's and boards nailed across the shutters. Our sheep and pigs, confused and stubborn, were chased out of their stable and into Zia Lucia's, which had been abandoned for years; and my grandfather was once again placed on the church's rack, amidst groans and curses, and moved to Zia Lucia's as well, back into the house where he'd spent his childhood. He was set in a small ground floor room that looked out onto the spine of Colle di Papa, while my mother and I, together again in the last days, slept upstairs in Marta's room, Marta sleeping for the time in the kitchen on the flowered mattress that had been mine.

It was only when the last scrap of furniture had been removed from my grandfather's house, leaving my mother's packed trunk to sit alone in the middle of the kitchen floor, that our leaving took on in my mind the visible form of a truth. But in the few days that remained before our departure I could not bring that truth into any focus. I walked through the streets with a strange sense of lightness, as if at any moment I might simply lift up and walk on air; and houses, faces, voices seemed to fade away from me, to lose their power to impress me with their presence. But though my mind was filled with images of America, of tall buildings and wide green fields, of the dark-haired man I remembered as my father, I could not believe in the truth of them, even my father now seeming merely like someone I had imagined in a dream; and all I could see clearly of the future was a kind of limitless space that took shape in my head as the sea, and a journey into this space that took direction not from its destination but from its point of departure, Valle del Sole, which somehow could not help but remain always visible on the receding shore.

~~~

XXII

A few days before our departure I saw Fabrizio, as I came out of school, chasing his father's sheep through the late-winter mud and slush of via San Giuseppe. He looked frailer and thinner than he had in the fall; but he was still in his knickers and cap, swaggering as he walked, wielding his sheep stick like a sceptre. I waited at the top of the steps until he'd rounded the corner at the edge of town, so he wouldn't see me; but later that afternoon, tending the sheep down in the Valley of the Pigs, where the snow had all melted, I looked up to see him coming towards me from the direction of the cemetery. He came up without saying a word, plucking a stem of dead grass to chew and lowering himself cross-legged onto the ground beside the rock I was sitting on.

'My father says it's no use sending someone like me to school,' he said finally. 'He says I'm as stupid as a mule. The only way you can make a mule understand is with a whip.'

He stretched out his legs on the damp grass and leaned back on his elbows, holding his body with the studied nonchalance of a young man.

'Rompacazzo sent me home because I threw a

stone at a rat and made a hole in a bag of wheat. Pom!
across my face, just like my father. He says, *"Ma che sei,
scimunoit?"'*—Fabrizio put on the thick accent of Rocca
Seccans—*'"ma che sei, impazzoit?"* My father wanted to
crack my skull.'

He spit out a piece of chewed grass, then sat up
again and rubbed his goose-pimpled calves with his palms.

'Anyway, it doesn't matter to me,' he said. 'You
don't have to know *matematica* to stick a seed in the ground,
my father says. *E quella maestra'*—Fabrizio bloated his
cheeks and lifted out his arms, making a jogging motion
like a fat person walking—*'quella maestra* gave me a pain in
the ass. "Fabrizio"'—taking on the teacher's falsetto—
'"tell me, Fabrizio, ma chi sono le tre persone in Dio?" Addio,
quella porca!'

The sun had begun to set already, hovering cold
and red just above Castilucci. A gust of wind whipped
down sharply from the snow-covered upper slopes of the
mountains, rattling the bare branches of an old apple tree
nearby. A bird let out a few solitary notes; I searched for it
amidst the tree's branches but could not make it out.

Fabrizio was holding a cigarette out to me. I
hesitated, then took it, leaning forward towards Fabrizio's
proffered match.

'In America everybody smokes like chimneys,'
Fabrizio said. 'Sometimes you can't even see where you're
going because of all the smoke.'

'That's not true,' I said suddenly.

Fabrizio cocked his head and looked at me oddly,
squinting because of the sun.

'I was only making a joke,' he said finally.

He picked up a clump of dirt and slowly crushed
it in his fist, the dirt trickling in a fine powder onto the
pocket of his knickers. When a small mound had formed
he leaned forward and blew gently into the centre of it, the
dirt retreating from his smoke-filled breath in an ever-

widening circle.

'When you go to America,' he said, 'you can write me a letter and tell me what it's like. When I have enough money you can call me over.'

But I didn't know what to say to him, didn't know if I wanted to write a letter to him or call him over or even if I could; and I didn't know why I was angry at him now for coming to talk to me, as if *he'd* been the one who had done something wrong to *me*.

'We have to go home,' I said. 'It's going to get dark.'

'You promise to send me a letter? No joking?'

'*Sí.*'

He set his cigarette down on a stone.

'Then we have to make it good. Spit into your hand.'

'Why?'

'Just spit, you'll see.'

I spit into my palm. Fabrizio took my wrist and brought my hand towards his mouth; before I could pull away his tongue had lapped up the gob of spit cradled there.

'Why did you do that?'

'It's to make us brothers,' he said. 'Like we had the same blood. A person can never hurt someone who has the same blood. Here, you now.'

Fabrizio wiped his gritty palm on his knickers and spit into it.

'Go on,' he said, holding his hand up to me. 'It's only spit. Your mouth is full of spit all the time, it's the same thing.'

But when my tongue touched against Fabrizio's wet palm I felt myself beginning to retch. I closed my eyes and lapped the spit up quickly, trying to shunt it off to my cheek, hoping to spit it out again when Fabrizio had gone; but my stomach lurched again, forcing bile up into my throat, and I swallowed deeply to quell it.

'It's done,' Fabrizio said, grinning. He reached into his pocket and pulled out his jack-knife, the one his uncle had brought him from America. 'I want you to take this. That's to make sure I'll come to stay with you.'

In all the time I had known Fabrizio he had never gone anywhere without his jack-knife; it had seemed like a part of him, like his knickers and cap, as inseparable as a finger or toe. I could not have imagined him giving it away, any more than I could have given away my lucky one *lira* coin.

'*Grazie,*' I mumbled, taking the knife awkwardly in my hand. I ran my thumb over the smooth silver casing.

'Don't lose it,' Fabrizio said. 'You have to give it back when I come.'

He had not really given me the knife, then. It could be the same thing with my coin—I could get it back from him later, if I gave it to him now. But Fabrizio had already picked up his cigarette and stood, brushing dirt away from the seat of his knickers.

'I have to go,' he said, starting away. 'I have to get the sheep out of the pit before it gets dark.'

When he had already begun to grow dim in the twilight, he turned in mid-stride to wave.

'Ho, Vittò!' he bellowed out. '*Buona fortuna in America!*'

He was almost half-way to the cemetery now; but I had taken my one *lira* coin out of my pocket, held it cradled in my palm.

'Fabrizio!' I called out.

He turned again; but he did not wait for me to speak.

'Don't forget to send me a letter!' he shouted. '*Numero tredici, via Giovanni Battista!*' He turned and walked on, stopped a moment to grind his cigarette butt into the earth with his heel, half-turned to wave again, then

dipped his hands into his back pockets and disappeared
finally in the darkening twilight.

~~~

XXIII

On my last day of school, the teacher kept me behind after classes. It was Antonio Girasole's turn to sweep—since the New Year *la maestra* had ceased to single me out, and the readings from the *Lives of the Saints* had dwindled—and for several minutes I sat silently beside the teacher's desk while she waited for him to finish. Seeing the teacher's eye on him, Antonio swept furiously, continually casting side-long glances up to the front of the room; but he never seemed to move away from a small patch of floor in the back corner, enveloped there in a cloud of dust.

'Go on, Antonio, you can finish in the morning,' the teacher said finally. 'Anyway I've told you a thousand times to be more gentle. All you do is move the dirt from one place to another.'

'*Scusi, maestra,*' Antonio said, head bowed, 'but I can't come in the morning. My mother is sick with di-arrhoea, and I have to make the food for my brothers and sisters.'

'Liar. I saw her on the street only this morning.'

'She got sick this afternoon.'

'Get out of here,' the teacher said, 'before I break your skull for your lies. And if you're not here first thing in the morning, the devil himself won't want you when I'm done with you!'

But when Antonio had gone, *la maestra*'s anger melted.

'Come here, Vittorio,' she said, motioning me around her desk; and when I had come close enough she reached out suddenly with both arms and pulled me against her, burying my face in her bosom. She held me a long moment, tight, rocking me back and forth, beginning to sob; but all I could think of was the way Fabrizio had called her *quella porca* a few days before, and ballooned out his arms in imitation of her.

When she drew away from me, finally, she pulled a handkerchief from her skirt pocket to daub at her eyes.

'Ah, Vittorio, *figlio mio*,' she said, pulling in her breath. 'You see what babies women are? Here, there's something I want you to have.'

She reached down under the desk and pulled her *Lives of the Saints* from her leather bag.

'I hope you'll live by it,' she said, handing the book to me. 'I hope you'll follow their example.'

I clutched the book guiltily under my arm.

'*Grazie.*'

'You know, Vittorio,' she said, 'I had a son once too. He would have been your age now, but he died when he was a baby, and the Lord hasn't seen fit to give me another one.'

I stared at the floor. I had not imagined that teachers had babies, too. Suddenly *la maestra* seemed a stranger to me, as if she had split before my eyes into two separate people: one who had babies that died, the other who appeared as if from nowhere every morning in our classroom, and who faded into some shadowy limbo when school was over.

'Go on now,' she said, beginning to cry again. 'I've already made a fool of myself. Go on home. Maybe you'll send me a letter from America, no?'

'*Sí*,' I murmured.

She wiped at her tears.

'Here, give me the book,' she said. 'I'll write my address on the front page, so you'll know where to send it.'

'*Signora* Gelsomina Amicone,' she wrote, in her large, careful script, 'Piazza del Tomolo No. 3, Rocca Secca'; but I still could not make any sense of it, could not connect her to a name and address, to a table and chairs in some dim kitchen, to a bed. I had an image of her going into the market in Rocca Secca to buy her vegetables, like the other big-boned women there, talking like them with the traders, haggling over the price of a cabbage or bag of onions; but the image did not fit.

'Go on now,' she whispered finally, still wiping at her tears.

She leaned forward and planted a last silent kiss on my forehead.

'*Buona fortuna.*'

~~~

XXIV

The eve of our departure, after supper, my grandfather called me into his room.

'Close the door,' he said.

In his own house my grandfather's room had looked over the valley, always airy and bright; but Zia Lucia's house was on the hill side of the street, cut into the slope, and the only window in his room now looked onto a sloping wall of rocky earth. Seeping moisture had coated the wall under the window with frothy white sediment, and the room smelt of damp and rot, like an old blanket left too long in a corner.

My grandfather's face had grown pale and gaunt from his confinement, loose skin draped over sharp, thin bones that looked frail as a bird's. He lay propped on a pillow now, his cast bulging beneath the sheets like the last vestige of some former larger self.

'Open the drawer in my table,' he said, his voice already hoarse with emotion, 'and give me the case with my medals.'

His hand trembled as he reached for the case I held out to him.

'I've had these medals since the first war,' he said, clicking the case open. 'The first two are nothing, half the men who fought then have the same ones. It's only the last one that has any meaning. Here, look at it.'

He handed the case back to me, impatiently almost, as if he were anxious to be rid of it. The medals were pinned to a backing of faded red velvet; the one he pointed to bore a medallion of bronze engraved with a laurel-wreathed star and the inscription '*Al valore militare.*' A ribbon of thick blue cloth hung down from the medallion.

'That's what I got for a wasted life,' my grandfather said, taking the case back from me. 'That and a small pension that couldn't keep a goat alive. And I was so foolish as to think it was enough. Do you know what I got this medal for? For saving the life of a coward. A man who if he was standing before me now I would put a bullet between his eyes. I carried him a mile and a half, on my back, by God, because his muscles were so stiff with fear he couldn't move, and when the bomb fell that ruined my legs he left me to rot in the mud. He left me to die there, *per l'amore di Cristo*, after I had saved his life, and no one came back for me until one of our own horses had finished the damage and left me a cripple. I lay there in the mud for what seemed a thousand years, bombs falling everywhere, wishing only that I would die. And now I curse God that I did not.'

Tears had begun to trickle down his cheeks; but his voice was still dry and bitter, his words hanging in the air like frost.

'Here,' he said, closing the case with an air of finality and handing it towards me, 'take them. Maybe they'll mean something to you some day, when you're older. I have no one else to leave them to. When I die I'll leave the house to you, if you ever come back for it. But now you're lucky to leave this country, because it's a place of Judases and cowards. That's what killed Mussolini. Now everyone is brave, everyone denounces me in the streets, because I've been made a fool. But who was brave then, of those asses and cowards who laugh at me now? Who complained when the school was built, when money came from the government to buy land? All my life I've been surrounded by traitors and fools. Even my own daughter has betrayed me.'

His voice was choked now with emotion. He tried to pull himself up in bed, pushing his fists against the mattress, his jaw tight with pain, until finally his cast shifted slightly under the sheets. He closed his eyes and leaned back against his pillow, the muscles of his face loosening finally like a fist slowly unfolding. When he opened his eyes again he brought a hand up and brushed it against my cheek.

'Take them, *figlio mio*,' he said. 'I hope they bring you better fortune than they brought me.'

~~~

XXV

The morning of our departure from Valle del Sole dawned wet and cold. I heard the rain coming in the early hours before daybreak, first the wind, which dragged some object on the balcony across the metal rail and hurled it with a muffled clap to the floor, then the first dull splats of rain against the window. As the noise built up to an insistent drone, grey light began to filter through the curtain and give form to the objects in the room, the chair at the foot of the bed, a rickety table, a crucifix on the wall. I had spent the last nights in almost constant wakefulness, listening to the measured rhythms of my mother's breathing, conscious always of the warm bulge at her belly, which seemed to hum with a strange, electric energy; but tonight my mother had tossed and turned the whole night, her breathing broken and quick.

'Get up, Vittorio,' she said, when she'd dragged herself up from sleep. 'It's time to go.'

We had breakfast with Zia Lucia and Marta in silence, a small fire burning in the hearth and the rain still falling heavily outside. My mother seemed tense and irritable. She brought some breakfast in to my grandfather but they didn't speak.

'Don't trouble yourself about him,' Zia Lucia said, in her calm, ancient voice. 'Marta has no one else to look after. He'll be her father and her son.'

There was a glint in Marta's eye, of pride or insolence; for a moment it made her seem almost lucid, almost competent. But then she rose up suddenly from the table and moved towards the door.

'Where are you going, in this weather?' Zia Lucia said.

'I have to feed the pigs.'

'*Dai*, you can do it later.' But Marta had already pulled on a shawl, and she slipped out of the room like a shadow.

A small group of well-wishers, Giuseppina and her husband, Silvio the postman, a few neighbours and cousins, began to collect in Zia Lucia's kitchen after breakfast. Di Lucci arrived finally as well, draped under a wide rain poncho, restrained and solemn; but after a moment of sombre greeting he unveiled a small parcel he carried in a plastic bag.

'A camera,' he whispered to my mother. 'Just a few pictures before you go. *Per ricordo*.'

'Please, Antonio,' my mother said, 'not this morning.'

'*Ma scusa*, Cristina, if not this morning then when?'

Several others had come bearing parcels, holding them clutched in their hands or tucked under their arms as if embarrassed by them; but finally Giuseppina approached my mother, holding out a small brown bundle neatly tied with white string.

'It's just a little something for my husband's cousin,' she said. 'If you don't have room for it—'

My mother sucked in her breath.

'I'm sorry, Giuseppina,' she said. 'I'm not taking anything. It's nothing against you, but I'm not the one to send as your messenger. Three months ago, if I'd gone, not one of you would have come to see me off. I don't know why it should be different now.'

But Giuseppina remained for a moment where she stood, as if confused, her parcel still held out before her.

'I don't know what you're saying,' she said finally.

'You know damn well what I'm saying,' my mother said. 'You and the rest of you.'

Giuseppina shot a glance around the room, her face flushed.

'If that's how you feel I don't know why I bothered to come at all,' she said.

'Then go.'

My mother had already turned away, packing some food for the journey into a hamper. Giuseppina, as if still hoping she'd misunderstood, remained for a moment in the centre of the room, her parcel clutched protectively to her now; but finally she seemed to gather her pride around her like a cloak, and turned towards the door.

'Let's go, Alberto,' she said coldly. Her husband hesitated a moment, staring down into his cap; but finally he followed Giuseppina out the door into the rain.

A silence fell over the room, and a few others moved towards the door as if preparing to leave. But a clatter of hooves outside seemed to distract them, and a moment later my uncle Pasquale was standing large and wet in the doorway. It had been months since we had had any contact with my father's side of the family; but my uncle simply tossed aside the plastic sheet draped over his shoulders and strode smiling towards my mother without breaking his stride.

'So finally going to America,' he said, bending forward to kiss her cheek, natural as rain. 'You should have let us know. Mario didn't say anything in his letters.'

But my mother turned away from him awkwardly.

'Everything was decided in a hurry,' she said. 'Here, you must be soaked through, I'll make you some coffee. There's still some warm on the fire.'

'No, no, it's all right, I have to get to the market.' He pulled a parcel from a hunter's sack draped over his shoulder and held it out tentatively towards my mother. '*Mamma* wants you to bring this to Mario, a shirt or something, as if they don't have shirts in America. If you don't have a place for it I'll bring it back. It's only a token.'

But my mother took the parcel from him quickly.

'It's all right,' she said. 'I'll find a place for it.' She stuffed the parcel into the wicker hamper where she had been packing food. But the tension in the room was thick now; even my uncle seemed infected by it, an awkwardness breaking through his genial surface.

'Is Mario meeting you at the port?' he asked.

'No,' my mother said. 'We'll take the train ourselves. We'll find our way.'

'Ah.'

He stood for a moment in the centre of the room, staring at the floor.

'Maybe I'll take that cup of coffee after all,' he said finally.

The other visitors began to leave now, my mother saying her goodbyes from half-way across the room, her arms folded sternly across her chest, as if only impatient for the leave-takings to be over. Finally only my uncle remained, sitting stoop-shouldered beside Zia Lucia in front of the fire, and Silvio and Di Lucci. Marta had returned from the stable, as furtively and silently as she had left, and was cleaning away dirty glasses and cups. We waited several minutes in silence, my mother and I seated at the table, Di Lucci and Silvio at the door, until finally we heard the sound of a horn above the patter of rain outside— Cazzingulo, who would be taking us into Rocca Secca. In a moment his truck pulled up in front of the house, and he popped his head through the door.

'Oh, is this the house? *Crist' e Maria*, it's raining

like a bitch out here. We'll have to hurry if you don't mind, *signora*, I have a dozen people in the back of my truck who want to break my balls.'

Silvio and Di Lucci carried our one suitcase and our hamper of food out to the truck, then went up to the old house to help Cazzingulo with the trunk; but my uncle stayed behind, coming slowly across the room to join my mother at the table.

'Vittorio, go in and say goodbye to your grandfather,' my mother said. My uncle had rested his elbows on the table; he leaned forward slightly now towards my mother, staring down at his hands. Marta, washing cups at the sideboard, tilted her head almost imperceptibly towards us.

'You're not going to him,' my uncle said, barely audible. 'I saw it in your eyes the moment I came in.'

But my mother turned away.

'Vittorio, damn it, I told you to go in to your grandfather.'

I hovered a moment by the table; but my mother rose suddenly and prodded me with an abrupt push into my grandfather's room. As we came in my grandfather's eyes shot sharply towards her; but she stepped out of the room almost at once, closing the door behind her.

I was in my grandfather's room only a minute. Without speaking he reached out and drew me towards him, pressing his grizzled cheeks hard against my own. When he pulled away his eyes were rimmed with tears.

'I hope to God she doesn't ruin your life the way she's ruined hers,' he said.

When I came out I heard my uncle just starting up his cart outside; he had not waited to say goodbye to me. There was a silence in the room like the ringing silence after an argument, though I had not heard any loud voices while I had been in with my grandfather. Zia Lucia was still staring into the fire, her back to me; Marta was still wiping glasses dry in the corner. My mother rose from the table when I came out, stepping past me into my grandfather's room without looking at me and closing the door behind her.

'Oh, are you coming?' Cazzingulo had popped his head in the front door. 'The bus from Rocca Secca leaves in half an hour.'

Now Silvio and Di Lucci crowded in behind him, Di Lucci, huddled under his poncho, still clasping the plastic bag that held his camera. For the next few minutes we waited in silence in Zia Lucia's kitchen while a low hum of conversation reached us through the door of my grandfather's room.

'What do they have to discuss in there?' Cazzingulo said. 'A kiss on each cheek and it's finished.'

'Sit down for a minute,' Zia Lucia said. 'Let them make their peace.'

Di Lucci moved towards the fire, bending to warm his hands; but my grandfather's voice rose up suddenly sharp and loud from behind his door.

'Have you gone mad? If you go through with this, so help me God, I'll pray every day of my life that you rot in hell!'

'And what would you have me do? Go to the hell that's waiting for me there?'

'You'll face your sins, and pray that God will have mercy on your soul!'

'I've paid for my sins a thousand times over!'

'And the boy,' my grandfather said, shouting a full voice now, 'what'll become of him? You'll not take him away from me like this!'

'I'll take my own son where I damn well please, and not you nor anyone is going to stop me.'

'Then get out! Get out of this house! And if you ever step through that door again I swear by God I'll throttle you with my own hands!'

The door to my grandfather's room flew open, and my mother stormed into the kitchen.

'To hell with you all!' she shouted. She pulled her shawl off a hook by the door and flung it around her shoulders.

'And you,' she said to Cazzingulo, 'don't stand there like an ass.' She pushed her way past the men at the door and into the street.

'Vittorio! Get your coat and let's go!'

In a moment I had run out in the street after her, afraid that I would be left behind. From the back of Cazzingulo's truck half a dozen people, their knees jammed up against our trunk, stared at us blankly as we came towards them; but my mother marched up to the cab, and a man sitting there quickly gave up his place and hurried through the rain to join the others in the back.

Cazzingulo, flanked by Silvio and Di Lucci, still stood staring after us at Zia Lucia's door.

'*Per l'amore di Cristo*, what are you waiting for?' my mother shouted back to him.

But all along via San Giuseppe, I saw now, on the balconies, on the stoops, huddled under jackets or shawls in the street, the villagers had come out to watch us, the men and women, small children, the old people who never moved the long day from the chairs where someone had set them, all of them watching us now so still and rapt they might have been posing for a portrait, offering us a final frozen image of themselves, only the hard drone of the rain relieving their still silence. For an instant my mother, her hair curling down now in glistening coils, her dress glued to her belly and thighs with rain, seemed suddenly small and defeated: something like fear seemed to flash through her eyes, and she drew the edges of her shawl more tightly over her chest.

'Fools,' she muttered to herself. She turned back to the open door of the truck, drawing me towards her protectively. 'Go on, Vittorio, get inside.'

But before she had lifted me into the cab she whipped suddenly around again, one hand still clutching my shoulder.

'Fools!' she shouted now. 'You tried to kill me but you see I'm still alive. And now you came to watch me hang, but I won't be hanged, not by your stupid rules and superstitions. You are the ones who are dead, not me, because not one of you knows what it means to be free and to make a choice, and I pray to God that he wipes this town and all its stupidities off the face of the earth!'

When she had finished an eerie silence fell over the street, even the rain seeming suddenly hushed. The villagers stood still as stone, seemed to have merged with the rock of the houses and pavement, become finally themselves simply crags and swells in the hard mountain face of the village.

My mother hustled me into the cab.

'Get in and drive!' she shouted back to Cazzingulo. She climbed in beside me, dripping now with rain. She whipped her head to one side to draw her locks from her face and her hair sent a spatter of rain against the side window.

In a moment Cazzingulo had slid into the driver's seat.

'*Ma scusi, signora*,' he said, scratching his chin, 'I know that as long as I get paid it's none of my business—'

'Then drive!' my mother said. 'The only mistake I made was that I didn't leave this hell a dozen years ago, when I had the chance. Drive!'

Cazzingulo seemed about to speak; but finally he shrugged, reached forward to start up the engine, and lurched into gear. Through the rain-streaked side-view mirror I had a last glimpse of the villagers—some of them had begun to move now, drifting like wraiths towards the edge of town; though no one raised a hand to wave goodbye to us, the way they did when other families left the village. But in a moment we had gained the high road, Cazzingulo taking the curve without stopping and shifting into a higher gear, and Valle del Sole had disappeared from view.

~~~

XXVI

To the sea, to the sea. A bus ride down pitted, mountain-slung roads, the bus stopping in every town and village until it was crammed with other passengers, day labourers in home-spun jerseys and cracked hobnailed boots, freshly shaven soldiers in sharp-creased khaki, adolescent town girls who covered their mouths when they spoke, to hide their lipstick. Long switchbacked descents into rain-drenched valleys, then the sudden grinding churn of the gears and groan of the engine as the driver urged the bus up another rise, up and up, into gloomy cypress forests and small stony villages still crusted with snow.

After several hours of hard mountain the land began by slow degrees to ease into gentle rolls, and finally the bus rumbled onto a wide highway of smooth black. Above us the clouds which had followed us the whole journey gave way now to widening swatches of blue; and beside me the hardness in my mother's eyes melted slowly into runnels of quiet tears, which she hid by turning to the window and bringing a discreet hand up to wipe at her cheek. 'Napoli 13' a sign read, and in the distance the almost perfect lines of two great triangles of earth rose up towards the sky, the Vesuvius; and moments later we were into the outskirts of the city, driving past billboards and streetside markets and great smouldering heaps of garbage. Gradually the streets narrowed, hemmed in by mottled pink buildings a dozen stories high and increasingly crammed with cars and carts and people, until finally the bus came to a lurching stop in an enormous square where the traffic formed almost a solid sea, and where boys my own age, crooked-toothed and barefoot, went from car to car hawking cigarettes and fruit and glossy-covered magazines.

We spent the night in a dim, brown-walled hotel room, a picture of the Last Supper hanging over the bed and curtains of dirty red velvet draped over a window that looked onto a garbage-strewn alleyway. My mother had hardly spoken since we'd left Valle del Sole, and all night long she twitched and turned, as if wrestling a phantom, the bulge of her belly dragging the sheets away from me and leaving me exposed to the room's cold. Towards morning I slipped into a familiar dream, one I had had a hundred times before in Valle del Sole: my mother and I were in a dark passageway, slowly feeling our way along the walls in search of a way out, hoping to slip unseen past the hunch-backed guardian who inevitably barred our way. Tonight, though, the hunchback did not come; but at some point, reaching out into the darkness, I realized with sudden horror that my mother was no longer beside me.

But someone nudged my shoulder then—my mother, still in bed next to me.

'Wake up, Vittorio,' she whispered. 'It's time to go.'

Outside, it was still dark. My mother and I had a breakfast of bread and cheese from the food she had packed, then went down to the lobby. My mother exchanged a few words with the man behind the counter there; he went out into the street and returned a few minutes later with a small, gaunt-faced man with a clot of blood in one eye.

'Oh, *signó*,' he said, grinning at my mother and winking his bloody eye, 'so you're going to America, eh?'

The two men dragged our trunk from a storage room behind the hotel counter, carrying it out into the street and lifting it onto the roof of a battered Cinquecento, where they secured it with ropes passed through the car's open windows.

The gaunt-faced man drove us through the city, keeping up a steady stream of banter in a thick, rounded dialect I couldn't understand. The city was quiet now, great *palazzi* looming up out of the morning shadows on either side of the streets like silent sentries. I drifted off to sleep in the car's back seat; when my mother woke me our driver and a man in a stiff red cap were lifting our trunk off the roof onto a cart. We were at the port: not a hundred yards from us, at the pier, was a great ship taller than any of the buildings I had seen in the city, a leviathan of blue that stretched half a mile along the pier. Beyond it, under a pale early-morning sky, was a crisper blue, stretching smooth and picture still as far as the horizon, the blue of the bay and the sea.

My mother and I followed our porter to a counter where a numbered label was pasted onto our trunk and it was hauled away by two thick-armed men who grinned at my mother through rotting teeth and called something out to her I couldn't understand. Despite the early hour the port was alive with motion, blank-faced porters in their red suits and stiff caps crisscrossing the pavement with trolleys and handcarts, moustached men in work clothes lounging at dockside on wooden crates, black-toothed vendors peddling *castagne*, baked chestnuts, shouting in their thick, rounded accents, 'Oh, *castà! Cald' e saporí! Venite signó e signó'! Castà!*' Amidst the porters and workers and vendors moved a floating mass that seemed cut adrift, lost and directionless, men in stiff dark suits and white shirts, women in bulging flowered dresses, children in Sunday outfits that strained at their wrists and ankles, rope-tied suitcases and overstuffed handbags and lumpy burlap sacks strewn all over the pier like the ruins of a war. Here and there whole families were bedded down on the dirty pavement with bundled undershirts for pillows and thin coats for blankets; and from all along the mile-long pier came the great collective wailing of a thousand agonized goodbyes, women and men alike crying and clutching their sea-bound relatives as if seeing them off to the very bowels of hell.

'*Scusi*, do you know where we board?' My mother had come up behind a pale-khakied *carabiniere* who was leaning against a steel post, one thumb cocked under the strap of his rifle. Without looking over at us he made a vague gesture with his chin.

'*Di là, signó*.'

But now his eye had caught my mother's swollen belly. He turned slowly, then leaned forward finally to pick up my mother's suitcase.

'*Venite con me*.'

He led us down the pier, along the length of the great blue hulk parked there. Yard-high white letters spelled out a name along the ship's flank: *SATURNIA*. But the paint around it was cracked and peeling, splotched here and there with lesions of rust.

'What class?' the soldier said.

'Third.'

We stopped finally near the ship's stern, at the foot of a gangplank crowded with boarding passengers.

'So *la signora* is going to America,' the soldier said.

'*Sí*.'

The soldier looked my mother up and down a moment, nodding slightly, then shifted the strap of his rifle with a broad slow swing of his elbow.

'*Beh*,' he said finally. '*Buona fortuna*.'

'What a precious one he was,' my mother said,

when he had gone. 'He might at least have offered to carry our luggage up to the deck.'

But it was a long time before we had made our way up the gangplank, the line ahead of us, five or six feet abreast and tangled with bags and hampers and suitcases, moving at a snail's pace. When we'd finally reached the deck my mother moved to the side of the line, the other passengers making way for her to pass, and collapsed exhausted onto her suitcase. We could see now what was causing the delay: the boarding area had been cordoned into a funnel, at the head of it two tired-eyed young officers in blue uniforms and stiff caps checking documents as passengers filed through a narrow gap in the ropes.

As my mother and I watched, a squabble broke out. While one of the officers inspected the papers of a grizzled old man in a coarse black suit, a muffled cackle arose from the large covered hamper the old man carried under one arm. When the officer removed the hamper's lid, a chicken popped out its scrawny head.

'*Scusate, signore,*' the officer said, in polished Italian, 'but you're not allowed to bring live animals aboard without a special permit.'

But the old man did not seem to understand, and hugged the hamper obstinately to his breast. The officer explained the regulation again, and placing a hand on one of the hamper's handles he gestured out towards the pier, suggesting the man try to sell the chicken to one of the traders there. But the old man seemed to grow suddenly frightened, as if he'd understood that he would not be allowed to board, and grasping at his hamper he tried to make a dash through the narrow gap in the ropes. The officer tugged sharply on the handle he still held in an effort to restrain him, and the hamper tore free from the old man's arms. In a moment its contents were flying across the deck—grain, clothes, a loaf of bread, a *provolone*, and the scrawny-headed chicken, which flapped its wings wildly in a vain effort to remain airborne, sending up a flurry of downy feathers, before it crashed finally with a squawk to the deck and began scrambling between the legs of the oncoming passengers, its claws slipping and scraping against the deck's metal floor. In a moment the deck was in an uproar, the officer and the old man pushing their way furiously through the crowd, women and children shrieking and shrinking back from the chicken's mad flapping.

But beside me my mother was laughing, a full-bellied laugh that brought tears to her eyes.

'Look at you,' she said to me when the chicken had been caught and the commotion was over, 'always so serious!' She made a face of exaggerated seriousness, eyes squinty, lips pouting, then burst into laughter again and hugged me towards her, pressing her cheek against mine.

'E' scimunita tua mamma,' she said, drawing away and wiping at her tears. 'Come on, we'd better do our business and find our room, before they throw me off the boat for a madwoman.'

My mother heaved herself up from her suitcase. But as she stooped to pick it up a man in a blue uniform and cap suddenly towered up like a phantom beyond the cordon behind us and leaned swiftly forward to close a thick hand around the suitcase's handle.

'Allow me,' he said, lifting the suitcase easily over the cordon. For a moment I was afraid my mother's joke had come true, and we were being thrown off the boat: the man standing over us seemed grim and severe, despite his smile, his hard jaw jutting forward like a threat. But in an instant he had scooped off his cap and seemed suddenly transformed, his severity softened by the flecks of grey in his hair, by the wrinkles which brimmed the corners of his eyes like laughter.

'My name is Darcangelo,' he said. 'Antonio Darcangelo. I'm the third mate. May I carry la signora's luggage to her cabin?'

'*Grazie*,' my mother said, hesitant. '*Tanto gentile.*
But you don't show the same kindness to all the passengers.'

'Not all the passengers have quite as heavy a load
as you do.'

'*Beh*, you have a point.'

And a few minutes later, on a nod from Darcangelo, we had passed unhindered through the gap in the
ropes. On the other side, Darcangelo checked quickly
through my mother's papers.

'*Molisana*,' he said, looking up from her passport.
'I thought so, when I heard you talking to your son.
Though you speak very well for someone from those
parts.'

'You mean for a peasant?' my mother said.

Darcangelo blushed.

'*Scusi*, I only meant—you see I know very well the
Italian they speak there. I come from Termoli.'

'Ah, Termoli,' my mother said, smiling. 'You have
some nice beaches there, I hear.'

'Oh, yes,' Darcangelo said quickly, but then added,
recovering his calm, 'that is, if you like beaches. Actually,
when I left home I was so sick of the sea that I wanted to get
as far away from it as possible. So I travelled all the way
across the country, and before I knew it, there was the sea
again. I couldn't get away from it. It was my fate, I
decided.'

Darcangelo glanced at my mother's ticket.

'Room 409?' he said, surprised. 'But that's third
class.'

'We were told this was the proper boarding place
for third class,' my mother said.

'Well, yes—but in your condition. Third class is
worse than a hospital. You'll be with half a dozen strangers
and their screaming children. And you'll have to share a

bathroom with half the ship.'

'That's better than just sticking your backside over the rails,' my mother said.

For a second time Darcangelo blushed; but finally he let out a short laugh, as if he were suddenly amused by his own embarrassment.

'*Beh*, we can't stand here holding up traffic all day,' he said, switching into dialect. 'I'll show you your room.'

But half-way down a stairwell that led into the ship, Darcangelo stopped.

'You know, I've just had an idea. We might have an extra cabin in second class. Two beds, one for each of you. And a private bathroom.'

'It's kind of you to be concerned,' my mother said, 'but I really can't afford that kind of luxury—'

'Oh, there's no question of cost. You see, the captain usually keeps a room open in second class for— well, let's say a friend. But I don't think his friend will be coming aboard this trip. Come, follow me.'

Back on deck Darcangelo led us down a wide aisle flanked with grey doors and small curtained windows, then up a rusty stairwell which led to an upper deck. The aisle here, lined with a long row of dirty white boats that hung in the air like gulls, was bustling with uniformed crew members. Darcangelo led us towards the bow, and knocked at a door on which '*Capitano*' was stencilled in black.

'*Avanti.*'

The room we stepped into was windowless and small and dim, the walls covered in dark wood panelling and the floor in thick brown carpeting. Here and there the panelling had warped away from the walls in long, undulating waves, giving the room a dizzying feeling of motion. On one wall, above a shelf of books and a wooden model of an old sailing ship, hung three large clocks, each showing a different hour.

Behind a huge wooden desk sat a balding, greying man with wind-burnt skin and heavy jowls, a large chart spread out before him. He squinted as we came in, as if the sudden light had caused him discomfort, then brought a hand up to rub the back of his neck. He wore the same blue uniform as Darcangelo; but a double row of gold buttons ran down the front of his jacket, and four gold stripes circled his cuffs to Darcangelo's two.

'What is it?' He surveyed my mother and me with narrowed eyes, as if we might be stowaways Darcangelo had found in the hold, among the olives and *provolone*.

'Captain,' Darcangelo said, looking not at the captain but at a point somewhere above his head, 'this good woman has tickets for third class. I thought, however, that in her condition she might do with a little privacy. I've suggested we put her in 213.'

'Eh? 213? But my wife—' But some thought made him suddenly pensive. He leaned back in his chair and brought a hand up to rub his grizzled chin. 'Hmm. Yes, Darcangelo, I see your point. What room are you in now, Mrs.—?'

'Innocente. Room 409. I appreciate all this trouble, captain, but I'm sure I could manage—'

'409? That's below the water line. It's an inferno down there. Too close to the boilers. *La signora* is travelling alone?'

'As you can see I'm travelling with my son.'

'Yes, yes, I was referring of course to your husband.'

'My husband is waiting for me on the other side. He's been in Canada a few years now.'

'Oh?' The captain's eyes shifted to my mother's belly. 'But you've seen him recently?'

'He comes and goes.'

'Yes. I see. And he knows, I take it, about the little surprise you're bringing with you?'

'Oh, yes,' my mother said, smiling. 'But I'm sure it was a surprise.'

The captain cleared his throat.

'How long, ah, Mrs. Innocente, before the baby is due?'

'Five weeks, six—it's hard to say. With Vittorio I was three weeks late. Maybe this time I'll be three weeks early. I hope you have a midwife on board. Or a good doctor.'

'Eh? Oh yes, we have a doctor all right. Yes.' The captain stroked his chin, distracted; but then he leaned forward again, suddenly peremptory.

'All right, Darcangelo, give them 213, the key is with the steward.' He turned back to his chart with an air of dismissal. 'Good day, Mrs. Innocente, and a pleasant trip. Officer Darcangelo will be glad to help you with anything you need.'

~~~

XXVII

Room 213 was small and tidy, a strong perfume smell overlaying a faint whiff of mould and rot. The furnishings—a two-tiered bunk up against the inside wall, two slender-framed armchairs with flowered cushions, a round coffee table with an old brown map veneered over its top, the countries and continents all distorted from the shapes *la maestra* had taught us—were bolted to the floor, the bolts and clamps plainly visible above the floor's grey carpet, as if they had been added as an afterthought. On one wall hung a heavy-framed painting of St. Christopher crossing the river, the baby Jesus sitting placidly on his shoulder, a gold sceptre in one hand and a small globe of bright blue and green in the other.

In the bathroom, bright porcelain and chrome gleamed under the white clarity of an electric light. A chain above the toilet sent a rush of water swirling into the toilet's bowl, and silver taps over the sink and tub brought hot and cold water gurgling down from the faucets at a turn.

'Don't worry,' my mother said, 'for the next two weeks you'll get your fill of water. *Acqua, acqua, dapper-tutto.* When you get to America you won't want to see another drop of water for a hundred years.'

My mother closed herself into the bathroom to wash and change.

'When I'm through we'll go upstairs to watch when the ship leaves.'

On the far wall of the cabin two curtained portholes looked over the sea. By standing on one of the armchairs and leaning over its back I was able to peer out one of them into the bay. From here the sea, about a dozen feet below me, looked not blue but murky green. Out on the bay a large black ship was just heaving into port, a crowd of small dinghies bobbing precariously in its wake.

But someone pounded on our door now, hard and frantic.

'*April! Senti!* Open the door, I know you're in there!'

It was a woman's voice, angry and shrill. My mother came out of the bathroom in her slip, wiping her face on a towel.

'*Ma chi è questa?* There must be some mistake.'

More pounding.

'Open up, I know who you are! Open so I can see your face! So I can see the face of a whore!'

'This woman is mad,' my mother said, paling; but she went to the door and drew it open.

In the doorway, blocking it like a mountain face, stood a short older woman of generous proportions whose too-tight dress seemed ready to burst with the pressure of its owner's trembling, red-faced anger. But as my mother drew the door fully open, the blood seemed to drain away suddenly from the woman's cheeks.

'*Madonna!*' she cried, clapping her hands together like a penitent. 'She's pregnant! My God, it's come to this!' Then, catching sight of me hovering near my mother's side, her eyelids drooped as if she were about to collapse.

'Another one! God help me!' And pushing past my mother and me she lunged across the room and fell heavily into an armchair, her chest heaving.

'Two children, I never imagined, not in my worst dreams. And four at home who never see his face!'

'*Scusi,*' my mother said slowly. She shifted the strap of her slip and crossed her arms over her chest, hugging her shoulders protectively. '*Ma chi è Lei?*'

The woman drew a handkerchief from her bosom and patted at her forehead.

'What does it matter, who I am,' she said, still struggling for breath. '*Nessuno.* I'm no one. Two children! I can't, I can't, I can't go on like this any longer. I'll kill myself.' She blew loudly into her handkerchief, then broke finally into heaving sobs. '*Trent' anni!* Thirty years I've worked like a slave for him!'

'*Scusi*, but I don't understand,' my mother said, still hovering uncertainly near the open door. 'Who have you worked like a slave for?'

'Who, who, you know as well as I do, who,' the woman said, her chest still heaving. 'What's the use in hiding it now? When the cook's wife told me I didn't believe it, I thought it was *invidia*, because her own husband has been running around with a tramp. But then I found the key in his pocket, room 213, just like she said—ten years! Ten years this has been going on, and no one told me a word. If you knew what I have to put up with—' but she broke into sobs again.

But a look of sudden understanding had crossed my mother's face, and she moved towards the woman now and crouched down beside her.

'*Calmatevi,*' she said gently. 'I think you've made a mistake. I'm not the woman you're looking for.'

'*Ma come,* what are you saying?' the woman said, still sobbing. 'It's this room, I know it, it's always this room. I wanted to wring your neck, but now I see how things are with you, two children, he's probably ruined your life too—'

'*Scusate, signora*,' my mother started again. 'We've both been tricked—the captain's friend isn't coming aboard this trip, they must have put me here to confuse you. I don't know anything else about it, except that they tried to make fools out of both of us.'

The woman looked over at my mother now with new attention, her sobs subsiding.

'*Ma è vero?*' she said, daubing at her eyes. 'You're not trying to make fun of me?'

'*Sí, è vero.*'

'And the children?'

'Whoever they belong to, it's not your husband.'

The woman looked from my mother's face to mine, then back to my mother's.

'Oh, thank God!' She let out a great sob and clasped thick arms around my mother's neck. 'Thank you, *signora*, thank you, you don't know what a burden you've taken off me! *Beh*, you can imagine when I came in here and saw you bloated up like a whale, and then the little boy, his eyes are just like my husband's—'

But a foghorn sounded now, drowning the woman out, and the floor beneath us began to tremble like a huge stomach growling.

'*Signora*, I think they're starting the engines,' my mother said. 'If you don't want to follow us to Canada, you'd better get off the ship.'

'*Sí, sí, grazie.* I hope you'll excuse me for the way I lost my head but you can imagine how a woman feels—'

'Hurry now,' my mother said, helping the woman to the door. 'If I have a chance I'll have a few words with him for you.'

'*La ringrazio, signora, grazie tanto*,' she said, backing out the door and clasping my mother's hand; but a moment later, as she hurried away down the hall, she was cursing again. '*L'ammazzo!* I'll kill him! I'll kill them both!'

'*Addio*,' my mother said, watching her go. '*Pove-*

retta.' But a smile was playing around her lips. 'Well, at least we got this room out of it, eh Vittorio? Come on, I'll put on a dress and we'll go say goodbye to Italy.'

Up on deck the gangway was just being pulled up, newly boarded passengers abandoning their suitcases and bags to flock to the rails and wave their final goodbyes. All along the port side the rails were lined three and four thick with people exchanging shouts with those they'd left behind on the pier or simply casting their goodbyes to the wind.

'*Addio Italia! Salve America!'*

My mother managed to squeeze us through to a place against the rails just as the ship was churning away from its moorings. On the pier people were shouting last minute instructions, raising enough noise to wake the dead.

'Tell Giovanni the army is looking for him!'

'Say hello to President Eisenhower! And send me back an American woman!'

'Tell your father that when I get my hands on him, I'll break his balls!'

Then, amidst the noise, I made out a boyish shout of 'Ho, Vittò!' and my eyes scanned the crowd until they lighted on a familiar face peering out from the shadows of a corduroy cap. My hand shot up instinctively to wave.

'Who are you waving to?' my mother asked.

But I shrugged in embarrassment—the corduroy cap had come up now, in response to my wave or someone else's, to reveal not a boy but a small, ancient man with a wrinkled face and blackened teeth.

As the gap between the rails and the dock widened, the ship's horn boomed above us, drowning out the shouts from the shore. Slowly the ship, like a great tired whale, pulled back into the waters of the bay and began to turn its nose to the sea. At last the people on the pier had become a single undulating wave, their shouts barely audible, and as the ship slipped away from them I felt a tremendous unexpected relief, as if all that could ever cause pain or do harm was being left behind on the receding shore, and my mother and I would melt now into an endless freedom as broad and as blue as the sea.

We stood at the rails until most of the crowd around us had filtered away. Gradually the wind stiffened, the smells of the shore, of Naples, of the crowds, giving way to the briny smell of the sea. For a few minutes my mother cried silently beside me.

'Is grandfather going to die while we're away?' I asked her, when she'd stopped crying.

'Maybe.'

'Do we have to live with my father when we get to America?'

'Do you want to?'

'I don't know.'

When we went down to our room, finally, the Bay of Naples was no larger than a cup you could hold in the palm of your hand, and we were on the open sea.

~~~

XXVIII

My mother settled quickly into the life of the boat. Though it was only mid-March each day dawned warm and cloudless, and the air and sun seemed to bring back to my mother a warm radiance, as if the crisp blue of the sky and sea had seeped inside her. She had soon made a number of friends: Mr. D'Amico, a bent, bespectacled man in the room across from ours who was going to America to visit his son, and who greeted me every morning when we went up to breakfast with him with a *'Salve, dottore!'* and a hearty salute; a honeymoon couple down the hall who asked every day after my mother's health, as if nothing could be more precious or fragile than a woman in maternity; a grey-eyed German from first class who spoke only broken Italian but who bought my mother an English grammar book in the magazine store and gave her lessons sometimes on the sun deck or at the side of the ship's tiny indoor pool. For the first day or two we did not see Antonio Darcangelo again; but then a box of chocolates arrived from the gift shop with the enigmatic note, 'My deepest apologies for Naples—I had not realized the full extent of the problem. Antonio.' The next day the ship docked in a small port overlooking a dusty sun-drenched town of white adobe, and Antonio appeared at our door.

'We've stopped to pick up some oranges and the

captain has given all the officers four hours of shore leave. Will *la signora* and her son join me for a Spanish lunch?'

Thereafter we began to see much of Antonio. He'd slip away from his rounds sometimes to join my mother and me on the sun deck, regaling us with gifts of sweets and ice cream; occasionally he came to our table in the dining hall, bringing a special dessert over for me from first class. Around the other crewmen Antonio was always formal and aloof, issuing orders with a crisp precision; but my mother would tease him.

'Heil, *Herr Kommandant!* Always so stiff! The war was over more than a dozen years ago, you know.'

She got him once to take us down to the engine room, despite his protest that women were not allowed to go below. We looked down from a high railing into a dim cavern that stank of steam and coal; everything seemed larger than life, as if made for giants, the huge pipes that ran overhead and along the walls, the great outsize boilers that rose up like vast oxen. Below, men in grey overalls stoked coal or watched over gauges and valves. One of them looked up and caught sight of my mother.

'Oh, *signó*! Look, the third mate brought his mistress to visit us!'

The other men had turned to look up now.

'Oh, Andò, you made quick work of this one, eh? Two children! *Crist' e Giusepp'!*'

But Antonio had taken my mother by the arm.

'Let's go, Cristina. I told you I didn't want you to come down here.'

'There's no need to get angry,' my mother said. 'You're the boss, why don't you tell them what's what?'

But Antonio had already hustled us back to the stairwell.

'You can't say anything to those men. They live like animals down there.'

'I don't know,' my mother said. 'One or two of

them seemed rather handsome. Why is it that all the handsome men go out to sea?'

But Antonio had flushed with anger.

'Everything is a joke to you, isn't it? And the baby you're carrying, is that a joke? Maybe you know all about men like those down there.'

My mother pulled suddenly away from him, her smile gone.

'We'll find our own way upstairs.'

But that evening there was another box of chocolates for my mother, and a bottle of wine; and the next day she and Antonio were laughing together again on the sun deck, while around us the sea lay bright blue and placid, stretching away in every direction, it seemed, to the very ends of the earth.

~~~

XXIX

Since the start of the trip the captain had appeared only
seldom among the passengers, coming down once or twice
at supper to sit briefly at the head of a large table in first
class, stiff and gruff, and disappearing long before the meal
had ended. Once Antonio had taken me up to the bridge,
and I had stood only a few feet from him; I had expected
him to turn to me, to show some sign of recognition, but he
had continued staring squinty-eyed towards the sea as if he
hadn't noticed me, his hands thrust deep into his pockets,
his jaw set so firm and hard he seemed to be nursing some
ancient grudge, mulling it over and over in his mind until
it made him burn with anger. He had about him an air of
distant authority which made me think of the politicians in
Rome that people in Valle del Sole always complained
about, men who directed our lives from afar but were
never seen, like spirits from another world.

But a week or so after we had left Naples, Antonio
came down to our room with an invitation.

'The captain would like to know if *la signora* and
her son would join him at his table this evening.'

My mother raised her brows.

'To what do we owe this honour?'

Antonio cleared his throat.

'The captain wishes to make amends—for the

little incident which occurred at Naples.'

'I see,' my mother said. 'And was this gesture entirely the captain's idea?'

'I admit I may have dropped a word or two—'

'And did you also tell the captain what I thought of his little joke?'

'I beg you, Cristina—don't say anything embarrassing to him in front of the other men. For my sake.'

'Well, we'll see how he behaves himself.'

The captain's quarters were just down from his office, and had the same aura of faded elegance—dark panelling on windowless walls, heavy wood furnishings, worn velvet upholstery. To one side, beneath a brass chandelier hung with dozens of glass pendants, sat a long white-clothed dining table, most of the chairs around it filled. The captain, at the head, rose as we came in, the other men around the table following suit.

'Darcangelo, I take it, has conveyed my regrets for the confusion over your room.' He bowed slightly towards my mother; but the gesture had an air of condescension about it, as if he considered the matter hardly worth mentioning. On the wall behind him, though, I noticed now four pictures of children, hung in large oval frames, and in the centre of them one of a woman who looked like a younger, prettier version of the woman who had stormed into our room in Naples.

Antonio had begun introductions. There were twelve or thirteen of us in all, most of the other guests in officer's uniforms, crew-cut and blue-jacketed and tight-collared, almost indistinguishable from each other. One guest, however, stood out from the rest, a corpulent man with thin, greasy hair and a network of broken blood vessels on his cheeks. He was dressed completely in white, from the tips of his collar to the toes of his shoes; I had noticed him once or twice before in the dining hall, moving from table to table in the first class section, his voice always louder than the rest, a glass always in his hand.

'Il *dottor* Cosabene,' Antonio introduced him, 'who tends to the ship's sick and dying. Which means he usually has nothing to do.'

'*Piacere*,' said the doctor, extending thick fingers to take my mother's hand and bring it to his lips.

The table had been set with white china and gleaming silverware, napkins of red cloth billowing from the mouths of wine glasses like exotic flowers, bottles of red wine set out along the table like columns along a boulevard. The place settings, with their three-tiered arrangement of dishes, a large plate at the bottom, a soup bowl, a small antipasto dish with bits of celery and carrot, black olives, slices of *prosciutto* and *provolone*, seemed like tiny models of the fountains I had seen in the squares in Naples.

We took our places, and the captain bowed his head briefly in silent grace. When he had finished he wished the table a gruff '*Buon appetito*,' and the officers fell to as if a spring had been released in them, spreading napkins on their knees and bearing down silently on the small bits of antipasto before them. Stewards, meanwhile, invisible as ghosts in their white gloves and serving jackets, had come into the room with steaming bowls and covered trays which they set on a serving trolley at the side of the room. One of them worked his way around the table uncorking bottles and filling glasses.

'*Grazie*,' my mother said, when her own glass had been filled. Her voice rang out strangely in the room's strained silence. 'Maybe you can get some *gassosa* for my son.'

My mother had held back from eating, looking from face to silent face as if waiting for her own cue to begin.

'*Dai*, Vittorio, let's eat,' she said finally. She cracked a roll over her dish, stuffed a slice of meat into it with her fingers, and handed it to me. She made another roll for herself and bit into it, then raised up her glass.

'*Saluti.*' A hurried chorus of toasts went up around the table, dying down again into an awkward silence. My mother set her glass down again.

'*Scusate*, captain, but is it forbidden to talk at your table?'

Around the table a dozen mouths abruptly ceased their chewing. The captain looked up suddenly from his dish and brought his napkin to his lips, his face flushed.

'Forbidden? Why do you say that?'

'No one has said more than a dozen words since I came in. I feel like I'm at a funeral.'

But now the captain smiled sourly, as if he had suddenly understood.

'I merely like to observe a little formality,' he said. '*La signora* of course is free to talk if she wishes.'

The captain picked up his glass, and despite his invitation it seemed we would pass once more into a strained silence; but after he had drunk, he turned back to my mother and smiled again his grim smile.

'Once upon a time a captain had absolute power at sea,' he said. 'Now everywhere he turns he finds a union. These little rituals are all we have left.'

'And at home?' my mother said.

Antonio, sitting beside her, shifted uncomfortably in his chair, picking his napkin up suddenly and bringing it to his lips.

'*Scusi?*' the captain said.

'At home. Does a captain still have absolute power at home?'

A nervous laugh went up around the table. The captain smiled, less sourly. Antonio set down his napkin.

'*Ma certo,*' the captain said, almost genial. 'At least until wives have unions.'

The laughter now was less restrained.

'Tell me this,' my mother said, beginning to pick

again at the contents of her antipasto dish, 'doesn't it worry you to spend so much time at sea? What do you think your wife does when you leave her alone like that? Even a woman has an itch she needs to scratch once in a while.'

Another round of laughter. But this one died away awkwardly: the captain was not smiling.

'What she does is her own affair,' he said gruffly. He turned back to his plate as if the matter were closed.

'I see,' my mother persisted, 'but I also see that your children'—she gestured with a tilt of her chin to the pictures hanging behind the captain—'all have your features. Maybe for that you should be grateful.'

The captain set down his fork, and the tension in the room thickened; but finally he shook his head and made a sound that was half grunt and half laugh.

'You've won your point, *signora*,' he said. 'I've already been accused of being a tyrant. I won't be accused of being a poor sport as well.'

The tension in the room seemed to break now, and slowly conversation began to flow more freely. While the soup was being served, some of the officers asked permission from the captain to take off their jackets, which he granted with a slight nod of his head; and by the pasta course many of the officers had loosened their collars as well and rolled up their sleeves, the conversation punctuated now by peals of laughter. Empty wine bottles had begun to accumulate on the serving trolley, the stewards filling glasses with a heady regularity. Dr. Cosabene, sitting across from me, kept a bottle at his elbow for ready service, his glass always brimming; and once or twice, while my mother wasn't looking, he winked broadly at me and reached over to pour a quick shot of wine into my *gassosa*, so that soon the room had begun to revolve slowly around me, like a great globe spinning idly on its axis. Only the captain seemed unaffected by the wine: he downed his glass as regularly as the others did, but the wine seemed only to harden him, the way drink hardened my grandfather, to make him draw more and more into himself like an animal into its lair.

Dr. Cosabene had been trying to edge himself into my mother's conversation since antipasto. Now, as the stewards were dishing out meat and vegetables, an opening occurred, and the doctor slipped into it.

'*Scusi, signora,*' he said, leaning his bulk across the table with an air of confidentiality. 'You know, normally I can pick out an accent right down to the province and town. But all night I've been listening to you and still I can't place you.'

'I was born in the king's palace at Caserta,' my mother said, talking more towards Antonio than the doctor, as if to close the doctor out of her joke. 'But my mother gave me to the gypsies, to save me from the republicans.'

'Ha, ha,' the doctor laughed. 'And now, no doubt, you're running to America to save yourself from the gypsies.'

'Something like that.'

'Tell me, *signora*, if I may ask a personal question, how long before you deliver that little parcel in your lap? I ask, of course, out of professional interest, as a postmaster to a postman, so to speak.'

'Who can say?' my mother said, shrugging. 'You know how the mails are.'

'Ha, yes, very good. But only three months ago, you see, I delivered a baby on this very ship. A Calabrese woman. Two weeks early—the motion of the ship, you know. The water broke, and plop! The baby, unfortunately, was stillborn—'

'Doctor, please.' Antonio had edged towards my mother protectively.

But the doctor opened his hands in a gesture of helplessness, as if the comment had been unavoidable.

'*Scusi,*' he said, 'I didn't mean to upset *la signora—*

but I wonder why a woman in her state would travel? Why not wait another month or two, and have the baby at home?'

'Sometimes it's easier to carry a baby in your belly than in your arms,' my mother said.

'Ha, ha, you may have something there, it's true. But still it must be hard for you—you're in your last month, no?'

'What a lot of questions you ask, doctor. Perhaps at one time you were a priest?'

'Ho, ho, oh no, never a priest! Not even an altar boy—I'm much too honest for that kind of work. Though after all we work together, they take over where I fall short, heh, heh.'

As the stewards were clearing away our last dishes and setting out fruit, our meal was interrupted—a boyish crewman, apprehensive and grave, his sailor's cap clutched in a white-knuckled hand, came into the room with a message for the captain.

'There's a storm, sir, we just had a wire from the *Vulcania*. The first mate thought you should have a look. Sir.'

'All right.' A look of fatigue crept into the captain's eyes. 'Tell him I'll be up in a minute. The rest of you have ten minutes to get to your posts. *Signora*, you'll excuse the interruption—Darcangelo will see you to your room after your coffee.'

Conversation died down quickly now. One by one the officers took their leave, offering apologies and goodnights to my mother, and in ten minutes only the doctor, Antonio, and my mother and I remained, and the stewards had begun to clear the table. The doctor was still drawing regular draughts from a bottle of wine in front of him; when a steward reached for it, the doctor made a sudden move to stop him and the bottle toppled forward, spilling out onto the table. My mother quickly drew back, but before she could get clear a bright stream of wine had spilled into her lap.

'*Addio*,' she said, rising abruptly. The steward, a boy of not more than fourteen or fifteen, hurried over mumbling apologies and began wiping at my mother's dress with a napkin.

'Watch where you put your hands,' the doctor said. 'After all, the lady is pregnant.'

'Oh, *scusi, signora!*' the steward said, blushing. 'I didn't mean—'

'It's all right,' my mother said. She took the napkin from him. 'The doctor is just having his little joke.'

'I was merely thinking of *la signora*'s health,' the doctor said.

Dr. Cosabene stood and reached towards the other end of the table for a bottle that still had most of its contents intact. His glass in one hand and the bottle in the other he walked unsteadily towards a grouping of couches and low armchairs on the other side of the room.

'I remember,' he was saying, 'a storm in '33 that came out of the sky just like that, one minute it was blue and the next black as night, and this on an old ship left over from Caesar's time. We had to tie ourselves to the deck so we wouldn't get washed overboard. Nowadays on these big ships you could sleep through a storm and never notice a thing—'

He had eased himself now onto one of the captain's couches and leaned forward to untie his shoes, his voice hoarse and strained.

'We'd better go,' Antonio said, taking my mother's arm. 'The storm may be hitting soon, and anyway you'll want to get out of that dress. And the doctor, you can see, does not make a very pleasant after-dinner partner. *Buonanotte, dottore.*'

'Eh? But it's early still, why are you running off?' The doctor had stretched himself out now along the couch, his white-stockinged feet protruding over one end. His bottle and glass he'd set on a low table in front of him, a larger replica of the table in room 213, with the same old brown map veneered over its surface, Europe abnormally bloated and large, America just a thin strip of bush across an endless ocean. Antonio had begun to lead us towards the door, but when the doctor saw us moving past him he reached out suddenly for the bottle he'd set on the table and held it towards us.

'Oh, stay and have another small glass,' he said. '*Dai*, the doctor insists. No? *Beh, va bene*, go to the devil then. *E buon viaggio alla signora*! Let's hope that—' But we were already out the door.

Outside, Antonio pointed to a patch of sky towards the horizon where the stars seemed abruptly to end.

'It looks like we're going to run right into the middle of it,' he said. But beyond the rails the water seemed calm and still in the moonlight, only the waves from the ship's motion disturbing its surface.

'Should we put on our life jackets?' my mother said.

But Antonio had become suddenly serious.

'There's no danger, really,' he said. 'All the same, it's no fun to pass through these things. This is an old ship—all we have to control the rolling are tanks. They're not nearly as good as the fins on the newer ships.'

'You worry about the tanks and fins,' my mother said. 'I just want to know if I can get a good night's sleep.'

'Keep a bucket by your bed.'

At the door to our cabin, Antonio paused.

'Cristina, I don't want you to leave your room during the storm. In your condition—'

'Yes, yes, I'm tired of hearing about my condition. I'm not sick, I'm pregnant.' My mother touched an orange she'd carried away from the captain's table to Antonio's nose. 'Go, I'll be fine. Go play with your toys, like a good boy.'

While my mother took a bath, I watched from a porthole for the coming of the storm. The sea had grown choppy now, sending up glints of reflected moonlight like secret signals; as I watched the waves began to swell higher and higher, with a thrilling suddenness, until they were lapping up as high as the portholes. The light of the moon and stars drained away, as if a canopy had just been drawn over the sky, only the glint of deck lights and other portholes shining out in the darkness. Heavy drops began to pelt against the porthole glass, and by the time my mother came out of the bathroom the window had become a steady wash of rain and sea, the dizziness I'd felt earlier from the wine Dr. Cosabene had poured in my glass beginning to give way to a new dizziness, one that started in the pit of my stomach.

'I think the storm has hit,' my mother said. 'All that wonderful supper is going to go to waste.'

Holding the frame of the bunk bed for support she eased herself onto the lower bunk. But as she settled onto the mattress she drew in her breath sharply.

'*Addio*. Now my back is starting to go. I'll be glad when I get this extra weight off of it.'

I abandoned my place at the porthole and went to my mother. The floor was listing noticeably now, the furniture beginning to creak against its bolts. The orange my mother had placed on the coffee table had begun to rock slightly back and forth, reluctantly, as if some tiny insect beneath were continually hurling its weight against the orange's uneven bulk, trying to overcome its mute inertia.

'St. Christopher will protect us,' my mother said, taking me in her arms. 'Look how he's staying straight in the storm.'

But the painting of St. Christopher was moving too, scraping against the cabin wall in fitful jerks.

'He's not staying straight,' I said.

'It's not the picture that's moving, it's the wall.'

'*Mamma*,' I said, 'I feel sick.'

I was the first to start emptying my supper into the toilet. But not long after my mother followed, and soon the cabin had begun to reek with the smell of our vomit. The rolls of the ship had grown so steep now that it was impossible to stand upright without some handhold for support. Every few minutes another wave of nausea would wash over me, and finally I gave up stumbling up and down the ladder to my bunk and settled in my pyjamas on the bathroom floor, one hand clutched to the door frame for support and the other to my stomach, my feet gripping the floor to keep myself from sliding with the ship's rolls. The bathroom light had begun to flicker like lightning, making my head swim; to blot it out I closed my eyes and listened for the low rumble of the orange still rolling to and fro on the coffee table, imagined it crossing and recrossing the misshapen oceans and continents veneered on the table's surface, waited for the moment when it would exceed its bounds finally and drop with a dull thud to the cabin floor.

Every few minutes my mother lurched through the bathroom doorway, hands scrambling for supports, and eased herself down in front of the toilet. One hand clutching her back she'd begin to retch, with a violence that frightened me, her body jerking like a whip with each heave; in the flickering light she looked like a wild animal howling in a storm. But by her third or fourth visit she seemed to have coughed up the dregs of her supper, her heaves coming up dry. Her breathing had grown shallow and quick, and with each heave she threw her head back with a groan, as if a pain were passing up her spine. Finally her visits to the toilet stopped altogether, though I still heard her shallow breathing through the doorway, and every few minutes a pause and a groan.

Though the floor was still listing sharply, the

churning in my own stomach had begun to subside; a long time had passed since I had last had to crawl to the toilet. My mother was muttering, words I couldn't make out, her groans growing more drawn out and frequent, like the creak of a great branch slowly breaking beneath the weight of a storm. I had an image of her stretched out on her bunk with her swollen belly and matted hair, her head rocking back and forth; but I didn't want to leave the bathroom to look at her, remained huddled on the floor there instead counting the number of times the ship rolled between each of her groans, now twenty-three, now twenty, now eighteen.

Finally she called out to me. She was lying with her knees up and her hands clutched to the bedposts; as I watched another pain passed through her and she squeezed her eyes shut.

'*Addio,*' she said when the pain had passed. 'I wish we could do it just the two of us, without that drunken idiot.'

She smiled weakly, but tears had formed in the corner of her eyes. She squeezed my hand.

'There's nothing for it,' she said. 'You'll have to go for the doctor. Tell him—tell him the pains are only a few minutes apart. Take the stairs up to the main deck and go to the infirmary, next to the swimming pool. There should be a nurse there or someone who'll know where he is.'

I stood irresolutely a moment.

'Go on.' She squeezed her eyes shut again and groaned. By the time the spasm had passed I was at the door.

'Put on some shoes,' she called weakly, but I was already running, weaving unsteadily towards the stairwell that led up to the deck.

~~~

XXX

The hall on the main deck was deserted, the silence there broken only by the tumble and creak of furniture and loose objects shifting and straining behind closed doors. Even the maintenance staff, who usually began to come out at this hour, had kept to their rooms—in the stairwell I had had to step over a few pools of vomit that had simply been left to congeal where they had fallen. The lights on the main deck were not flickering, but the infirmary, its door propped open with a rubber wedge, was dark. When I looked into the reception room, which held a few uphol-stered chairs and a large metal desk, I found it deserted; but it gave onto another room, beyond a partition of frosted glass, from which I heard a low moan. Inside, from the dim light filtering in from the hall, I made out about a dozen high tubular beds tilting precariously with the ship's roll, their bolts creaking; and on one of them, facing away from me, lay a small woman in a nurse's bonnet and uniform, her stomach pressed to the mattress.

'*Scusi,*' I said from the doorway. But the woman did not turn towards me.

'*Scusi,*' I said, louder. 'My mother's sick.'

The woman on the bed moaned.

'Everybody's sick,' she said finally, her voice slurred and muffled by her pillow. She moaned again, then brought a foot up lazily to scratch her calf, her toe hissing like static against her nylons.

'My mother told me to get the doctor,' I said.

'The doctor's sick,' the nurse said. 'He's probably throwing up in a closet somewhere, like everyone else.'

I stood uncertainly a moment, clutching the frame of a bed for support.

'She said the pains are only a few minutes away.'

'She's lucky,' the nurse said. 'Mine are here right now.'

But I was suddenly sure where I would find the doctor, stretched out like a beached whale on one of the captain's couches where we'd left him a few hours before, and already I was out the door and running again. I knew only one way to get to the upper deck, by the outdoor stairwell, and I headed towards the double doors at the end of the hall that led outside to the sun deck.

The ship was still rolling steeply, erratically, pitching sharply forward or back sometimes in the middle of a roll; but I had grown so used to the movement now, lulled by it almost, that I'd lost any sense of the storm outside that was causing it. The portholes on the doors that led out to the deck were thick with rain, but they were too high for me to peer through, and preparing myself merely for the prospect of getting wet I pushed down on one of the bars that released the doors' catches. But the door wouldn't budge. I tightened my feet against the floor and leaned into the bar with my full weight, then again, harder; but still the door held firm. I stepped back about ten feet and made a running lunge; but though the door frame creaked as if about to splinter, the door did not give. Then on my second running lunge, the sea gave me a sudden boost, the ship pitching sharply forward and flinging me hard against the bar; and with a crack the door suddenly gave way, and I was hurled out into the storm.

I found myself sprawled on a deck thick with rushing water, my eyes blinded by wind and rain and my head reeling. I tried to stand but the ship was tilting to port, and a torrent of water caught me at the knees and flung me to the rails. For perhaps five seconds I stood pinned there by the roll of the ship and by the rush of water at my back, staring helpless as the ship completed its roll and the sea opened up before me like a jaw, so close I could have thrust my fist into it, the great wall of a wave building over me in a lengthening curve. But in the brief instant before the wave fell, all my fear suddenly drained away and I felt a tremendous power surge in me, as if I had grown god-like and could command the movement of the world at will; and for a moment it seemed the world had obeyed me, had become suddenly silent and still and calm again, frozen in an instant that might stretch on endlessly, give me time to crawl into the sea's belly and find whatever spoils of storms and tempests lay half-digested there. Then as if in a dream the wave finally closed over me, and the world went black.

When I came to I was lying on the other side of the deck, my pyjamas pulled half-way down my buttocks, my feet only a yard from the rails. Through some instinct my hand had reached out to clutch a handhold; when I pulled myself up by it I found myself at the foot of the stairwell that led to the upper deck. The ship was just beginning another roll to port, but I managed to pull myself up the first few steps, free of the flood that was rushing again across the deck. I sat a long time clutching the stairwell's railing, coughing up salt water and bile until it seemed I had torn my insides. Slowly my mind emerged from its stupor and I became conscious again of the wind and rain lashing at me, and when I had gotten my breath again I stood and lurched upstairs to the upper deck.

The captain's door slammed inward when I turned the handle; a flurry of wind swept into the room, setting the glass pendants of the chandelier chiming wildly. I could not get the door closed again and left it banging against the wall. But two white-stockinged feet were protruding undisturbed over the end of one of the captain's couches: the doctor was snoring there peacefully as a lamb, an empty wine bottle clutched to his chest and a thin stream of spit drooling from a corner of his open mouth.

I clutched the arm of the couch to support myself against the ship's roll and nudged the doctor's shoulder.

'Doctor,' I said, shouting to be heard above the wind and the banging door, 'my mother wants you to come.'

The doctor twisted his shoulder away from me.

'Leave me alone,' he muttered. Little beads of sweat glistened on his forehead.

I nudged again, harder.

'My mother wants you to come.'

'Leave me alone,' he muttered again, rolling over heavily towards the back of the couch. 'I did the best that I could.'

'Doctor, my mother's sick.' I shook him now with both hands. 'She said you should come.'

'Hmm? . . . Who is it?' He rolled flat again, bringing both hands up to rub his eyes. His bottle tumbled to the floor with a thud.

'My mother's sick.'

'Eh? . . . Why are you shouting like that, *per l'amore di Cristo?*' The doctor wiped at the stream of spittle on his chin with the back of his hand, then raised himself up on his elbows and peered at me through squinting lids. '*Ma chi sei tu?*'

'Vittorio.'

'Eh? Look at you—stand back, you're dripping all over my suit.' He began to ease himself up slowly from the couch. '*Ma sei scimunito?* What, have you been out in this weather? In your pyjamas, *che stronzo.* And all this wind, you didn't even close the door—were you born in a stable? . . . Who, Vittorio?'

'Vittorio Innocente. My mother's sick, she said you should come.'

'Sick?' The doctor rubbed the back of his neck with a grimace. 'It's just the weather. Go shut the door, for the love of Christ, I have a headache that would kill a whale.'

'I couldn't get it closed,' I said. I'd begun to tremble now with cold. My body ached as if a thousand hammers had been pounding at it.

The doctor rose with a curse and lurched towards the door.

'You're that woman's son, aren't you, the pregnant one who thinks she's a princess. Look at the mess on the floor now.' He slammed the door shut with a heave of his shoulder; immediately the room became calm, and the pendants on the chandelier gradually ceased their mad ringing. Leaning against the door the doctor pulled a small bottle from the inside pocket of his jacket and took a swig of the golden liquid inside, then lurched back to the couch.

'*Beh*, so what is it?' He fell heavily onto the couch and reached down for his shoes. 'Look, now my socks are soaked. *Addio*.'

'My mother told me to call you,' I said, my teeth chattering. 'She said to say about the pains. She was throwing up and making noises even after she stopped. I was throwing up too but I wasn't making any noises, anyway not the same ones.'

'Noises? Look at you without any shoes. If you die from pneumonia you'll have yourself to blame.' He'd stood now and was moving towards a doorway opposite the one I'd come in through. 'Everyone gets sick in a storm if they're not used to it, nothing to worry about. I'll give you some pills. Nowadays they have pills for everything—constipation, diarrhoea, malaria, hangovers. Pretty soon they won't need doctors any more, only pharmacists.'

The door we went through led into a narrow hallway that ran the length of the upper deck, a high line of windows looking onto the sea—I remembered now having been down the hall once with Antonio, when he'd taken me with him on his rounds. But I did not see Antonio now among the crewmen and officers who were lurching in and out of doorways or hurrying down the hall in one direction or other, casting backward glances at me as they passed.

'Where did you pick this one up, *dottore*? Don't tell me he's been outside in this weather—if the captain finds out he'll have someone's balls.'

'There's no problem,' the doctor said casually. 'Everything's under control.'

The doctor led me down an indoor stairwell and we came out on the main deck not far from the infirmary. The door I'd opened to get outside was closed now, though the hall was still deserted.

'How did you get outside?' the doctor asked. His body swayed like a great bending sail as he walked, though he kept to the centre of the hall, ignoring the handrails along the wall. 'I don't know what got into your head to go out there. Why didn't you go to the nurse? Louisa!' The doctor flicked on the lights as he stepped into the infirmary's reception room. He popped his head into the ward. 'Louisa! What, are you sleeping? You're on duty tonight, get up, and with half the ship probably trying to find you. How can anyone sleep in weather like this?'

The doctor pulled a key from his pocket and opened a door behind the reception desk. Through the doorway I caught sight of a bed-like table upholstered in black, a dark lamp stretching up from the table's head like a blind eye.

When the doctor came out he was holding a small glass pill bottle.

'Here,' he said, handing it to me. 'Tell her to take a couple of these every few hours. And change out of those clothes.'

'But she wants you to come,' I said, close to tears;

I was beginning to despair of ever getting him down to the room. 'She's making noises. She said you should come. She said to say the pains are only a few minutes away.'

'The pains?' A roll caught the doctor by surprise and he stumbled backwards against the reception desk, its bolts groaning under his weight. 'What pains?'

I shrugged helplessly.

'She said to say about the pains.'

'*Madonna*,' the doctor said, paling, 'she's having her baby. Louisa! Louisa, *per l'amore di Cristo* get out of that bed! We're having a baby!'

The doctor hurried back into the room behind the reception desk. I heard him rummaging through drawers, heard cupboards slamming shut, and a minute later he emerged again carrying a small black bag. A bleary-eyed Louisa—she was little more than sixteen or seventeen, I saw now, a small slip of a girl with large black eyes and a tiny upturned nose—was standing in the doorway of the ward, her uniform creased and puckered and her bonnet askew.

'A baby?'

'Bring some ether, Louí, *sbrigati*. And a basin!'

The doctor and I were already rushing headlong down the hallway. A moment later I saw Louisa following behind us, a basin clutched to her chest with one hand and her other still reaching down to slip on a shoe as she stumbled out of the infirmary doorway.

~~~

XXXI

My mother lay in the same position I'd left her in, knees up and hands clutched to the bedposts. Her breathing, though, seemed calmer than before.

'A few minutes more,' she said weakly as we came in, 'and I would have had to do it myself. The water broke.'

The doctor felt the mattress between my mother's legs. His hand came away wet.

'How long ago?'

'A few minutes.'

'The baby's early?'

'About a month.'

'Louisa, we'll have to put her on the floor. Spread some blankets out. And you'—the doctor turned to me—'stand over there in front of St. Christopher and keep out of the way. And get out of those clothes.'

Louisa stripped the upper bunk and arranged the blankets and pillow in the narrow aisle between the beds and the sitting area. The lights had stopped flickering now and the rolling of the ship seemed to have eased, though rain and waves were still lashing at the portholes. Louisa had set the basin she'd brought with her on the coffee table; a quart-sized silver canister was shifting inside it with the ship's roll, metal against metal.

With the doctor and Louisa each taking one of her arms, my mother rose slowly from her bed and settled

herself onto the blankets Louisa had set out for her. She
was still breathing steadily but her face was stippled with
sweat.

'Get her ready, Louisa,' the doctor said. He took
off his jacket, turning away from my mother to slide out his
bottle and take a quick pull from it. He draped the jacket
over a chair and rolled up his sleeves, then reached into his
black bag and pulled out a thick bar of brownish soap
wrapped in clear cellophane.

'Do you want me to shave her?' Louisa said. She
had knelt between my mother's legs and reached under her
night-gown to pull off her underwear. The underwear was
dripping wet.

'There's no time,' the doctor said, stepping around
my mother to the bathroom. 'The baby could start coming
any minute now.'

As if on cue, my mother's breathing became suddenly quick and sharp. Her body tensed and she stopped
breathing for a few long seconds, her fists clenching the
blankets beneath her. Finally a long, open cry passed out of
her, dying down in slow degrees, like a wave spending
itself on a shore. Her breathing did not calm down now,
though, and only a moment passed before she cried out
again.

The doctor had come out of the bathroom.

'Give me my bag.'

When Louisa had handed it to him he pulled out a
small package and tore it open with his teeth. The package
held a wad of cotton; the doctor poured some of the
contents of the silver canister onto it and knelt at my
mother's head.

'What are you doing?' my mother said, between
breaths. 'You smell—like a liquor factory.'

'It's just the anaesthesia.'

'No. No anaesthesia.'

'*Signora*, be reasonable,' the doctor said, his hand

still hovering above my mother's head. 'Why would anyone want to put herself through this pain?'

'I want—to see—everything.' But another spasm gripped her, and the doctor brought the cotton down over her face. Her cry came out muffled. The doctor held the cotton to her for a long moment; finally my mother's body seemed to relax a little, the muscles around her eyes easing as if she had fallen into a troubled sleep, her breathing growing more calm and rhythmic.

'Louisa, come up here and give her a dose of this every few minutes.'

The doctor knelt between my mother's legs and pushed her night-gown up to her belly, then slipped a hand under each knee and spread her legs apart until it seemed he would split her open. He pulled a slim package from his bag and slipped out two gloves of thin, translucent plastic; these he drew over his hands with two deft tugs, the gloves stretching over his thick fingers and palms like an extra layer of skin. He leaned forward and began probing with his fingers in the dark spot between my mother's legs. I looked away.

'The head is already starting to come through. Thank God it's not a breach like that damned Calabrese.'

My mother was still moaning, not the open cries of before but the half-stifled groans of someone crying out from a dream. Several minutes passed when everything was quiet except for these half-cries; even the ship's creaking had died down, the rain and waves no longer pounding at the portholes. Everything seemed poised at a point of stillness, on the edge of some yawning chasm.

The hunch of the doctor's broad shoulders blocked my view of my mother; but when he shifted position I saw that his gloved hands were clutching the top of a cheesy bluish-black sphere that was pushing itself out from between my mother's legs like an egg.

Louisa, seeming now tired and dreamy, her long

eyelashes drooping, was still kneeling at my mother's head, bringing her wad of cotton down every few minutes.

'Go easier on the ether,' the doctor said. 'It's not coming out.'

But when several more minutes passed and nothing happened, the doctor seemed to grow impatient.

'Get my forceps from my bag,' he said.

Louisa rummaged with her free hand in the doctor's bag.

'They're not here.'

'They're there, I put them there.'

Louisa set down her wad of cotton and searched more thoroughly.

'I can't find them. Do you want me to go up and get them?'

'No, I want you here,' the doctor said, irritated. 'I'll send the boy. *Come ti chiami, ragazz'*?'

'Vittorio.'

'Yes, yes, that's right. *Beh*, Vittorio, I want you to go upstairs to the infirmary and into my examining room, the room at the back. Inside the third drawer of the first cabinet on the right you'll find something that looks like two big spoons joined together so you can open and close them like a mouth. Like this.' He pulled his hands from between my mother's legs to flap them open and closed like jaws. 'Understand?'

I nodded.

'O.K., go. And be quick. And when you come back change out of those clothes.'

Maintenance people had begun to come out into the halls now to mop up floors and run wet rags along railings and walls, grey-overalled men who grinned at me through crooked teeth and thick-waisted women in hair nets and rubber gloves.

'Oh, *giovanotto*, where are you going in such a hurry?'

But I kept running, breathless by the time I reached the infirmary. The walls in the examining room were lined with cabinets and cupboards; but the doctor's instructions had gotten jumbled in my head. I began to search through each drawer and cupboard, desperately seeking the mouth-like spoons. I found scissors, packets of cotton, odd glasses, strange instruments of polished steel; and, at the bottom of one drawer, a small magazine whose cover pictured a dreamy-eyed woman wrapped in a shroud of translucent gauze. But no mouth-like spoons. Finally, using a small step-ladder I found wedged in a corner, I climbed up onto a counter to check the cupboards above it. Here were all manner of bottles and metal containers, arranged in wooden racks that held them in place; but no spoons. But with the third cupboard I opened a loose bottle came rolling off a shelf; it struck the edge of the counter and then shattered finally on the white-tiled floor, splattering a reddish-brown liquid that filled the room with a strong sickly-sweet smell.

In a panic, I scrambled to the floor and ran back down to room 213.

'I can't find it!' I cried as I opened the door, bursting into tears. But another cry answered my own from the bathroom, small but strong. The doctor looked over at me from where he still knelt between my mother's legs.

'Some assistant you are, eh? You're lucky your mother was only playing with us. She gave an extra push, and that was that.'

Louisa came out of the bathroom carrying a small bundle swaddled in a sheet.

'Say hello to your sister.' She leaned towards me, and I started back. Only the bundle's face was showing, small and ugly, the skin sickly blue and wrinkled like a dried olive; but I was flooded with relief to see that all its features were human, the tiny nose and eyes and ears, that it was not the snake-headed child that Alfreddo Girasole had warned me about.

When Louisa brought the face up closer to me so I could have a better look it screwed up into a grimace and let out a cry. Louisa laughed.

'She doesn't like you,' she said. 'Brothers and sisters never get along.'

'Bring it upstairs and make up a bed for it,' the doctor said. 'And bring down some new sheets.'

My mother was lying peacefully now: she seemed asleep, her eyes closed, her head rolled to one side on her pillow. The doctor was still crouched between her legs, holding a dark tube that coiled down inside her, his gloves stained with brownish blood and with a white substance that looked like soft cheese. Beneath his hands sat the metal basin Louisa had brought.

'*Che spettacolo*, eh?' the doctor said. 'Now we're just waiting for the dessert.'

We waited for a few long moments without speaking or moving, my mother lying peacefully on the floor, her breathing now calm and steady, the doctor on his knees with his fist closed around the dark cord. Finally, as if he could bear waiting no longer, the doctor gave a small tug, as slight as a twitch; immediately a fleshy mass, dark and bloody, flowed out from between my mother's legs into the waiting basin. I turned away, my stomach churning.

'It's done,' the doctor said. 'She might bleed a little, but it's nothing to worry about.'

Louisa came in now with the sheets.

'*Madonna*, what a mess you made up there! He spilled iodine all over the floor—I'll never get those stains out.'

Louisa made the beds, then helped the doctor lift my mother, who was still sleeping peacefully, into the lower one. It seemed a long time had passed; but outside the portholes the sky was still night-dark. The storm, though, seemed to have passed completely, a thousand stars glinting again overhead. It all seemed a dream now, the storm, the few terrible minutes I'd spent on the deck; but my skin still itched under my damp pyjamas, as if tiny worms were crawling beneath it.

'For the last time, get out of those clothes,' the doctor said. 'Take a hot bath and then go to bed. I'll come in the morning to check on your mother.'

He turned to pick up his coat from where he'd draped it, but stooped suddenly to pick something off the floor: my mother's orange.

'Breakfast,' he said, peeling into it. A gush of juice squirted up at his shirt and he wiped at it with a curse. When he'd finished peeling he portioned the orange out among us; for a moment the three of us stood silently eating in the centre of the room, like farmers taking a rest in the fields.

'A good night's work,' the doctor said, on his way out. As the door swung shut I saw his hand go to Louisa's behind for a quick pinch.

In the bathtub, lulled by the water's warmth, I twice nodded off; now that I could finally go to bed a great tiredness had overtaken me. Afterwards I pulled on a pair of long underwear and a thick long-sleeved undershirt. But before I had climbed up to bed my mother called out to me softly.

'Is it done?' she whispered.

'*Sí.*'

'A boy or a girl?'

'A girl.'

'Lie down beside me.'

My mother's belly felt soft and flabby now, and her hair was still dank with sweat; but I nestled close against her, drawing myself into her warmth. She kissed me on the forehead.

'*Figlio mio,*' she whispered.

Almost as soon as I closed my eyes, I was asleep. I slept for what seemed a long time in an utter darkness, without thoughts or dreams; then I dreamt that I was lying in a pool of warm water and I awoke with a start, afraid that I had fallen asleep again in the bath. But no, I was still in bed with my mother—I was conscious of her lying warm and still beside me in the darkness, her breathing so calm and faint now it was barely audible. I thought at first that I was back in my mother's room in Valle del Sole, then remembered the ship, then thought that I was somehow on the ship and in Valle del Sole at the same time; but the effort of piecing out the truth seemed too great. I wanted only to go back to sleep; but though I felt a heavy tiredness closing over me again, I could not sink under it, felt suddenly as if the whole night a hand had been constantly nudging my shoulder. My body now was making a hundred claims on me—my limbs were stiff and sore, as if covered with bruises; my bladder ached; and all along my back and thighs I felt a warm stickiness, as if I had forgotten to change out of my sea-soaked pyjamas, or I had wet the bed. Still thinking I was back in Valle del Sole, I rose out of bed to go behind the stable to pee. I had already turned on the bathroom light before my mind clicked with a little shock and I realized where I was, and that the warm stickiness I'd felt was blood—all along one side my clothes were soaked in it, some of it already beginning to dry and crust.

Mr. D'Amico was just stepping out his door when I came into the hall. His face paled when he saw me.

'For God's sake what's happened?' Then through the open door of the cabin he saw my mother still lying in bed, and he went in quickly and pulled back her covers.

'Gesù Crist' e Maria.'

He took my mother's wrist in his hand briefly and then hurried back into the hall, closing the door behind him.

'Are you all right?'

'Sí.'

'Go wait in my room. I'll get the doctor.'

From Mr. D'Amico's room I saw the doctor come, still in his pyjama top, Louisa behind him with his bag. A few minutes later Mr. D'Amico returned with Antonio.

'Look after the boy,' Antonio said. He went into my mother's room and closed the door.

In silence Mr. D'Amico poured a bath for me. When I had gotten out of my clothes he bundled them into a tight ball and set them in a plastic bag he pulled from one of his suitcases. For several minutes he left me alone in the bathtub; I heard Antonio come into the room and talk briefly with him in a low voice. When Antonio had gone, Mr. D'Amico came into the bathroom and lowered himself with a grimace onto his knees in front of the bathtub, his eyes clouded behind his spectacles. He took the washcloth from me and began to scrub my back, dipping the cloth continually into the water to clean it, the water crimsoning gradually with blood. Finally he pulled up the tub's plug and the water swirled slowly down into the drain. He wrapped a towel around my shoulders, then took off his glasses and rubbed his eyes with one hand as if he were tired. But I saw that he had started to cry.

He leaned towards me finally and I thought he was going to lift me out of the bathtub; but instead he clutched my shoulders with his hands and pressed his cheek hard against mine, his body trembling now with his quiet crying.

'*E' morta tua mamma*,' he whispered finally, as if telling me a secret. '*E' morta*.'

~~~

XXXII

The next few weeks I passed in a delirium. I had contracted pneumonia, and spent the rest of the voyage, and some time after it, in a high fever. It seemed I had fallen into the world of dreams, where no object or image had the meaning normally assigned to it, hid some secret about itself that I must discover; and all day and night my mind raced, working out complicated schemes and theories that might account for all the disparate facts, that might piece them together at last into a final magical solution. But just when the solution seemed near, an odd image would intrude: the face of Dr. Cosabene peering over me, distorted like an object in a curved mirror; a white room whose rough ceiling had become the surface of the moon; two spoons the size of young men leaning tiredly against a wall, rifles slung over their shoulders; a large orange balloon floating calmly by in the sky, and someone in a basket beneath waving goodbye, goodbye to a friend on the earth.

Later, in a hospital ward where a thousand wild voices babbled incoherently around me, I had two visitors. The first did not take me by surprise, really: I had seen him only once before, and then only fleetingly, but his eyes, blue flames, had burnt themselves into my memory then, and I recognized him at once when he came to stand over my bed, his presence fitting into place like the final sum of one of *la maestra*'s arithmetic questions. But I was only just coming out of the delirium of my fever then; and afterwards I could not say for certain whether he had actually stood over me, or whether I had merely imagined him.

It was the second visitor, who came after the first, that I had not expected to see: a stranger who was my father, and after all not the black-haired ogre I had imagined but a tired-eyed man whose hair had begun to grey and whose burly shoulders and limbs seemed to fit him awkwardly, like the Sunday clothes the peasants in Valle del Sole wore to mass. He cried without shame when the nurse brought him to my bed; and every day afterwards, until my fever had finally broken, he came to sit beside me, though he never spoke a word, only peered at me through his watery eyes, his cap clutched in his hands like a talisman. When I was let out of the hospital we rode together on a coal-dust-filled train, my father holding the baby in his awkward arms while we rolled across a desolate landscape, bleak and snow-covered for as far as the eye could see.

But all these later events happened in a mist. Before the mist set in, though, I was granted a few final moments of clarity—time enough to witness my mother's funeral, which took place the morning after her death, and which I was allowed to attend because no one, not even myself, had noticed that I was burning with fever. The funeral was held at the ship's stern, where the sun deck normally was, though all the chairs had been cleared away now. The sun was just edging above a still sea, the air cold but the sky stubbornly clear; and despite the early hour a small crowd of passengers attended—the ones my mother had befriended, Mr. D'Amico, the grey-eyed German, the honeymoon couple, and several others who I did not recognize, and who stood a ways back as if they were afraid of being turned away. Antonio was there, and the captain, hats in hands, as well as a few of the other officers, the ship's chaplain, Louisa, a sombre and sober Dr. Cosabene.

But only Louisa and Mr. D'Amico and the honeymoon couple cried through the service; the others retained a stony silence, stiff and awkward, as if the bright sun and clear sky made them feel unnatural in their mourning.

My mother's body, enclosed in a canvas sack and covered with an Italian flag, lay on a small platform that rose up above the rails and pointed out to sea. After the chaplain had read from his missal Antonio gave the eulogy. But I wasn't following—there had been a mistake, the kind of thing where dead people were not dead or where they could sometimes come back to life again, like that, the way the wheat around Valle del Sole, snow-covered in winter, could suddenly be green again in the spring. In a moment, I was sure, my mother's head would pop out of her sack. 'Vittorio,' she'd say, eyes all squinty and lips pouting, 'look at you, always so serious!' And everyone would laugh.

But now Antonio, his voice hoarse with emotion, was ending his eulogy; and after a long moment of silence a young frail-eyed officer began to play a song on a bugle, while we stood with our heads bowed. When he had finished the chaplain made a sign of the cross, and on a nod from the captain Antonio's hand slipped over a lever beneath the platform that held my mother, hesitated there a moment, then finally wrenched the lever back, hard. The platform tilted sharply towards the sea and the canvas sack slid out suddenly from under the flag; but before I could hear it strike the sea's surface my knees buckled beneath me, and my mind went black.

~~~

XXXIII

That evening I lay white-gowned in the infirmary, with a temperature of a hundred and four. The day nurse, Maria, older and more matronly than Louisa, her hands ruddy and thick and her uniform smelling of starch, roused me from sleep to feed me a bowl of chicken soup. The soup seemed to curb my fever, because some time after I'd eaten it I felt suddenly clear, clear enough to look around the room and realize where I was, and to see the one bed in the corner whose barred sides had been raised and whose occupant had been enclosed in a large plastic cube, two small grey tanks breathing coiled tubes into its canopied air. Maria had gone—she was not in her chair by the entrance, or behind the reception desk; and seeing that I was alone I climbed out of my bed and went to the one in the corner, wedging my face in between two bars to get up close to the cube. The baby was staring up at its plastic ceiling, waving its wrinkled limbs as if reaching for something above it. I tried to get its attention, tapped on the plastic, made small gurgling noises, and finally it turned towards me, spittle dribbling down its ruddy cheek. I made a face to make it laugh, but its small grey eyes—they were not yet the vivid blue they would become—seemed to stare right through me.

       Maria had not returned yet. I saw now that the clothes I had worn to the funeral were hanging on a rack near the doorway; I went over and pulled my pants on over my gown, then slipped through the reception room into the hall. A couple was coming in from the sun deck but they paid no attention to me, and I passed outside without resistance, through the same door that had cracked my bones the night of the storm. On the sun deck all the canvas chairs had been set out again in their orderly rows, as if nothing had happened; but it was supper hour, and the area was almost deserted. I skirted around the chairs until I came to the stern. At the other end of the ship the sun was only just setting; but beyond the stern the sky was already a deep blue, and it was hard to tell where the sky ended and the sea began.

My fever had begun to creep up on me again, my head starting to spin and my knees growing weak. The words of a song were floating into my head, surfacing like sunken relics from a place that was no longer visible on the horizon, that had been swallowed into the sea:

Vorrei far ritornare un' ora sola
Il tempo bello della contentezza
Quando che noi giocando a vola vola
Di baci i' ti coprivo e di carezze.

I realized with a start that I'd been singing out loud, a small mumble that died now as I became aware of it. I glanced behind me to see if anyone had heard. My mother's grey-eyed German friend had just come onto the sun deck with a young woman; but they eased themselves into deck chairs without noticing me, laughing and talking in a language I couldn't understand.

In my pant pocket, where I'd put it that morning before the funeral, was my lucky one *lira*, and I pulled it out now to look at it. The coin was shiny and slick from handling; but the imprint had not worn away, as it did sometimes on older five and ten *lire*—the lines were still visible on the eagle's wings, and the mark where Luciano had said a bullet had hit. But when I flipped the coin over to look at the bust on the other side, it slipped through my fingers—easily almost, without resistance, as if I had not tried to stop it, or had not believed it could fall; though now that it was falling my limbs seemed to have grown too thick and slow to stop it. For a long instant it tumbled down, winking darkly at me in the dying light as if to send me some final secret message, some magic consolation, if only I could make it out; but at last it fell with a hollow clang to the deck, where it rolled for a moment in a wide slow arc before tilting fatally toward the rails, and tumbling out to sea.

———————————

A NOTE ABOUT THE AUTHOR

Nino Ricci was born in 1959 in Leamington, Ontario, Canada, of Italian parentage, and holds both Canadian and Italian nationality. After completing studies at York University in Toronto, he taught for two years at a boarding school in Nigeria, then travelled widely throughout Africa and Europe. He spent a year in greenhouse farming before entering graduate studies in Montreal, at Concordia University, where he subsequently taught Canadian literature and creative writing. Recently he completed a year of study at the University of Florence. He is an active member of International PEN. *The Book of Saints* is his first novel.

A NOTE ON THE TYPE

This book was set in Palatino, a typeface designed by the noted German typographer Hermann Zapf. Named after Giovanbattista Palatino, a writing master of Renaissance Italy, Palatino was the first of Zapf's typefaces to be introduced in America. The first designs for the face were made in 1948, and the fonts for the complete face were issued between 1950 and 1952. Like all Zapf-designed typefaces, Palatino is beautifully balanced and exceedingly readable.

Printed and bound by Fairfield Graphics, Fairfield, Pennsylvania

Title page and binding design by George J. McKeon